ONE HORSE OPEN SLAY

ELLEN RIGGS

BOUGHT-THE-FARM
MYSTERIES

FREE PREQUEL

Rescuing this pup could bring Ivy a whole new life... if it doesn't kill her first.

Discover how big city executive Ivy meets Keats, her crime-solving sheepdog, in A Dog with Two Tales. Ivy Galloway doesn't know how desperate she is to escape the big city and her soul-sucking corporate career until she meets a sheepdog in need of rescue, too. This short prequel to the laugh-out-loud Bought-the-Farm Mystery series is a page-turner for lovers of animals, humor and spunky amateur sleuths. Join Ellen Riggs' author newsletter at **ellenriggs.com/opt-in** to get this FREE prequel.

One Horse Open Slay

Copyright © 2025 Ellen Riggs

ISBN 978-1-83410-185-9 D2D Paperback
ISBN 978-1-83410-184-2 D2D eBook
ISBN 978-1-83410-180-4 Book
ISBN 978-1-83410-182-8 AudioBook
ASIN B0FXN168GC Kindle
ASIN 1834101816 Paperback

Publisher: Ellen Riggs
www.ellenriggs.com
Cover designer: Lou Harper
2512231316D2D

CHAPTER ONE

Keats trotted ahead of us through Clover Grove town square, slowing to sniff around the base of a massive fir tree that stood waiting for its official lighting ceremony.

"Don't even think about it, mister," I called after him. "That tree isn't conveniently placed for dogs to do their business." My border collie was normally at least moderately obedient, but in coat season, all bets were off. My genius canine loathed his smart black parka with a fiery passion. The glance he gave me with his blue eye showed he had loathing to spare for me for making him wear it, even on a night so cold my teeth ached. Snow was coming. I could feel it in my bones. A white Christmas was almost guaranteed.

Keats half-cocked a leg and directed a sullen mumble my way. It sounded like, "Try to stop me."

"Back away from the pine, Keats," I called. "It needs to be perfect for its big moment tomorrow night. This magnificent fir represents town unity and community."

"That's a lot of weight to put on a tree, Ivy," said Jilly Blackwood-Galloway, my best friend. "Even a huge one. But she's right, Keats. Keep that leg down. We already give people enough to talk about."

Edna Evans cackled behind us. Our octogenarian prepper neighbor gave up worrying about appearances years ago. "It's nearly dark already. Who'd know the difference?"

"I would." Reaching up, I touched Percy, my fluffy ginger cat, who perched on my shoulder like a pirate's parrot. "The tree lighting embodies everything I love about a small-town Christmas. Especially after our disastrous stint in the choir."

Two years ago, a choirmaster had been murdered, and a stray donkey led us to the killer. In between, Keats had saved the life of our mayor, Meryl Martingale.

"That choir was the highlight of my non-military career," Edna said. "I'd have taken up the baton again this year if I weren't so busy."

Despite her camouflage fatigues, Edna's military career existed only in imagination. She was a retired nurse whose abrasive personality and passion for injections had scared off the town's songbirds. The choir had shrunk to a mere quintet of carolers, and Edna's prodigious ego forced her to walk away.

"We're too busy, too," Jilly said. "Christmas is the one time of year Runaway Inn can count on guests, and we only have a few more days. Let's keep this visit short, Ivy. When we're done, I need to bake more shortbread."

"You got it." We hurried a few blocks up a side street to an old red brick building that once housed the post office. Over the door hung a new sign that read, Clover Grove Museum. "We're just doing our bit to support family."

Iris, second in line of the five Galloway sisters, was not only a fine hair stylist but also the curator here. Over the past few months, she'd overseen a move from the previous tiny site to this vast space. Mayor Martingale had supported the transition by granting the lease, boosting funding and encouraging local families to donate items for display. It was a win all around for culture and something positive for townspeople to think about when headlines turned sour. Today's cocktail reception marked the museum's grand re-opening.

"Will there be actual cocktails?" Edna asked.

"Probably mocktails," Jilly said. "Too much Christmas cheer could lead to broken artifacts. You don't drink anyway."

"A little brandy in the mulled cider would make this event more palatable. Old things give me the creeps. The same will happen to you one day."

"Already has," I said. "This is just a family duty. I'm glad to have support from Keats and Percy to get through it." My dog turned back to face us from the top of the stairs and mumbled something grumpy. His blue eye gleamed with the reflection of multicolored Christmas lights. Local businesses had pulled out all the stops with seasonal décor this year. Even Keats' warm brown eye sparkled. Normally, it was nearly invisible after sunset, which happened so early now.

Jilly reached up to touch the cat's fluff. "You're sure Percy is welcome?"

"Pers-onally invited." I grinned at her. "See what I did there? Iris said the mayor wants the boys to be mascots. They're so photogenic."

My best friend rolled skeptical green eyes. Neither pet enjoyed posing, and it was nearly impossible to get a good shot of them.

"Meryl's not expecting trouble, is she?" Jilly tried to pluck Percy off, but he dug his claws into my best wool coat. I'd exchanged my hobby farmer uniform of overalls and work boots for nice jeans and heels. No one could say I wasn't a team player tonight. Christmas worked its magic even on mavericks like me.

"Of course not," I assured her. "What could go wrong at a museum opening?"

Keats mumbled again, and Edna drowned out the sound with another cackle. "Iris has gathered treasures from the town's founding families. Some of our forefathers were godfathers of the criminal variety. I bet there's a stash of stolen diamonds in there somewhere. Christmas and bloodshed go hand in hand."

Jilly's hand left Percy to smack Edna's sleeve. "Don't say that. It's a big night for Iris. Let's go inside and be nice."

"Do you know me, Jillian? Nice isn't in my repertoire."

Maybe not, but Edna was my second-best friend now and had saved my life on several occasions. Nice was overrated. "We just need to be civil," I said. "Half the people here hate me, anyway."

Jilly sighed as I followed Edna inside. "That's not true. They're just scared of you."

"Like that's any better." With the help of my pets and my friends, I'd contributed a lot to this town in the form of volunteer crime-solving. Most people only remembered the outrageous lies reporter Justine Schalow printed in her salacious rag, the *Clover Grove Tattler*.

"Focus on Christmas, Ivy." Jilly stepped into the vestibule and bumped shoulders with me. "It's the most wonderful time of the year. Cliché for good reason."

Keats mumbled again, more happily. There was something here that outweighed the featherweight burden of his parka. His cheery tone made me scan the large main gallery quickly. Generally, only trouble took my dog's mind off his winter wear.

The scene was exactly as I had expected. Sedate mingling. Murmured conversation over paper cups of mulled cider. Objects on stands and in glass cases that spoke to our community's agricultural roots. Butter churns. Crockery. Metal tools. That era had circled back more recently with an influx of homesteaders, some of whom attended tonight in hand-knitted hats and mittens, and thrift store coats. I admired their spirit but preferred to embrace modern conveniences. Jilly and I adored our fancy espresso maker and couldn't last an hour without our cell phones.

Iris had done her very best to make the museum inviting. There was a warm glow throughout from carefully chosen lighting.

Garlands framed natural oak window frames and doorways, giving off a piney scent. Somewhere, gingerbread cookies issued a siren's call to my rumbling stomach. Cocktails had little appeal for me. Sweets were my undoing.

Edna patted her pockets to take inventory. They contained a utility knife and pepper spray at bare minimum. "Iris has done a good job. Let's make sure no one ruins the moment for her."

Pride swelled in my heart for my sister. Iris had always been the most polished of the six Galloway siblings. After college, she'd cobbled together a living between odd jobs and stints at various hill country museums. More recently, she'd opened a unisex salon named Bloomers with our feisty mother, Dahlia. They'd lasted over two years in business without detonating. All credit went to Iris. Mom was the main reason I'd stayed in Boston for a decade. We got along better these days, but it was still hit and miss.

Jilly leaned in and whispered, "We're here to blend in and support Iris, remember. No drama."

"I'm not the one packing a taser," I whispered back.

Edna smirked as she eavesdropped. "Just a precaution, and a wise one with vultures in attendance."

The vultures in question wore matching khakis and puffy black jackets. Heddy and Kaye Langman weren't twins, but they usually dressed alike, and their gray hair was cut in the same utilitarian style. After inheriting The Langman Legacy antiques store from their father, they started attending any event featuring vintage objects of potential value. It was never clear whether they secured invitations to weddings, christenings and funerals or simply crashed them. They weren't above casually dropping a business card on a casket or attaching one to gifts and floral arrangements.

Keats' mumble turned into an irritable grumble. The sisters Langman had given us plenty of trouble in the past. On top of tacky tactics, they'd stolen objects of sentimental value from Edna's best friend, Gertie Rhodes. I'd suspected them of worse crimes, but

Kellan Harper, Chief of Police and love of my life, hadn't been able to put them away yet. Touching Keats' soft ears, I put him on notice. My other hand drifted up to Percy on my shoulder. If the Langmans had one redeeming quality, it was that they loved cats. My savvy ginger sleuth often seduced them with feline wiles.

Iris was deep in conversation with Meryl Martingale when we came in and, for once, someone outclassed the mayor. My sister wore a tailored dress of forest green with her dark hair swept into an elegant twist. When she caught sight of us, her professional smile warmed into something more genuine, and she excused herself to hurry over.

"You came!" She hugged me and then Jilly. Her arms reached for Edna and then dropped, knowing that our warrior friend considered public displays of affection weakness. "Thank goodness you brought the boys. Meryl's been asking about our mascots."

Percy head-butted the hand my sister offered. "The place looks amazing, Iris," I said. "Impressive yet welcoming."

It was true. The refurbished main hall featured high ceilings with crown molding, polished hardwood floors, and glass display cases arranged to create a natural flow through the exhibits. Holiday decorations complemented rather than overwhelmed the artifacts, with red bows, jingle bells and poinsettias placed tastefully throughout. The crowd was a mix of civic representatives, local business owners, history buffs and regular folk who came for the free food and gossip.

A flicker of worry crossed Iris' face. "I'm just glad we reached the finish line. Renovating and filling the larger space was challenging." Pulling a chamois from her pocket, she buffed fingerprints off a glass case. "I've been running on coffee and fumes for weeks."

"Anything we can do to help?" I asked.

"Just mingle and remind people that their tax dollars have been well spent," Iris said. "Oh, and do your best to avoid Hester Belcher. Do you remember her?"

Hester was the museum docent who pre-dated not only Iris' tenure but some artifacts on display.

"How could I forget? Hester collared Asher for knocking over a bourbon barrel while chasing me around during a school visit at the old site."

Iris squinted toward a wiry senior who wore a herringbone pantsuit, glasses with heavy dark frames, and a ponytail so tight it offered a facelift, too. Hester stood in a prominent position with a slight young man by her side. "Hester's mastery of historical records is unrivaled, but her people skills haven't improved. I'd like to keep her away from anyone who might become a benefactor. Can Keats help?"

I looked down at my dog. His ears were flat, and his tail puffed. If the jacket hadn't squished his hackles, they'd be rising, too. "He could, but I think he has Langmans on his mind."

My sister grimaced. "Heddy made me an offer on a porcelain Christmas platter, which the donor's family overheard and resented. It feels like there are landmines everywhere."

"Always best to assume that's the case, young lady," Edna said. Iris was closing in on 40, but Edna still considered us kids. "In Clover Grove, you need to step lightly. We'll do our best to defuse some of the bombs."

Iris squeezed my arm before stepping away. "We'll talk more in a bit. I need to check on the catering. Good thing I ordered for double the number of guests."

"She seems a little worried," Jilly said after my sister left. She tried again to detach Percy from my shoulder. The gesture told me Jilly was anxious, too. What's more, Percy's failure to comply suggested she had reason to be. Normally, the cat was delighted to lounge in my best friend's arms. What was I missing here?

"It'll be fine," I said. "Iris is like a duck. Unruffled on the surface and paddling like mad underneath. She'll pull it off. Always does."

Edna pushed into the small crowd ahead of us so that we could make our rounds. Clover Grove had formed in the early-1800s and the museum chronicled everything from its agricultural beginnings through a tourism-driven era and back to a homesteader focus. We'd practically come full circle. As much as I loved my town, I wondered if we'd made much progress.

Keats pushed ahead of Edna to take the role of tour director. His head swiveled as he scanned the room, probably cataloging exits and potential security risks.

He stopped suddenly. His right forepaw came up, and his ears twitched forward before flattening.

There was a steady clinking sound.

And then a tinkle as glass broke, hit the floor and scattered.

CHAPTER TWO

We rounded the corner into the next gallery and found the Langman sisters standing beside the remains of a display, their boots covered in shards of glass.

"Which of you broke that?" Edna said. "I heard the tap of a key on glass."

"A key? Don't be silly." Heddy's hand was buried deep in her parka pocket. "Besides, quality museum glass could withstand a key."

I stooped to hold Keats back by the collar, and Jilly finally managed to steal Percy off my shoulder.

Edna crunched over the glass and peered at the display. "That's the Christmas platter you tried to buy from Iris."

Kaye's eyebrows rose. "There are half a dozen holiday platters here, Edna. If we damaged it, of course we'll buy it. That's the policy, isn't it?"

"In a store," Jilly said. "Not a museum."

"You ladies running a con?" Edna said, as the slim young man who'd been standing near Hester a few minutes ago came in with a dustpan and broom. "If so, it's a bold one. Even for you."

"Always so extreme, Edna." Heddy leaned over the young man. "I do see a slight scratch, though. That'll reduce the platter's value."

Iris stood in the doorway with her arms crossed, observing. "The scratch was already there. And my security cameras will tell me how the glass broke. For the moment, everyone please move along so we can clean up."

The Langmans held back. "Iris, if you check your documentation, I think you'll see additional damage, and it's only right that we compensate you. We'll take this platter off your hands."

My sister had flushed to her hairline, a sign of barely suppressed fury. "Meryl Martingale is coming to speak to you, ladies. Take it up with her."

The Langmans turned together, grinding glass fragments into the hardwood. They hurried into the next gallery, the smallest room, and we followed. I didn't want to be cornered by the mayor, either. Meryl always wanted something from me. I figured she'd have plenty of time to hit me up while staying at Runaway Inn over the holidays.

Any concerns the Langmans had about either the broken display or the mayor faded as they fell under the spell of a sterling silver tea set, which was also behind glass.

"There's a buyer for this," Heddy muttered to Kaye while snapping a photo. The flash glanced off the glass and dazzled my eyes.

Edna snatched the phone out of Heddy's hand. "No flash photos in a gallery, Heddy Langman. Were you born in a barn?" She paused for effect. "Actually, you were. Doc Grainer and I were on the way, but your mother didn't make it back to the house in time. We wrapped you in a horse blanket and popped you into an old tin basin. Bet you've already sold it."

Heddy smirked. "Not yet. All yours if you can afford it."

"It's true about flash photography, Heddy," I said. "Apparently, it causes chemical reactions that damage artifacts."

Heddy rolled her eyes. "Modern phones don't have that effect. We know a thing or two about preserving antiques, don't we, Kaye?"

The elder Langman nodded. "That we do. We've made a good living from cherishing hill country's treasures. Like our father and his father. There's nothing special about this tea set historically speaking. Iris must be desperate to fill the space."

"She grew too fast," Heddy chimed in. "The Galloways are always too big for their britches. Especially Dahlia." Standing on tiptoe, she added, "Where is your dear mother?"

I rarely wished my mother was around to defend me, but she enjoyed going toe-to-toe with her former schoolmates. "Mom's holding down the fort at the salon. Everyone wants perfect hair for the holidays."

Edna patted her tight brown curls. "Booked my perm early. You're probably out of luck, Langmans."

Nylon rustled as both women shrugged. "We have more to worry about than hair," Kaye said. "It's a busy time, and getting away from the store isn't easy. Nothing says 'I love you' more than a fine antique."

"Nothing says 'I love you' more than a new pet," I countered. "I've asked Santa for a pony."

"Ivy, don't you dare," Jilly said. "Your ark is practically sinking already."

Heddy snatched her phone back from Edna and walked around the sterling tea set to take another photo. "This museum makeover is a bust. The mayor will probably pull the funding and send Iris back to the outskirts. Her original building is gone. Hopefully, someone has a spare garage to offer when the time comes."

The junior Langman was trying to rile me, and it worked. "My sister's done an awesome job here, Heddy."

Edna raised a gloved finger to let her take over. "Especially when you Langmans have already sold most of our regional history to outsiders."

Nylon-clad shoulders shrugged again. "Meryl can use tax dollars to buy it back," Heddy said. "Some might say we need a local medical center more. I'm not one of them."

Kaye pulled her sister away. "If you'll excuse us, there's only one piece here really worth seeing, and we've been waiting for a gap in the crowd."

Keats herded us along behind them. He was still disgruntled, and it was about more than his coat.

"This is the first year Heddy and Kaye have hired help at their store," Edna said. "Frees them to hit holiday parties and case out collectibles. Apparently, they've been handing out bottles of good brandy as hostess gifts. Getting people sloshed loosens their cabinet hinges."

We were laughing as we walked into the next room, where the Langmans had pushed as close as possible to a large display. Under a trio of lights sat an antique child's sleigh. It was painted red with a festive scene on the side. The runners were made of metal, and the seat was upholstered in green velvet that was either updated or very well preserved.

My sister was standing guard over the gem of her holiday collection. The Langman sisters fired off questions, which Iris answered or deflected with ease. Her steely self-control cracked only slightly when Heddy asked about the sleigh's price tag.

"It's not for sale, Miss Langman," Iris said.

"So rude," someone beside me whispered. "I can't believe it."

I turned to see a man in his mid-twenties with a head of curls. His brown eyes, behind round, wire-rimmed glasses, darted from one Langman to the other and then back to Iris. He was still holding a dustpan full of glass.

"Believe it," I said. "The Langmans want that sleigh."

"Won't happen. Not now, not ever." His voice was crisp. "It's on loan from the Millbrooks, Clover Grove's founding family. They had it designed for their daughter in 1858."

I stuck out my hand. "You must be Anthony Cork, the museum's assistant. I'm Iris' sister Ivy, and these are my friends, Jilly and Edna."

Anthony shifted the dustpan to shake my hand. His grip was gentle, perhaps because of his training in handling artifacts. "Iris speaks of you often. I'm sorry you overheard my comment. I was rude, too."

Jilly flashed her best smile to put him at ease. "The Langmans bring out the worst in all of us, Anthony. Tell us more about this beautiful sleigh."

"It would have cost a small fortune when it was made," he said, sliding the dustpan and broom behind a cabinet full of china. "The little girl only rode in it behind her pony a few times before she outgrew the sleigh, and it became more of a Christmas ornament. The Millbrooks kept it in the attic, basement, or shed, so it does show its age." Anthony's glasses slid down his nose, and he shoved them back up. "Miss Belcher says greatness is squandered around here." His lips pressed into a thin line and then he whispered, "That was rude, too. Sorry."

Edna chuckled. "Sounds like something she would say. Hester and I go back a very long way. I was the one to lance her first boil."

Now I pressed *my* lips together to hold back laughter. Even Keats relaxed enough to give a pant-laugh, his first since we arrived.

"Edna, stop," Jilly said. "We're on Hester's turf."

"Iris' turf," Edna corrected. "This lad works for her."

Anthony nodded. "Technically, yes. But Miss Belcher oversees me day-to-day. She's on site more."

The museum had basically become Hester's full-time volunteer job after retiring from her position as a legal secretary in Dorset Hills. Iris might have the title and accreditation, but Hester pretty much ran the place with an iron fist.

"Both my sister and Hester admire your knowledge and work ethic, Anthony. Neither is easily impressed."

"Thanks. That means a lot." Anthony's eyes tracked a tall, distinguished-looking man in his early seventies who approached the sleigh. The older man's tailored suit and confident air marked him as someone of importance, although I couldn't place him. The ruddy flush in his cheeks made me wonder if he'd spiked his mulled wine. Perhaps that's what gave him the courage to nudge the Langmans aside.

Gesturing to the sleigh, he said to no one in particular, "Magnificent, isn't it? An acquisition like this elevates our humble museum."

Anthony leaned in to whisper to me again. "Mr. Nobbs is our biggest benefactor. He privately funded nearly half the renovation."

Now I remembered Iris mentioning her patron. Powell Nobbs had made his fortune in real estate development and moved back to Clover Grove about five years ago. After restoring an old manor, he immersed himself in civic affairs. My brother Asher, a police officer, said Powell was prone to steamrolling anyone who opposed his vision for the town. Plenty did.

As if to confirm it, Edna muttered, "Old windbag."

Anthony looked startled, and a little confused. Edna had a decade on Powell and plenty of wind to spare.

"The workmanship is remarkable," Powell continued. "The Millbrook family has entrusted us with a great treasure." He glanced across the room at a petite woman who was a little younger than him. "Don't you agree, Miss Tupling?"

Aline Tupling looked up from the coin box she was offering to guests. I didn't know her well, but she frequently raised funds for worthy causes. In this case, it was the Christmas toy drive. The mayor would distribute gifts to children at the tree-lighting event tomorrow, so we were down to the crunch. Someone added a few coins to the box, and Aline smiled. "A treasure, yes," she answered. "We live in a generous town, Mr. Nobbs."

Jilly and I exchanged bemused glances. That wasn't always true, but Christmas brought out the best in all of us.

"I'm hoping to convince the Millbrook family to make this donation permanent," Powell continued. "I have a little pull with them, you see."

Iris turned on her best curatorial smile. "Please use it on our behalf, Mr. Nobbs. Perhaps you could convince them to donate a painting from their collection as well."

Aline's coin box jingled merrily. "That would be wonderful. I hear they have a piece that features a sweet brown pony in a snowstorm. A perfect addition to this little sleigh."

"I'll see what I can do," Powell said. "Art would be a vast improvement over taxidermy." He jerked his thumb over his shoulder to the only exhibit we hadn't visited. "Those beasts are taking up valuable real estate. It's the largest gallery."

My sister's smile became diplomatic. "You're our most generous patron, Mr. Nobbs, but not our only one. We were pleased to accept other donations."

"A stuffed moose doesn't belong here, let alone a bear, wolf or cougar. There are no such creatures in hill country."

Iris touched her hair, probably wanting to loosen her bun before it gave her a headache. "At one time, they owned the land, and that's the point of the natural history exhibit, Mr. Nobbs. Our local children will only get a chance to see these animals here."

He huffed indignantly. "I don't like it. While I'm hustling to find real exhibits, you're giving floorspace to stuffed beasts."

"Powell?" Edna waited until she had his attention. "Go stuff yourself."

A ripple of laughter filled the room, and people began migrating to the natural history exhibit. Powell had achieved the opposite of what he'd hoped. In fact, he was pulled along by the crowd under protest. Aline Tupling smiled as she joined the exodus, coin box jingling again.

We followed, but I stopped just inside the doorway of the darkened gallery to watch over Iris, knowing the Langmans would likely close in on her again. Keats sank into a crouch, ready to apply strategic nips to khakis. Percy jumped down to stage his own coup.

"Iris, you really should protect this sleigh," Kaye said. "Put it behind glass and control the climate. Did they teach you nothing at museum school?"

"I'm following the direct orders of the Millbrook family," Iris said. "They want people to have access to the sleigh. It was built to be used and was never packed away in cotton gauze."

Heddy leaned in for a closer look. "It's strangely well preserved, considering. If we were the type to believe in hexes—"

"We're not," her sister intervened. "I'd just like to see this fine piece given the respect it deserves, and we know exactly the right buyer to do it."

"The sleigh isn't for sale," Iris repeated. "It's on loan and goes home to the Millbrooks in January."

Heddy tipped her head. "Dear, naïve Iris. Everything's for sale, isn't it?"

"Actually, no." The words came from Hester Belcher, the docent. "Nothing here is for sale. So, scat, both of you."

Hester's glare cowed even the resilient Langmans. Kaye beckoned her sister and eased away. "We'll see about that, Hester. The Millbrooks' holiday open house is tomorrow. Perhaps some brandy will help them part with their family heirloom even before Christmas. You can fill the spot with dead raccoons."

A few moments later the front door slammed as the Langmans left.

Keats pressed me back a few steps but only to position me better to observe unseen. I nearly bumped into Anthony, whose eyes were glued on Powell Nobbs as the older man pontificated about the ins and outs of taxidermy.

"Kaye wasn't wrong, Iris," Hester said. "We should have that sleigh under lock and key. Not to mention climate control. What's the use of a big budget if it's spent unwisely?"

"I've allocated the funds as best I could, Hester." Iris sounded defensive. "This is a big place, and we've tripled our exhibits. It'll take time to catch up."

The docent crossed thin arms across her chest. "You need more help. Carve off some of the budget to hire someone permanent. I know just the right person."

I presumed she meant Anthony Cork and looked over my shoulder. There was no sign of the assistant now. He was probably defending a stuffed bear from Powell.

"It's fine," Iris said. "Growing pains are inevitable. Please lighten up, Hester. With the mayor here, it's already tense."

Hester straightened under her herringbone jacket. "I will not lighten up. On the contrary, I have an important matter to discuss with you. Things have been falling through the cracks, and it's my responsibility as a longtime docent to point out what you're missing."

Iris raised both hands to fend her off. "Let's sit down in the new year and brainstorm a way forward that suits us both."

"That simply won't do. It's urgent, Iris. You can only stick your bun in the sand so long."

"Hester, don't use that tone with me. We still have a chain of command."

I snapped my fingers, and Keats shot forward to intervene. Hester backed away from my sister and swatted at the dog.

"Don't hit my dog, Miss Belcher," I said. "I have a chain of command, too."

Before I could join them, there was a crash, and something rolled past me out of the natural history exhibit. The floor was uneven, and the piece picked up speed until it landed between Hester's sensible loafers.

I gasped as I recognized the object.

It was a skull.

A human skull.

There was no doubt in my mind. Once upon a time, I'd carried one in my handbag.

"Percy Bysshe Shelley, you stop that!" Jilly's voice soared over the noise in the crowded exhibit. "Come down here at once or I'll have you declawed."

Hester bent over to pick up the skull. "Now look what's happened. Pets have no place in a cultural institution, Ivy Galloway."

"I'm so sorry, Miss Belcher. If it's broken, I'll replace it."

Hester scowled at me. "Precisely the point. These objects are irreplaceable. Your cat belongs in a barn."

Percy sauntered out of the natural history exhibit ahead of Jilly. My best friend's face was flushed. "Iris, it's my fault," she said. "He was under my watch. Whose head did he get?"

Iris fought a smile that would only aggravate Hester more. "It's a replica of the oldest human remains in the area. Unbreakable. Percy chose well."

Jilly picked up the cat. "Still, I'm sorry."

My sister pried the skull out of Hester's fingers and offered it to Jilly. "See? Not a nick on it."

When Jilly declined the skull, Iris tried me. Keats gave a ha-ha-ha as I took a quick step back.

"Is that dog laughing?" Hester demanded.

"Of course not," I said. "Dogs don't laugh, Hester. He's panting because he's hot. He hates his parka."

"Then take him outside where he belongs."

Keats' lunge at Hester was more for show than anything else. He was always testy when the topic of outerwear came up.

"Remember, the mayor wanted Ivy's pets to be here, Hester," Iris said. She pulled her phone out of her pocket, and a series of pings got louder. "Uh-oh! A pipe burst at the salon, and Dahlia's about to follow suit." My sister's fingers flew on the phone, and then she peered up at us. "I need to go deal with this. Ivy, can you help Hester close the museum later? Bring Jilly and Edna."

"No thank you," Hester said. "The day I accept help from Edna Evans—"

"*Again*," Edna interrupted, rejoining us. "You didn't argue when I dealt with your carbuncles years ago, Hester."

I raised one hand. "Iris, you stay and we'll help Mom with the flood. This reception is a big event for you."

She sighed. "The salon's still my bread and butter. Mom's hysterical, and the clients are upset, too. I can be better spared here."

"That's exactly what I was talking about earlier, Iris," Hester said. "You treat this place like a hobby."

My temper bubbled, knowing how hard Iris worked to spin all the plates. "Miss Belcher, my sister is a dedicated professional. She's worked incredibly hard to make this reopening a success."

"A dedicated professional would know animals don't belong in a museum unless they're stuffed," Hester said.

"The Smithsonian used cats for rodent control for decades," Edna chimed in helpfully.

"That's untrue. I know everything there is to be known about the Smithsonian, Edna. You just stick to—"

"Carbuncles," Edna interrupted again, lifting a camo glove. "Fine, Hester. Have it your way."

Hester unlocked her arms and loaded more verbal ammo. Luckily, Anthony Cork reappeared before she could fire.

"Miss Belcher, could I have a moment in the natural history exhibit? Mr. Nobbs is deliberately misleading people. Moose aren't carnivorous. Miss Tupling was startled enough to drop her coin box."

"Aline is so gullible." Hester started after Anthony. "Keep your animals under control, Ivy, or I'll have the authorities remove every last one of you."

"My brother, the cop, would be glad to help," I called after her. It sounded like she dropped a curse, but that seemed unlikely.

Iris shook her head at me. "Leave Hester alone. She's brilliant, and she knows more about this town's past than anyone alive. Even you, Edna."

"Change is hard for many people," Jilly said. "The old museum was Hester's history."

After checking her phone again, Iris took a deep breath. "Okay. I'm going to see the mayor out and then go help Mom." Reaching into her pocket, she pulled out a key and handed it to me. "You guys circle back at eight-thirty and give Hester a hand. Anthony has the night off for a Christmas party."

"Got it covered." I gave her a little shove. "Go save the salon."

Keats weighed in with an ominous grumble.

"What's his problem?" Iris said. "Keats loves to work."

"Not when the job comes with a parka. He clocks out early in winter."

"I owe you one, Keats," Iris called back as she left.

His next mumble suggested that she very much did.

CHAPTER THREE

The museum looked different at night. As we walked up the front stairs, streetlights filtered through frosted windows, casting strange shadows among the exhibits. Even the holiday decorations seemed altered. Garlands drooped and the unlit Christmas tree became a blurred creature preparing to pounce. The cheerful chaos of the earlier reception had faded, leaving behind a stillness that made me shiver despite my warm cardigan and lightweight parka.

"Museums are creepy even in the daytime," Jilly said. "Now it feels like the building's watching us. It's dark in there."

Edna reached the door first. Finding it locked, she fished a jangling keyring from one of her many pockets. "Consider it a dress rehearsal for the end times, Jillian. At least you brought shortbread."

"Why do you have a key to the museum, Edna?" I asked.

"Why wouldn't I?" Her saucy tone made me wonder how many buildings in Clover Grove she could pass into and out of at will. Edna had been around a long time and knew a lot of people. Many of them had been on the receiving end of her hypodermics when she worked as a nurse in Doc Grainer's office. Perhaps she'd collected stray keys along the way.

I left that line of questioning for another time. "Hester's car is still here." I pointed to the small, sensible sedan sitting alone in the side parking lot, its shape softened by a mound of fresh snow. When we were finished inside, I'd help her clear it. "It's after nine, and she's probably wondering what took us so long. I should have accounted for last-minute shoppers, heavy traffic and slippery conditions."

Keats pressed against my leg and mumbled something that sounded like a warning. His fur bristled slightly around the collar of his jacket. Percy, back in position on my shoulder, stiffened too. He was wearing his bright yellow bomber, so I couldn't tell if his hackles were up, but his tail twitched in a way that spelled trouble.

"What's going on?" Jilly's voice slipped up a notch. "The boys seem on edge."

"Like you said, no one likes a museum at night." I tried to sound casual, but something about my pets' behavior made the hair on the back of my neck stand up. "The stairs are icy, so be careful."

Edna stuck out an army boot. "These could carry me up Everest. Again."

I was reasonably sure she hadn't climbed Mt. Everest or any other mountain, but I let that go, too. Edna fired out random comments when she was nervous. But she was so seldom nervous that it made *me* nervous just thinking about it.

She turned the key in the lock, and the door creaked open. It was warmer inside, but not as warm as it should be. A cool draft wafted through the room, carrying the scent of pine and a hint of cinnamon from the reception. Keats mumbled something terse. A warning, perhaps. Reaching up, I found Percy's tail had stopped twitching and now stood straight up, like an orange exclamation point.

"Hello?" I called out. "Hester? Hester! Sorry we're late."

The only answer was the tick-tock of a grandfather clock that had required a special team of its own to move. That sound would get on my nerves fast. Maybe it had been fraying Hester's nerves for decades and made her cranky.

"She must be in the office," Jilly said. "Or in the storage room taking inventory."

"Or planning where to stash more bodies." Edna's cackle was gleeful and jarring. When we turned to stare at her, she shrugged. "Taxidermy bodies, girls. What did you think I meant?"

We stomped snow off our boots on the mat in the vestibule and then moved through the main gallery, footsteps clunking on wooden floors. The motion sensors triggered lights as we walked, creating pools of brightness that somehow made the shadows deeper. Percy jumped off my shoulder and darted ahead, his orange tail still high and bristling.

"Percy, wait!" The cat had already vanished into the next gallery.

Keats shot me a look with his eerie blue eye and declined to pursue his feline colleague.

"Is it just me," Jilly whispered, "or is this starting to feel like one of those holiday horror movies?"

"It's just you," Edna said. "I'm no fan of old clutter, but that's all this is. Plenty of homes in the area have even more. The Langmans visit all the hoarders regularly."

I patted my best friend's sleeve. "We'll be done here in a few minutes. Then we can head home for the hot cocoa you promised."

"There's a chicken pot pie warming in the oven, too. Asher will be hungry when he gets home. He burns an extra thousand calories on cold days."

There was nothing unusual about her words. Only an expert in Jilly Blackwood would know her throat was trying to clamp shut. Maybe she'd noticed the broken ornament on the floor near the collection of snow globes. I wasn't going to point it out, but Keats did it for me, with one white paw rising and a mumble to make sure we all caught it.

"Iris won't be happy about a smashed bauble," I said. "Guess that's what happens when people—and pets—ignore Hester." I craned toward the back room. "She's probably getting a dustpan. Or drinking heavily to ease the loss."

"Hester doesn't drink," Edna said. "The world might be a brighter place if she did."

"You don't drink, either." I shooed Keats away from the glass fragments. "You used to like a grapefruit juice martini now and then."

Edna flipped up the flaps on her camo cap. "That was before I realized it's vital to stay alert in this town." Her sharp eyes darted around the room, taking in details I probably missed. "When the apocalypse comes, it won't find me twirling a tiny parasol."

A garland had come loose from the frame over a doorway, and its end coiled on the floor like a bristly snake. Several display tables and cabinets seemed to have shifted slightly, too. Maybe the reception had gotten rowdy after we left. Hester wouldn't have liked that one bit.

Percy's eerie meow drifted back from the next room. It was a summons.

"Doesn't sound good, does it?" Edna's voice was still cheerful, probably because the mission had spared her from a night of knitting mittens in her recliner. She'd made dozens of them for Aline Tupling's toy drive. While not technically toys, mittens supported outdoor play. Edna was a fan of anything that ripped kids away from the electronic devices that supposedly rotted young brains. "Bet you ten bucks your cat found something interesting."

"I'll keep that money, thanks." I already knew Percy had found something interesting because Keats had moved in front of us to control our pace. It was a defensive strategy.

Maybe Edna came to the same conclusion, because she fumbled in her pockets. I always worried a pistol would emerge, but so far, it hadn't happened. Mace? Yep. Brass knuckles, also yep. Firearms, no. I liked to think she respected my "no bullets around my animals" rule, but Edna had her own guiding principles.

We rounded the corner to find Percy standing exactly where the child's sleigh had sat just hours ago. The treasured artifact Iris had been so proud to showcase was gone.

"That's strange," Jilly said. "Hester must be locking up the sleigh for safekeeping."

Edna finally found what she was groping for and switched on a powerful flashlight. "Not so sure about that, Jillian. Take a look at what the dog found."

I knelt beside Keats to do the honors. His white paw was up again to point out speckles on the hardwood.

Red speckles.

Paint, I hoped.

"I think the sleigh got dinged," I said. "Iris is going to flip."

The flashlight beam bounced around in Edna's hand. "Maybe I was wrong about Hester and booze. It's looking like she went on a bender. Maybe someone spiked the cider as a prank after we left."

"If it's a prank, it's not funny," Jilly said, reaching for Percy. The cat slipped out of her grasp, jumped down and stalked into the darkness ahead. This time, Keats joined him. The dog's ears flattened and hackles rose around his collar. The white tuft at the end of his black tail turned into a beacon to help light the way.

"Hester?" I called her name louder this time. "Are you here? Jilly brought cookies for you."

Cookies fixed a lot of problems, but I suspected they wouldn't do the trick tonight.

The draft I'd noticed earlier got colder and stronger as we followed the pets to the service entrance. It was no wonder, because in the museum's glorified mudroom, the rear door was ajar. Powdery snow had blown in from the alley, and footprints packed it down on the mat.

"That's not right." Jilly's voice dropped to a hoarse whisper.

"Hester would never leave a door open. The humidity could damage the collection."

I nodded. "Plus, someone could rob the place. Maybe she went out to dump the trash and slipped on ice."

Percy and Keats were already outside, and an eerie meow urged us on. We stared at each other in the mudroom in the circle of Edna's flashlight.

"Stay here," I told my friends. "I'll check on the pets."

"As if." Edna spun the light in a little circle. "I'm the one with the equipment. Jillian has shortbread, and you're empty-handed."

I patted the front of my jacket. "I have a utility knife and I'm not afraid to use it."

Edna pushed the door all the way open with a cackle that had lost half its oomph. "Perfect. You can carve your initials into a tree with the chief's."

There were no trees in sight, as her high-powered beam soon revealed. A bedraggled wire mesh fence separated the alley from farm fields. Closer to us, tire tracks ran down the lane and around the far side of the building, away from the parking lot with Hester's sedan. Snow was already filling the tracks, along with a scattering of footprints. It looked like there'd been a skirmish, perhaps among three people. Had Hester battled the Langman sisters for the sleigh? It wouldn't have been a fair fight, but Hester was the type to swing hard for the museum cause. That's why Iris put up with the docent's prickliness, which had intensified after retiring from the law firm.

Something caught the flashlight's beam. A glint of glass or metal near the bottom of the steps. Keats was in a point yet again. I hurried down the stairs to join him, holding the railing tight.

Bending, I found dark-rimmed eyeglasses in the snow. One arm was broken, and a lens was gone.

Hester's glasses.

"Oh, dear," Jilly said, joining me. "Hester must have fallen."

Edna swept her light in a wide arc. "Or been attacked. Something strange happened out here."

Keats raced ahead of us over the tire tracks and around the corner of the building. His sharp bark sent icy crystals of fear through my veins. A threat was close by, and he was ready to protect. Percy responded with a chilling yodel.

Reaching out, I took Jilly's free hand in its wool mitten. The container of shortbread was secure under her other arm. Edna tried to avoid letting me grab her camouflage glove but eventually surrendered. The three of us moved forward in a friendship chain, with Edna's beam bouncing off red brick walls, the wire fence and tracks in the snow. There was only a single bulb over the back door to combat the winter darkness. This alley was one of the few places in town without a string of merry Christmas lights. We supported each other across the slippery surface, trying to avoid trampling the footprints.

Finally, we turned the corner. The flashlight found Percy near the recycling bins. His orange paws flashed busily over a dark blotch against the wall.

Reaching him, we saw Hester Belcher lying face-up, her herringbone pantsuit providing contrast to the fluffy white backdrop. A fir-tree stickpin in her lapel glinted dully in the flashlight's beam. One bare hand stretched out as if reaching for something.

The Millbrook sleigh, perhaps.

Percy pronounced Hester dead with his classic ritual. Sometimes the "litter" was invisible, but tonight, snow churned up in a cloud and landed lightly on Hester's permanently startled expression. I groaned quietly while watching him perform this familiar ceremony for someone I had known, someone I had argued with just hours ago about keeping my pets away from the exhibits.

The sight hit me harder than I might have expected. Despite our differences and Hester's rigid ways, she'd been a fixture in our town and a longtime guardian of Clover Grove's history. That this happened at Christmas made it all the worse.

Edna's flippant attitude switched off, and the professional RN came online. "I'll check for a pulse." Her movements were swift and sure as she knelt beside the fallen woman, but we all knew it was too late. The unnatural angle of Hester's legs told us everything Percy wanted us to know.

Jilly set down the shortbread and pulled out her phone. "I'll call the police."

I pulled out my own phone and switched on the light to take stock of any details that could help determine what happened here. Without the other tracks, it could have been a tragic fall. Instead, it was more likely an ambush.

Someone—or sibling someones—put Hester out of commission and stole the sleigh.

My light found more speckles on the snow. Some were red paint, I was sure. Others appeared to be blood. Hester's bare, clawed fingers showed signs of a fight, and her forehead was scratched, too. A pool of darkness under her arm had melted down to the asphalt. Also blood, most likely.

Keats moved around Hester to show me a clue.

In the snow lay a single jingle bell, a slightly crushed silver orb.

There was more. Something highly unusual for such a scene.

I bent to examine small circles more closely.

Hoofprints.

CHAPTER FOUR

E dna bent over to add both her stronger beam and opinion. "I don't need my track app to tell me that's a miniature horse. Like Clippers."

"Bigger than Clippers. Stockier." I snapped some photos. "The prints are wider and deeper. I'm going to guess a pony. And judging by the pattern, it's not on a lead rope."

"That's strange. Runaway livestock rarely venture so far into town."

"Bocelli met us in town square," I reminded her. The lonely donkey had led me to Clippers, in fact. Both animals currently lived happily with my grandparents. I hoped this pony would find a warm Christmas welcome, too.

Blurred boot prints aligned with the pony's in some places. I got up to follow them and found something even more interesting: two evenly spaced slices in the snow.

Sleigh runners.

"I should call Iris." My eyes shifted to Hester's hand, still reaching, still trying to tell us something even in death. "She needs to know."

Jilly would have told me not to call, but she was still providing details to police dispatch.

I ducked back around the corner and pressed my sister's number.

"Hey, what's up?" Iris said over the roar of the motor in her old car. "Did you get the museum closed okay?"

I looked at the door still propped open. "Not exactly. There's been an incident."

"An incident? What kind of incident? Was anything damaged?"

"I'm afraid so, Iris. You should come over. Where are you?"

"On the way home from Dorset Hills. Had to get a part for the plumber. No one works overtime at Christmas. Tell me what happened."

Jilly came around the corner and slashed her mitten across her throat. Her expression transformed into crime scene schoolmarm and put me on notice.

"Iris, just come," I said. "You can hear all about it from Kellan."

"Kellan? Why Kellan?" Her voice became strident. "Ivy, I deserve to know. That museum is my life."

And Hester's death, unfortunately. "I know, sis. It'll be okay. It always is." She launched into a shrill protest that made me pull the phone away from my ear. "See you soon."

Jilly linked her arm through mine and tugged me back toward Hester's cold resting place. "You shouldn't have called Iris. That falls under police purview."

"I know, but the museum basically belongs to Iris. This is going to break her heart."

Her mitten gave my arm a padded pinch. "It might get worse before it gets better. Some people overheard her argument with Hester."

I turned to stare at Jilly. "It wasn't a big argument. There's no way Iris came back here to commit murder and steal the sleigh, if that's what you're suggesting. She's afraid of horses."

"Horses? What are you talking about?"

"Hoofprints. They're all over, Jilly. Small ones. Like a Shetland pony. You know Iris isn't an animal fan. She avoids the farm when she can."

I couldn't believe that the Galloway clan could all be so different.

"I can't imagine what a pony would be doing here," Jilly said. "But I hope you didn't tell Iris anything important. You know what Kellan says about protocol."

I tuned out Kellan's lectures on protocol whenever I could. If there was an animal in danger, my mind went into overdrive and created a drone inside my head. It had been that way since I got a concussion saving Keats.

The dog came over to me now and nudged my glove. His presence was comforting, as always. It would be okay, just like I told my sister.

Sirens wailed nearby. Soon the alley would be full of police vehicles and flashing lights. Questions would need answering. Statements would need to be given. I had only a moment to do my own due diligence.

"Back in a sec," I told Jilly, dropping her arm.

"Where are you going?"

"Just checking out where the pony went when it left. Kellan won't mind that." She started to protest, and I interrupted. "If he complains, give him some shortbread. It's still over there in the snow beside Hester."

"I can't offer that to anyone now," Jilly called after me. "No one wants corpse cookies."

"Please. Anyone would be lucky to get your cookies. Just stay mum on their provenance. We're not museum staff."

She followed me, and I followed Keats through a gap in the fence. The tracks went out into a field. Hoofprints and boot prints together. The pony had been tethered at this point. Eventually, the sleigh runners stopped, and the prints diverged again. The thief had likely dropped the rope and picked up the sleigh to make better time.

The first police car pulled up to the corner, lights splashing the snow in alternating red and blue. Jilly and I turned back in time to see Kellan jump out. Asher was ahead of him and running toward us. My brother was perpetually driven by the fear that the wife he cherished more than anything on earth would be harmed. "Jilly?" Ash shouted. "Honey? You okay?"

"I'm fine, Asher." He came into the field to hug her and pat her down to make sure. "Unfortunately, Hester Belcher isn't."

"Ivy?" Kellan's voice was concerned but also wary. "Please tell me you're not trampling evidence."

A familiar tension rose between us. He wanted to do things by the book, whereas I just wanted to get the job done quickly.

"Probably am, Chief," I said, walking back. "There are tracks all over the place. We couldn't move without stepping on something."

"Then the answer is *not* to move, isn't it?" His voice was curt.

"Tell that to Percy." The cat had covered Hester's face almost entirely with snow from what I could see now. Very little of it melted because she was already cool. "I had to check on my cat. And then my dog found the hoofprints."

Kellan's eyes closed briefly, no doubt trying to maintain his slippery grip on protocol. "There was a horse on the scene?"

I was standing in front of him now. "It wasn't the getaway vehicle, if that's what you're thinking. A pony can't carry an adult killer. Not easily, anyway. It would be a slow and awkward fade to white."

He opened his eyes. "That's not what I was thinking, but thanks for the image."

"Someone came by car without a horse trailer." I pointed to the tire tracks. "But someone else walked into the field with the pony and stolen Millbrook sleigh."

My beloved rubbed his forehead and sent his police toque

flying. Keats picked it up and delivered it back to Kellan. The dog rarely bothered retrieving. He must pity all of us right now. What was obvious to a sheepdog's nose and sensibilities would take time for the humans to detect and assess.

"Jilly didn't mention a pony on the phone," he said. "But she did say Iris had a fight with the deceased."

"It wasn't a fight, although Hester was gunning for one. Iris kept her cool. I was there eavesdropping."

"How handy," he said. "Sleuthing before there was even a crime or an animal involved."

"There's always an animal involved somehow. I argued with Hester, too. Percy knocked a skull off a shelf."

Kellan raked a hand through his hair, tousling it adorably before yanking the toque back on. "We'll take your statement later. Just go home and get warm."

"I'm not going home when there's a pony at large. It's my duty as a rescuer to make sure she's okay."

"She? Was this pony wearing designer horseshoes?"

I started to laugh and then stopped. "Just a vibe I'm getting. Someone has the stolen sleigh and the pony, so she's in trouble."

"Ergo, she's with a suspect and you're not going after her tonight."

Edna joined us. "Ponies are built for winter, Ivy. Wonderfully thick coats. She'll be fine. We'll rally the Rescue Mafia and find her in daylight."

"The trail could be buried by then," I persisted. "There's not a second to lose."

Kellan's handsome features fell into a scowl. "This is a police investigation, I remind you both. I'll call the shots."

Edna pointed toward the trash bins, now surrounded by police officers and equipment. "Of course, Chief. You'd better get over there before they're all gone."

"Pardon me?" He looked confused.

"Corpse cookies, I believe Jillian called them. Your officers are sprinkling shortbread crumbs all over."

"They're not," Jilly said, "and I didn't call them that. Not for real."

"But I did call Iris," I muttered. "For real."

Kellan was already walking away, but his superior cop hearing picked up my words, and he turned. "You know better."

"She's my sister, Kellan. I didn't give her any details. Just told her to come directly here. She's been out hunting for plumbing parts."

His palm came up. "Don't want to hear it from you. Stick to ponies."

"Is that permission to—?"

The other palm came up to cut me off. "It's an order to proceed directly to Runaway Farm and park yourselves. For real. We'll get there as soon as we can."

Edna watched him go and then shrugged. "He's an irritable man. Are you sure you want to be tied to him for a lifetime?"

Keats gave a ha-ha-ha and took a dive for Edna's calf, which she sidestepped with ease. Meanwhile, Percy hit me square in the back and climbed onto my shoulder. The cat's work was done.

"This lifetime and whatever comes after," I said, as the three of us linked arms again to trudge away. "That cranky cop is the man of my dreams."

CHAPTER FIVE

We were half-way back to the truck when Iris' sedan skidded into the lane and nearly took us out like bowling pins.

"Just circle the car and keep going," Jilly said. "Leave this to Kellan."

Our *true* chief had a different opinion. Keats blocked us and then turned us back with quick dives at our cuffs. Jilly tried to resist, but it was futile. Ultimately, we escorted Iris around to the back in a double circle of headlights. She stayed well behind, perhaps afraid of what she might find at the end of her journey.

Kellan's "official business" mask was latched firmly in place when he rejoined us. That mask divided the man who loved me from the police chief who protected this town.

"I told you to go home, ladies. This is an active investigation."

I opened my mouth to argue, but Jilly clamped down again with her schoolmarm mitten. Kellan's clipped tone suggested he was reaching his level of tolerance for my brand of cowboy justice, even when there was an actual horse in the vicinity, albeit a small one.

"Keats wanted us to come back with Iris," I said. "The dog must have his reasons."

Kellan briefly slipped out of chief mode and rolled his eyes. "We don't take orders from Keats."

Edna cackled. "Since when? I take this dog's orders every day, whether or not I like it." Keats mumbled saucily, and she added, "I've made peace with it. What choice do I have?"

"Just leave the crime scene. Don't make me ask you again."

"This would be exactly the right moment to thank us," Edna continued. "We found the body, preserved the scene, called it in. You're welcome."

Kellan's eyes closed again, and I suspected he was counting to ten. Possibly twenty. "I appreciate that. Now please go home before you contaminate more evidence."

Percy, still perched on my shoulder, let out a defiant meow that made Keats mumble more sass. My pets weren't ready to leave, which meant I needed to stay.

"Just let me follow the hoofprints," I said.

The gloved palm came back up. "Once again, no. We'll document everything. That's what we do, Ivy. Properly. According to police procedure."

The unspoken criticism might have stung if Iris' reputation hadn't been hanging in the balance. I'd helped solve nearly two dozen cases in Clover Grove, but Kellan still viewed my methods as chaotic at best and dangerous at worst. That I'd nearly been killed a few times supported his argument.

"The pony is the key to resolving the crime. You know that."

His gaze was skeptical. "I know nothing of the sort. Yes, there's been overlap with animals in a few cases, but there are plenty more cases without."

Edna snorted. "You might want to rethink your wording, Chief. Sounds like you're bragging about the crime rate."

"That's the last thing I'd brag about." He glanced over our shoulders as the car door opened. "Ivy, I know you're worried about the pony. But right now, I need you to trust me to do my job."

Trust. There was that word again, the one that always seemed to land between us with a clunk whenever a case involved someone I cared about. This time, it involved my sister.

"I am worried about the pony," I said. "But I'm also worried about Iris. It feels like someone set her up. She needs an advocate. Someone to remind you that my sister wouldn't kill her longtime docent or expose a treasured artifact to winter conditions."

Edna's camo shoulder brushed mine as she shrugged. "What if Iris was getting blackmailed and needed to buy someone off?"

We all stared at her, but Jilly was the first to speak. "Not helping, Edna. Iris is innocent, and the police will establish that in due course. Right, Chief?"

"I'll be examining every possible explanation for what happened," he said.

His comment was too vague for my liking, and more importantly, too vague for my dog's. Keats charged at Kellan and delivered a nip that made the chief jump.

"That's going to leave a hole. I've got plenty in my fatigues." Edna turned to me. "You could stop him, Ivy."

Keats came back and leaned into my leg. I could feel his satisfaction. "Unlikely. There are studies that say border collies are more likely to nip than any other breed."

"Call it what it is," Kellan said, bending to rub his shin. "A bite."

"Sheepdogs nip," I continued. "No one reports it like they do with other breeds because it's not serious."

I had accomplished my goal, and perhaps the dog's goal, of distracting Kellan and even venting some of his chiefly steam with tiny pinpricks. As Iris walked up beside me, Kellan was still straightening, and his expression was more disgruntled than imperious.

"What's going on?" Iris asked. "Ivy wouldn't tell me anything. She said you'd fill me in, Kellan."

"Chief Harper," he corrected. "I'm here in a professional capacity. There was an incident."

Iris pulled on leather gloves. "That's the word Ivy used. An incident. But there are four police cars here. It's more than an incident."

"Or just a *big* incident," Edna suggested. "Maybe two of them. One bigger than the other."

"Again, not helping, Edna." Jilly sent over a schoolmarm glare. "Let the chief handle this."

Kellan nodded his thanks to Jilly. "Miss Galloway, where were you this evening?"

"At the salon until just after seven. Then I drove to Dorset Hills to look for a plumbing part. The pipes burst, but the plumber can't make the fix till the morning." She stared at Kellan. "Why do you ask?"

"Because I heard you had a confrontation with Hester Belcher this afternoon."

Iris tipped her head. "One of many, Chief. It's not unusual for two people passionate about history to argue. This was minor in the scheme of things. Tell him, Ivy."

The chiefly palm came up. "Ivy won't be speaking right now."

Keats gave a pant laugh, and I muttered, "Oh yes, I will."

This time Jilly's pinch felt like a certain sheepdog's nip. "Stop it. Both of you."

The dog just repeated his ha-ha-ha.

Iris waved her hands around. "Will someone explain to me why arguing with Hester today was a big deal? Tell me she didn't go to the police to complain about a curatorial difference of opinion."

"She did not," Kellan said.

"*Could* not," I said, pointing behind him.

Iris stood on tiptoe. She was several inches shorter than I was and looked petite without her heels. "What is going on? Did Hester fall?"

"In a manner of speaking, yes," I said. "She was probably pushed."

"Tackled," Edna added. "There were visible contusions. But as a medical professional, I can say with confidence that she didn't suffer long."

My sister's mouth dropped open, and leather-clad fingers covered her lips. "Are you saying she's—"

"Dead as a doornail." Edna didn't sound like a medical professional now. "If it's any consolation, she likely died preserving the Millbrook sleigh."

Iris gave a little screech behind her glove. Then the glove moved slightly, and she whispered, "You cannot possibly think I had anything to do with this, Kel— Chief Harper. Poor, dear Hester."

Edna snorted. "The 'dear' is overkill, Iris. Figuratively speaking."

Kellan swept his toque off and flung it deliberately this time. It was back before he knew it, in the same teeth that nipped him only minutes ago. "Desist, all of you. Miss Gallaway, you argued with the victim. Tell me more about that."

After collecting herself, Iris forged on. "Hester and I disagreed about recent changes to the museum. She wanted more security for the Millbrook sleigh. Climate control, a glass case, additional locks. Increased staffing." Her shoulders sagged. "I guess she was right. If I'd listened to her, maybe the Founder's sleigh would still be here and Hester would be alive to say, 'I told you so.'"

The guilt in her voice made my heart ache. Iris was often the first to take responsibility, even for things that weren't remotely her fault. It was one of her greatest strengths as a curator and business owner, but right now it was making her sound like she had something to hide.

"I can't believe the sleigh was stolen," she continued. "This is a disaster. The Millbrooks entrusted me with a priceless family heirloom, and now it's gone."

"We'll do everything we can to recover it," Kellan assured her. "So, how long would you estimate Ms. Belcher was alone here?"

"Maybe ninety minutes? It depends on whether any visitors came in after the reception ended. The security camera out front will show that. Anthony, our assistant, had permission to leave early to go to a friend's Christmas party. Hester wanted to stay later. She loved being alone here, cataloging or researching. Or at least she loved our previous site. We were still adjusting to the new location, but we would have been fine. Eventually."

Iris' voice cracked on the last word. It was probably the moment when she truly understood Hester was gone. The difficult, demeaning—and yet brilliant—woman who'd made Iris' professional life richer and more challenging would never be a thorn in her side again.

Unless you called leaving Iris on the hook for her murder being a thorn, which I did.

"We'll go over all of this in more detail," Kellan said, touching the phone in his pocket as it rang and then ignoring it. "That's all that needs to be said at the moment."

The pressure in my throat gave way. "It needs to be said that my sister is not a killer, Chief Harper." My words were so harsh and loud that all the officers turned, and Asher loped over.

"Chief? What's going on? I mean, besides the obvious." He directed the words at his *work* boss, Kellan, but his eyes were on his *life* boss, Jilly.

"Emotions are running a little high," Jilly said. "The Chief is pointing fingers at Iris. Receipts from the hardware store should take care of this, no?" She turned to my sister. "Iris, you just need to prove you were somewhere else this evening."

I was happy my best friend had taken over as lead investigator, because my emotions really were running high. That Kellan could consider Iris guilty for even a second distressed me.

Iris patted her pockets and squawked in alarm. "I paid in cash and didn't bother with the receipt. The plumbing part wasn't expensive."

Jilly forced a smile. "It's okay, Iris. The cashier will remember you. Or there will be security cameras." She turned to her husband. "Could you call right now?"

Asher looked at Kellan. "How about it, Chief? I know there's due process, but this is family."

"You need a new process," Edna suggested. "One that rules out family fast. This is hardly the first time. You Galloways are a busy bunch."

Kellan gave Edna a look that took her humor from a boil to a simmer. "Officer Galloway, take your sister to your cruiser and keep her out of the way."

Asher snapped his fingers. "Ivy, come."

"Not *that* sister," Kellan said. "The person of interest."

My brother shrugged. "They both argued with the victim, Chief. Ivy's more likely to kill than Iris, if you ask me." He tapped his head. "She's never been quite right, since—"

"*Asher.*"

Kellan's voice drowned out Jilly's, but only slightly. I let Keats deliver my rebuttal. The dog did so with such flair that my athletic brother nearly went airborne and flailed as he regained his balance.

"Let's go, Iris," Ash said. "We'll track down your cashier. Which hardware store was it?" He was oddly gentle with our older sister as he escorted her to the car. Then his voice drifted back, "There are only two hardware stores in Dog Town and neither is called 'Plumbing Plus.'"

Kellan sighed. "That doesn't sound promising."

"Find the proof quickly. Please," I said. "She's not a suspect."

"She's a person of interest. There's a difference."

The distinction felt meaningless when it came to my sister's reputation. In a town the size of Clover Grove, being questioned by the police was as good as a guilty verdict in the court of public opinion. Justine Schalow would have a field day with this. I could already see the *Tattler* headline: "Museum curator's career goes up in smoke after deadly disagreement."

"Let me see the museum," Iris called back before getting into Asher's vehicle. "I need to understand what happened."

"The museum is a crime scene," Kellan said. "You can't go inside right now."

"It's my responsibility—"

"Your responsibility is to cooperate with this investigation." Kellan's tone left no room for negotiation. "Let us do our job. We'll move as fast as we can. The stakes are high."

"Because there's a killer on the loose," Jilly said, watching Asher ease Iris inside the car and close the door.

"Probably two," Edna piped up. "Anyone know a dynamic duo with an interest in antiques?"

"We'll interview the Langmans, of course," Kellan said. His phone buzzed again. Annoyance flickered across his handsome features, which gave me an idea about the caller. "The security feeds will identify other possibilities."

"I bet the mayor is worried." I watched for confirmation on his face and got it. "Meryl will want this resolved quickly so the tree lighting can go on tomorrow as planned. It's the event of the year. The sticky pine sap that holds this community together."

Kellan's eyes narrowed. "Naturally, the mayor is worried about someone being murdered and a valuable artifact stolen. The tree lighting is the least of her concerns right now. And mine."

"You're a terrible liar, and I respect that about you, Chief," Edna said. "Meryl has her mayoral robes in a knot, and we all know it. Why not let us help you?"

"I have a trained team, thank you. The mayor has increased staffing twice in two years. We'll be fine."

"Do you have an expert in hoofprints on staff?" I asked. "Because I'd love to confer."

"The hoofprints will be documented and investigated thorough-ly." Kellan sounded exasperated. I was pushing too hard. "This is a murder investigation first and a rescue mission second."

Keats mumbled something that sounded like a suggestion to reverse those priorities. Percy's tail lashed in agreement around my left ear. Kellan might be in denial, but my pets knew the pony might be the key to everything.

"You've got to admit it's uncommon for a pony to canter into the middle of a crime scene," I said. "Someone brought her here and attached her to the Millbrook sleigh. When we find her—"

"When *we* find her," he interrupted, sweeping his arm back to his team, "We'll question her thoroughly about her whereabouts and intentions."

Edna cackled again. "Good luck getting information out of a pony, Chief. They're notoriously tight-lipped around authority figures. Far be it from me to indulge vanity, but Ivy usually gets animals to spill their secrets."

"If I need a pony-whisperer, I know where to find her. At Runaway Farm." His eyes shifted to me again. "Go home, Ivy. You're done here."

"But—"

"No buts." He stepped closer, lowering his voice so only I could hear. "Please. I know you want to help your sister. I know you're worried about the pony. But charging off into a snowstorm following hoofprints won't solve this case. It'll just give me one more thing to worry about."

The plea in his voice cut through my anger. Kellan wasn't just being difficult or territorial. He was genuinely concerned about my safety. Our safety. There was no telling what might happen if we encountered a murderer or two in dark fields.

But Kellan was also wrong. The hoofprints weren't just a curiosity or a side detail. They were the thread that would unravel this entire mess if only someone pulled hard enough. I'd been around the pasture enough times to know that.

"Fine," I said. "We'll go home."

Relief flooded Kellan's features. "Thank you. I'll call you later, okay? Once things settle down here."

I nodded, knowing I'd only dig myself deeper into a hole if I spoke.

My sister needed help, and the only way to do that was to find out who really killed Hester Belcher. The trail started with one runaway pony.

Jilly linked her arm through mine as we trudged back toward my truck with Edna. "Are we really going home?"

"Yep." I opened the back door and let the pets jump in. "I didn't promise to stay there."

"It was implied." Jilly's breath formed clouds in the cold air. "Chasing a pony in a blizzard would be dangerous enough even without a killer at large."

"That's why we have Edna."

The older woman perked up. "Exactly right. We need Gertie and Minnie, too."

"And Cori Hogan," I said. "The Rescue Mafia may even know where the Shetland pony belongs. With enough reinforcements, this could be a short expedition."

"An expedition Kellan explicitly forbade," Jilly said.

Edna hopped easily into the back seat and welcomed the pets onto her lap. "Jillian, it's a very simple equation. Horses over husbands." Closing the door, she called through the glass. "Let's deploy."

CHAPTER SIX

I finished my chores in record time the next morning, although farm manager Charlie wouldn't have awarded me a gold star for quality. My body went through the motions, but my brain was very much elsewhere. Sleep, or lack thereof, had done absolutely nothing to remedy what had happened last night. Hester Belcher was still dead. Iris was still a suspect. The pony was still missing. And Kellan was still furious with me for breaking what he considered a promise.

I'd promised to go home, not *stay* home. It was a technicality I highlighted for him in the metaphorical couples' handbook. Then I chastised him for not playing fair, either.

A large group of my rescuer friends had geared up, rallied about half a mile from the museum and marched into a farm field to begin the search for the pony.

We were prepared for darkness, snow and wintery hardship.

We were *not* prepared for headlights, motors and an instant ambush.

A battalion of snowmobiles surrounded us. The man in front on a police Ski-Doo flashed a smug smile through his visor. Then he circled closer and closer like a sheepdog till he'd cut me off from my herd. Concerns about my actual sheepdog's safety kept me from jumping onto my brother and pummeling him. Even Edna stood down quickly. She recognized several of the machines in Asher's crew, and they belonged to men who'd never be welcome in her bunker.

In short, we'd been outplayed.

But the game wasn't over. Far from it.

Kellan was up a point, but I could even the score with scones and casual sleuthing.

"We need information," I told the pets as I finished up in the barn and let them escort me to the truck. "Luckily, we know exactly where to start."

Given the heavy snow, it took 10 minutes longer than usual to reach Mandy's Country Store. Despite the urgency of the mission, I took a moment to admire the strings of white lights around the windows and along the eaves. The wreath on the front door was decorated with tiny hand-painted ceramic gingerbread men, pies and cupcakes. I recognized the work of my talented friend, Mabel Halliday. When I got a free moment, I'd stop by her store and commission a custom wreath with a farm theme.

Mandy McCain let us in and then locked the door again. We had about 20 minutes before she officially opened for customers, and I had to make the most of the time. No one in Clover Grove had better access to the grapevine than Mandy, and no one was more discreet about it. She shared information with me only because of her guilt over nearly getting me killed by her murderous grand-mother, Myrtle McCain.

"Your coffee awaits," Mandy said, gesturing to a cup the size of a bucket on the long counter by the window. "I'll get your breakfast. You want sweet or super-sweet?"

I stomped the snow off my boots and walked to my usual place. "No wrong answer. Surprise me."

She went behind the counter, moving quickly and with confidence. Before Myrtle departed in handcuffs, my childhood friend had been painfully shy and almost skeletal. Mandy was still very slim under that apron, but she looked healthy now. In fact, she seemed to grow happier by the day running this community hub and amassing an encyclopedic knowledge of everyone's business.

While we waited, Keats and Percy fanned out to do reconnaissance, cataloging the signs and scents of recent visitors. Mandy would translate relevant findings into words for me in due course.

A few sips of strong black coffee made me sit a little straighter on my stool. Kellan's sneak snowmobile move had stolen some of *my* confidence, but it would be replenished easily enough through my normal channels, including a massive intake of carbohydrates.

Mandy delivered a plate that held a couple of magnificent gingerbread people wearing overalls made of blue frosting.

"I can't eat those," I said. "They're personalized perfection. Art."

"Figured you'd say that, so I'll box them to go." She slid another plate in front of me with a gingerbread snowman, cranberry cake and a custard tart I hadn't tried before. "How's that?"

"Just right." Breaking off the snowman's head, I popped it into my mouth. "I need something spicy to get the wheels turning."

She slid onto the stool beside me and picked up her own bucket of coffee. "Sounds like you'll need the fuel, if my sources are correct. I heard about Hester and the stolen sleigh. How's Iris holding up?"

"Not great." I broke off more gingerbread and shook my head. "She didn't eat or sleep, according to her text earlier. Just kept going over everything that happened yesterday, trying to figure out where it all went wrong."

"Poor thing. Iris worked so hard on that museum expansion." Mandy glanced at the parking lot to make sure no one else had arrived. "I heard Kellan questioned her for hours last night."

"Two hours. He was professional about it, but you know how it looks."

"I know how it *feels*, remember. After what happened with

Myrtle, I spent plenty of time with the chief trying to figure out where it all went wrong." She tucked a tendril of blonde hair behind her ear and let her pale blue eyes wander. "Never did get it sorted."

I used the last chunk of gingerbread to point at her. "Myrtle's problem, not yours. Look what you've done to expand her small empire."

Forcing a smile, she pointed back at me. "You want to know about Hester."

It wasn't a question, but I nodded anyway.

"She was a regular here," Mandy continued, as I picked up a fork and moved onto the cranberry cake with its white chocolate chunks. "Came in every morning at eight sharp, ordered black coffee and a bran muffin, and started complaining. The coffee was too hot or too cold. The muffin didn't have enough raisins. Or too many raisins. The newspaper arrived late. Hester even found fault with a perfect sunrise. Too bright, she said."

"Lines up with what Iris shared about her." I swallowed the last bite of gingerbread. "But she respected her as a professional."

"Hester loved the museum. Talked about it constantly. The new exhibits, the expansion, the artifacts. It was her whole life after she retired from that law firm."

I tried the custard tart and found it a nice balance to the ginger-bread. There were eggs in it, and a little protein would keep me from keeling over mid-morning. Sustained sleuthing required energy. "Did she mention any problems? Conflicts with anyone?"

Mandy's laugh was sharp and short. "Ivy, Hester had conflicts with everyone. I'm honestly surprised someone didn't snap sooner."

My coffee cup paused halfway to my lips. "Go on."

"I don't like speaking ill of the dead, and Hester definitely had good qualities. She was brilliant, dedicated and passionate about local history. With people, however, she was like a porcupine juggling balloons."

The image made me smile. "Tell me about her enemies. Real enemies, not just people she dissed and annoyed."

Mandy straightened on her stool, eyes glazing as she pondered. Aside from baking, this was her superpower. She'd been hanging around the store since early childhood, charting the intricate social web of Clover Grove, keeping track of feuds and alliances, knowing who owed whom and why. "Well, your sister reached the top of the list recently, I'm afraid. Hester didn't approve of Iris' modern ideas about the museum. Thought she was pandering to the mayor and turning the place into a tourist trap instead of a proper historical institution."

My fork clattered on the plate. "Iris was trying to get more funding and visitors. Keep the museum doors open."

"I know, but Hester saw it as dumbing down history." Mandy ticked off fingers. "They argued about the taxidermy exhibit. Hester wanted the animals gone. They argued about the Christmas decorations. Hester thought they were too frivolous for a serious cultural destination. They argued about allowing pets inside—"

"That one I understand," I cut in. Percy was on a shelf in the grocery aisle now, trying to knock something off. It was his signature move.

"Most of all, Hester and Iris argued about security for the Founder's sleigh," Mandy picked up again. "Hester wanted it locked up tight. Iris wanted it accessible for the community to enjoy."

"That's what the Millbrooks stipulated, but keeping it accessible turned out to be a bad idea. If the sleigh had been behind glass, Hester might be here right now slagging your bran muffins."

Mandy tipped her head until her skinny ponytail flopped. "If someone wanted the sleigh enough to kill for it, glass and locks wouldn't have stopped them."

"I guess not. The Langmans keyed some glass there yesterday in the middle of the reception." My fork started moving again, slicing into the cranberry cake. "Who else?"

"Powell Nobbs." Mandy's expression turned as sour as the cranberries I chewed. "He bankrolled half the museum expansion and thought it meant he could dictate every decision. Wanted his name on plaques and signs. Hester detested him."

"I remember Powell from the reception. He hated the taxidermy exhibit, too."

"That changed Hester's mind about it. When Powell lobbied to have those animals removed and replaced with 'proper art,' Hester told him where he could stick his art, and it wasn't in a display case."

I nearly choked on my next sip of coffee. "She said that to a major benefactor?"

"In front of witnesses. Powell threatened to pull his funding if Hester wasn't removed from her position."

My investigative instincts, honed through quite a few murder cases, started tingling. "That's a solid motive."

"For him or for Hester?" Mandy shrugged. "Because it could go either way. He wanted her gone. She wanted him gone."

"But Powell's still here, which makes him a viable suspect to take over the limelight from Iris. I wonder if he has an alibi."

Keats returned from his exploration and directed his eerie blue eye my way. It encouraged me to keep Powell Nobbs at the top of my mental list. I might as well ask around, since Asher's snowmobile militia held me back from pursuing the pony. The trail would be buried by now.

"And then there's the dastardly sister duo," Mandy went on. "Can't discount them."

My fork drifted down again. Little could put me off my sweets, yet somehow the Langmans managed. "Heddy and Kaye were at the museum yesterday, like I said. After trying to liberate a porcelain platter, they hovered near the sleigh like vultures over roadkill."

"Apt description." Mandy sipped from her own massive mug. "They've been trying to get their hands on the Millbrook sleigh for years. I heard they made multiple offers to the family, all rejected. They even showed up at the museum expansion planning meetings, trying to convince Iris not to display it."

"Let me guess... Hester threw them out."

"With glee and strong language. The Langmans threatened legal action, claiming Hester was slandering them and interfering with legitimate business. Nothing came of it, but the bad blood was there."

I added notes to my mental list, creating an imaginary map of grudges and grievances. In my old HR job, I'd mediated conflicts between executives that made Clover Grove's feuds look like playground disputes. But those corporate battles usually ended in golden parachutes, not murder.

"Anyone else?" I prompted.

Mandy's eyes drifted to the window again, and she nodded. "Isaac Gherkin."

"The homesteader? What did he have against Hester?"

"It started out as a general protest against the museum expansion. Isaac believes all development is destruction. He thought the town should've spent that money on sustainable agriculture programs instead of celebrating our inglorious past."

"It's not all inglorious," I said. "There are plenty of good people among the gangsters."

"Absolutely. Their descendants gather at your inn to celebrate holidays. I don't think Isaac notices upstanding citizens."

I didn't have a good fix on Isaac Gherkin. Just a vague recollection of a gruff man in his sixties who lived on the outskirts of town and raised free-range heritage poultry.

"Isaac and Hester had shouting matches at town council meetings and he protested outside the museum with placards during the reno," Mandy went on. "He complained about wasteful spending and historical whitewashing. Hester called the police on him twice. The second time, she allegedly threw a cup of coffee at his head."

"Allegedly?"

"Hester claimed it slipped from her hands. The coffee was cold, so no harm done, but Isaac swore she'd 'get what was coming to her.'"

"That sounds like a legit threat."

"Kellan thought so. He brought Isaac in for questioning, but there was no evidence of anything beyond heated words and embarrassment."

Percy meowed, and we turned to find him perched on a seat at a corner table. It was his way of telling me to pay attention to something, but I wasn't sure what had caught my inquisitive feline's interest.

The message landed for Mandy, however. "Oh, right. Anthony Cork came for lunch yesterday and sat right there. He's the opposing voice on Hester Belcher. Anthony saw past her abrasiveness and said he was lucky to land a mentor like her."

"They seemed close when I was at the museum reception." I tried the cranberry cake again and then swigged some coffee. "There are two sides to every story. And who knows, maybe something was happening in Hester's life to make her so testy. Like a health problem."

Mandy nodded. "I always like to give the benefit of the doubt, having been misjudged myself for so long. I'm sure Anthony's devastated today. I don't think he..."

Her voice drifted off, and Keats prompted her with a poke in the knee.

"What?" I asked. "You can tell me, Mandy."

Getting up, she smoothed her apron and then went behind the counter to box my gingerbread farmers. "Anthony wasn't as fond of Iris. He didn't say so, but I sensed it and wondered if Hester had been planting seeds of discontent."

"I got the same idea when I met him yesterday. He said Iris wasn't around much. Later, Hester accused my sister of treating the museum like a hobby instead of a priority."

Mandy came back with the coffeepot. She nudged the custard tart toward me, and I shook my head. The unthinkable had happened. I was full after a serving sized only for three.

A sleek black sedan pulled into the lot outside and fishtailed before parking. Fancy wheels like that weren't practical, nor within a typical homesteader's budget. The tall man who climbed out wore a long wool coat and fedora. Even from a distance, I could tell his blue scarf was high end. There was something irresistible about the drape of cashmere.

Mandy walked over to unlock the door and then stopped. "Oh. It's Powell Nobbs. He's never been here before. Not in person, anyway. Sometimes he sends his housekeeper to pick up baked goods."

I stared out the window. "Bet he came hoping to hear the scuttlebutt. He'll get an earful when the place fills."

"That's for sure. He's already being tried and convicted over breakfast tables throughout town."

At the bottom of the stairs, Powell looked up and saw me perched beside the window. There was no way he sensed the vibration of Keats' low growl, but the timing was right.

The older man's face was ruddy under his fedora, and the flush seemed to deepen as he caught my eye. Raising one hand, I waved and then beckoned. What a great opportunity to interview a person of interest without going out of my way. Coincidences like these were easy to explain to Kellan.

Too easy.

Powell turned and hurried back to his car. Then, he shot out of the parking lot before I could even get my parka zipped. He skidded on the highway as he gunned it out of sight.

Mandy looked at me quizzically. "What was that about? Guilty conscience?"

I shrugged. "Possibly. I get that reaction sometimes. Cori calls me the 'first lady of law enforcement,' which probably puts some people off. Shame, though. I wanted to talk to Powell." After a second, I added, "Did you notice a limp?"

"Actually, yeah. He was so red it looked like he'd run a marathon and come out the worse for it. I'd say Powell Nobbs is stressed today."

I got up and gathered my things. "I would be too if I had to give up your baked goods. Luckily, the early sleuth got the sweets."

"Powell was heading towards town, so he'll visit the Berry Good Café instead. I lose a lot of business to them because of their prime location."

"They can't rival your baking, Mandy," I assured her, pulling on my gloves.

"Some would disagree. Scones are their morning mainstay, and I rarely make them. As a baker, I find them boring."

"Not much of a scone girl, myself," I said.

She signaled for me to wait at the door and went back to the counter. Then she handed me a box stained with deliciously promising grease spots. "For energy or bribes. I consider both fair use of good butter." When I reached the bottom of the stairs, she called, "Be careful, Ivy. Whoever killed Hester is still out there. They've already murdered once to get what they wanted."

"The Founder's sleigh?"

"Maybe the sleigh was just an excuse. A cover for something else entirely."

I reached down and found Keats waiting for my gloved fingertips to arrive on his head. He sensed my unease, but I already felt better than when I had arrived. Thanks to Mandy, I had a list to keep me busy. Heddy and Kaye Langman, Isaac Gherkin, Powell Nobbs. Four suspects, each with a motive. Iris' alibi remained weak, but my sister wasn't capable of murder, no matter how much Hester had provoked her.

All I needed to do was prove someone else *was* capable. That's where I'd focus my energy if the police still hadn't detained the killer by the time I located the pony.

As I waved goodbye to Mandy, my phone buzzed. Kellan's text offered a brief good morning followed by the actual message: "Stay out of this investigation. I mean it, Ivy."

"Just getting coffee," I typed back. "Very innocent. Much law-abiding."

His response was immediate. "I smell a lie."

The man knew me too well. It was both endearing and inconvenient.

After sliding into the truck after the pets, I typed, "Have you found the pony? Say yes, and you'll smell manure. Because I'll go straight home and make festive fertilizer."

I waited over a minute for a response and didn't get one. Then I pulled out and headed toward town.

"As always, boys," I said, "No answer qualifies as permission."

CHAPTER SEVEN

The Berry Good Café sat on a prime corner of Main Street in Clover Grove. Today, fresh snow covered its cheerful red awning, and the warmth from bodies inside fogged its windows. Unlike Mandy's Country Store, which drew a steady trickle of loyal regulars throughout the day, this spot commanded the morning rush. All the parking spots within a block were full, so I had to circle twice before I could try to wedge my truck into a questionable space between high snowdrifts.

"No sign of Powell's sweet ride," I said. "Maybe he decided to head home. Clover Grove in winter isn't the place for cars like that. Even with a truck, I'm grateful for chains."

Keats mumbled something that sounded like a command to hurry. Was I missing something? Probably. The boys were always a few steps ahead of me, even when I got an early start.

"Okay, let's go." I shoved the door with my shoulder to get it open because the cold was making it stick. "We'll make this fast. I want to head back out to the field to look for that pony. Cori and Edna will figure out a way to elude the snowmobile army. If Powell's not here, we'll just grab a coffee to go."

Keats mumbled something skeptical from the passenger seat.

"I resent your implication, buddy. I can be efficient when properly motivated. And I'm motivated."

The pets trotted along the sidewalk in the lead. Normally, no one hassled me if I took them inside for a quick visit. That's probably because I was here with Kellan often on date nights. Sometimes, being the first lady of law enforcement worked in my favor.

I paused at the front door to admire a wreath covered in tiny ceramic coffee mugs of different sizes, shapes and colors. Mabel had hit it out of the park again. I admired her craftsmanship and ingenuity.

Keats shoved in front of me and pushed me back as I reached for the handle. Then he circled to herd me across the storefront to the mouth of the alley. It led to a back patio that was typically closed in winter. Percy scaled to my shoulder as I walked down the alley ahead of the dog. When we neared the end, we found the entrance to the patio partially blocked by a commercial dumpster that was nearly overflowing. In its shadow stood two figures in matching khaki pants and black puffer jackets.

The Langman sisters.

Were they lurking here because they saw me drive past? Probably. It was nice to be popular.

"Percy, turn on the charm," I whispered. "Keats, you have my permission to nip if necessary."

The dog's exuberant ha-ha-ha suggested he didn't require permission to do what came naturally. His breed didn't earn top billing for nipping by listening to handlers.

Heddy and Kaye didn't notice us at first. Their gray heads nearly touched as they hunched over a phone. Kaye held the device while Heddy jabbed at the screen with bare fingers. Their mouths moved in what looked like heated disagreement, but I couldn't make out the words until I got a little closer.

"—telling you, we need to move fast." Heddy's voice echoed slightly in the alley. "Before someone else gets the same idea."

"I heard you the first three times," Kaye said. "I'm not an idiot."

"No? You're the one who thought we should wait."

"For a respectful interval. It's called decorum, Heddy."

"It's called losing out on the biggest score of our careers. Dad would be ashamed if we missed this chance."

I had hoped we'd get to hear more, but something alerted them to our presence, and they looked up, surprised and then annoyed at seeing me. Kaye pocketed the phone instantly.

"Hi ladies." My boots clomped over the last few yards. "Fancy meeting you back here. Guess you never know where Santa might drop the antiques. Wouldn't be your first time dumpster diving for treasure."

Heddy rolled her eyes. "Your mother sent us on a wild garbage chase, yes. I haven't forgiven her. How about you, Kaye?"

"Dahlia's unforgivable list is long," Kaye said. "For starters, she should have quit reproducing before you arrived, Ivy. Six kids? Excessive."

"Can't argue with that." I blocked the alley so they couldn't easily pass to get out. "It gets so noisy at family dinners. Yours must be so civilized. Just the two of you scheming over your phones."

"Scheming? Not at all," Kaye said. "When you run a successful business, there's always something important to discuss. I suppose you wouldn't know about that. Runaway Inn never took off, did it?"

The jab hurt, and I knew it showed. I truly wanted the inn to be a success and justify Hannah Pemberton's faith in selling it to me for a song. Unfortunately, it was marked by murder early on, and we'd had trouble shaking off the stigma. We were never rolling in cash, especially because I'd chosen the expensive hobby of animal rescue.

"Not yet, but it will," I said. "Maybe you two could give me some pointers. The Langman Legacy seems to be thriving, and you own that lovely country home where you stashed the cat you stole from Gertie Rhodes."

"We *found* Fleecy," Kaye said. "Cats always gravitate to us."

Percy set out to make the second part true. He jumped from my shoulder and landed lightly on Kaye's. Her eyes widened, but her hand came up to steady him. That's why I couldn't utterly detest the sisters. They were always kind to cats, even the one they stole.

"Your problem is you're too soft," Heddy said, patting Percy, too. I presumed she was speaking to the cat until she added, "Business requires a certain ruthlessness. You can't be a yes-man. Or woman, in your case."

I laughed. "Tell that to the Chief of Police. He doesn't find me particularly pliable. I'm planning to defy him today and go searching for a missing pony. Do you know anything about that, ladies?"

"A pony?" Heddy's brow furrowed. "Why would we know anything about your menagerie?"

I checked in with Keats and decided she was telling the truth. He had them pinned with his blue eye, but both paws stayed planted on the snow-covered asphalt.

Kaye reached up to pat Percy again, and the cat leaned into her bare hand. "Surely, you didn't come here expecting to find a pony on a café patio, Ivy. We all know you're easily confused after that head injury, but you're not entirely stupid."

"Aw, thanks. That means a lot, coming from someone whose sister pretty much called her an idiot."

Heddy glared at me. "It's a term of endearment for us. If it bothers you, that's more proof you're too soft."

She was discounting the various killers I'd tackled, not to mention the duel I'd once fought with the sisters themselves in an old mansion. I was soft on animals, hard on crime, and wouldn't hesitate to take the Langmans down if I found proof they were behind what happened to Hester. With this slippery pair, it would take some doing to get the facts.

Jerking a gloved thumb over my shoulder, I said, "I'm here on a breakfast run. Mandy was out of scones. Thought I'd find out what all the fuss is about."

"Waste of time and calories." Kaye's nose wrinkled. "Their scones are all fat, no substance. Rather like your sister's fancy museum expansion."

This jab hit home, too, but I hid it better. Keats leaned against my leg and released a low grumble some might mistake as a growl. In fact, Heddy stepped back. Kaye held her ground, perhaps because she had custody of my cat.

"That's a little harsh, don't you think?" I asked. "It's a good thing Percy likes you."

Kaye's features softened as she stroked the cat's chin. "Such a handsome boy. Aren't you the clever one?"

He purred and leaned into her fingers. Strategist or traitor? Time would tell.

"Percy's always had excellent taste." I paused before adding, "In people he can manipulate."

Kaye laughed. "Fair enough. He's playing me, and I'm letting him. That's the feline way, isn't it?"

"Definitely." I noticed Heddy assessing the space around me to see if they could push past. They could, but it would mean dealing with the canine gatekeeper. Just the same, I'd have to pick up the pace before they bolted. "You both seem very chipper, given what happened last night."

Kaye's hand stilled on Percy. "What do you mean?"

"Oh, please, Kaye. No one's better connected than you two. You know about the incident at the museum."

Her gray hair brushed against the cat's fluff as she nodded, picking up some static. "Hester Belcher was murdered. How tragic."

"Yet you and Heddy look positively radiant."

The sisters exchanged a look that lasted a fraction of a second too long. They were so close they didn't need to use words. I couldn't say the same about my own sisters, but Jilly and I were masters of silent communication, and it came in handy.

"It's cold today, which brings out color in anyone," Kaye said. "We're both saddened by a death in the community."

"Hester's death. By foul play," I reminded her.

Kaye's hand dropped away from Percy, and she crossed her arms. "I won't pretend to be overcome by grief for Hester Belcher. She was a miserable woman who went out of her way to slander us and make our lives difficult."

"If I heard right, she was just protecting the museum's collection from sale to the highest bidder," I countered.

Heddy stepped forward and took over. "Hester hoarded pieces that belonged in the hands of proper collectors. The Millbrook sleigh, for instance. Do you know how many times we approached the Founder's family about acquiring it? Years of carefully cultivating a relationship torpedoed by Hester's poison."

"She told them we were crooks and con artists," Kaye added. "Spread vicious rumors about our business practices. We're women of honor."

"You keyed a glass case only yesterday. Where was the honor in that?"

Keats gave a pant laugh, and Heddy stared down at him, perplexed. She snapped her fingers in his face. "Stop your weird noises."

Kaye pulled her sister back a step. "Don't let them knock you off balance, Heddy. That's part of Ivy's game. She's just trying to deflect suspicion from the obvious killer. Everyone knows the chief grilled Iris last night. I don't envy him the job of putting her away. Prison time is hard on the whole family."

Keats nudged my hand to keep me grounded. Reading people was my specialty, and I couldn't give in to emotion. Right now, I was sensing these two were nervous despite their bravado. They were standing here without hats and gloves and seemed immune to the cold. Like reptiles, only less sluggish.

"Kellan won't have trouble proving Iris is innocent. My sister had no motive. Losing her longtime docent is a professional and personal blow. Meanwhile, you two had heated run-ins with Hester and made a blatant play for the sleigh yesterday. Witnessed it myself."

"Good thing we have a bulletproof alibi." Heddy pulled out her phone and then swiped through screens with swishes and taps. "We were both home all evening and can prove it."

Kaye pushed the phone down. "We don't owe Ivy any explanation. She's butting in where she doesn't belong."

"True, but she's persistent and annoying, Kaye. We have enough on our plates without sidestepping her. Let's show her the proof."

Heddy didn't wait for her sister's agreement before turning her phone around. The screen displayed what looked like the feed from a security camera marked with a timestamp from yesterday evening. Leaning in, I saw footage of the interior of The Langman Legacy antiques store. Both sisters moved through the frame, checking displays, adjusting inventory, locking up for the night. It looked choreographed. Too tidy by half.

"After that, we went upstairs to our apartment over the store," Heddy said. "We have time-stamped footage showing both of us at home during the entire evening." Her smile was smug. "Satisfied?"

"I'm not the one you need to satisfy."

"The chief will be more than satisfied, I'm sure," she said.

Kellan wasn't the one they needed to satisfy, either. The judges were here with us in the cold alley, dressed in fur and little parkas.

The judge leaning into my leg wasn't at all satisfied. Keats didn't need security footage to know the Langmans were lying. Maybe not about killing Hester, but about something. The canine mumble that followed confirmed it.

"Video footage can be faked," I suggested. "I've seen it with my own eyes."

"We're antiques dealers, not tech wizards," Heddy said, putting her phone away. "Let's leave this to your very capable brother to confirm. We spoke to him this morning. Voluntarily, I might add."

I reached out for my cat, who eluded me. Percy wasn't done yet. "Because you knew you'd be at the top of the suspect list? It's smart to get ahead of the story. That's what a good businessperson would do. Someone who isn't soft, like me."

Heddy simply smiled. "We're not soft, but we're not guilty. End of any story you might want to tell."

Percy hopped to Heddy's shoulder, perhaps sensing she was the weak link. She was usually the less discreet of the two sisters. The cat rubbed against her cheek, purring so loudly I could hear it through the cable knit hat pulled over my ears. Heddy's jaw slackened as he worked his fluffy wiles. There was already a lot of orange fur on her scarf. Percy must be pumping it out with the purr.

"My cat is quite the judge of character," I said. "You must be innocent."

"Of course we are." Kaye's whitening fingers reached for him again. Any more feline charm and she'd have frostbite. "We may have wanted Hester out of our way, but murder had no part in the plan."

"So, there *was* a plan?" I asked. "To get Hester out of the way?"

Heddy shook her head. "Nice try. Our plan was to outlive her, which should have been easy. She must have been eighty."

"Not that old," Kaye said. "Though she looked it. Bitterness ages a person."

I mused about their possible plan. "You *really* wanted that sleigh so it must have been very valuable. Maybe you hired someone to steal it and things went wrong."

"Such a vivid imagination, Ivy. Sounds like a thriller movie." Heddy's laugh was brittle. "We may be good businesswomen, but the antiques trade doesn't cover thieves and hitmen."

Percy kneaded his paws against Heddy's shoulder, claws catching in her puffer jacket. She didn't seem to mind, continuing to stroke him gently.

Kaye thrust her hands in her pockets and stared at me. "Why waste time harassing us in an alley when you could be finding the real killer? And more importantly, finding the Millbrook sleigh. Make no mistake, we'll absolutely try to buy it once it's recovered. The piece deserves to be cherished by a responsible owner. It shouldn't be left to disintegrate in a municipal museum without proper climate control."

"That's a decision for the Millbrook family," I reminded them. "Last I heard, the sleigh wasn't for sale."

"Everything's for sale at the right price," Kaye said. Her sister had used nearly the same words yesterday. It was obviously the family motto.

Percy jumped back onto my shoulder, calling it quits on the Langmans. Keats still wasn't happy, but there wasn't much we could do in this alley.

It was time to regroup. I'd leave these good businesswomen to the police and refocus on my main priority, which was the pony. My belief that the small equine was the key to the mystery hadn't changed. I was just stalling until I could get back in the field without having the rings on my left hand repossessed.

"Well, we agree on one thing," I said, backing away. "The sleigh needs to be found."

Kaye brightened as I gave them some space. "Two things. We also agree that your cat's the bomb."

I laughed. "Three things. Scones are overrated."

"Four," Heddy said. "You know you're soft, too."

"Ouch. Was that necessary, Heddy?" I asked. "We were having a moment."

"There was no moment." She snapped her fingers at me. "You basically accused us of murder."

"We were just having a nice chat beside a dumpster until you ruined it." I had backed halfway to the sidewalk and needed to raise my voice. "I might tell Dahlia you were mean to me. Then she'll want to stop by your store. You know how protective she is."

Kaye actually flinched at the threat, something that would make Mom very proud. "Dahlia's banned from the store after an insultingly low offer on our most stunning vase. I think she was planning to give it to you for Christmas."

Knowing my mother, the lowball insult was the goal of the visit. "I'll remind her to take her holiday shopping elsewhere."

Heddy snapped her fingers again. It was surprising they still worked in the cold. "A little tip before you go, Ivy. Speak to Isaac Gherkin."

My boots stopped. "The homesteader?"

"The radical," Heddy corrected. "He threatened Hester multiple times. Even threw a cup of coffee at her."

"Other way around," I said. "Hester threw a cup at Isaac by accident."

"Is that what she told the poor, deluded chief of police? Hester had excellent aim for an old lady. Ask us how we know." Heddy snickered. "It was another reason for Isaac to want her dead. She'd obstructed his free speech about the museum expansion, and she never shut up about the Millbrook sleigh."

"Why would Isaac care about a child's sleigh?"

Kaye picked up the story. "Because it represents everything he abhors. Generational wealth. Historical preservation that ignores environmental costs. Glorification of a past built on exploitation. I can't remember the rest of his rhetoric, but I'm sure he'd be happy to recap the speech he gave at the planning meeting. He's furious about your sister's pet project."

"Furious enough to kill her docent?" I asked.

The sisters shrugged in unison, another move that looked choreographed but was probably embedded in muscle memory.

"That's for the police to figure out, if you ever let them do their jobs," Kaye said. "Can we please leave before we freeze to death out here? I don't want to stay for coffee anymore."

I stepped out onto the sidewalk, and she deliberately elbowed me as she passed. That earned her khakis a nip from my bodyguard.

Kaye dodged out of reach. "Give poor Iris our regards. Tell her we hope this mess gets cleared up soon. It would be such a shame if the museum had to close due to scandal."

Her words hung in the cold air between us, but I pulled out my best HR smile. "The town's seen bigger scandals. The museum will be fine, and so will Iris."

Turning, I walked toward the door of the Berry Good Café. Kaye may not want coffee, but I sure did. "Well done, boys," I said. "Especially you, Percy. Can't be easy to fraternize with enemies like them."

Percy's purr suggested quite the opposite. He had no compunction about dumpster flirtation for a good cause. That was the beauty of cats.

My phone buzzed, and I stepped to one side to allow a couple to leave the café. The text from Kellan read, "Where are you?"

I stared at the screen, wondering how he had time to keep close tabs on me. Normally, he was too busy after a murder to keep in touch. "Getting a second breakfast," I texted back. "Always hungry in cold weather. Want anything?"

"The truth would be nice."

"Will a scone do?"

There was a longer pause this time. Then: "Ivy. We need to talk."

"Agreed. Let's have a chat just as soon as we know the missing pony is safe and warm."

Keats gave a brisk ha-ha-ha.

It was time to play hardball. Kellan was keeping me from my rightful calling as a rescuer. Until he disbanded the snowmobile militia, scones were all I had to offer this relationship.

Dropping the phone in my pocket, I walked inside.

CHAPTER EIGHT

The warmth of the Berry Good Café enveloped me in a welcome hug. After the bitter cold of the alley and a tense encounter with the Langman sisters, the hum of voices, hiss of steam and smell of baking felt soothing. Despite last night's heavy snow, the place was packed. Homesteaders in hand-knitted hats and parkas rubbed shoulders with downtown business owners in wool coats. The quest for caffeine and carbs united us all.

I scanned the room for Powell Nobbs and came up empty. Either Mandy had guessed wrong about his destination, or he'd come and gone in record time. Given Keats' irritable grumble and flattened ears, I suspected the latter. There was something in here the dog disliked more than the sister duo we met outside. Powell must have left a sour scent trail.

Before lining up at the counter, I glanced around again. This time, my eyes landed on a head of disheveled dark curls. At a corner table, a man took a swig of coffee and then scribbled in a spiral notebook.

Keats pressed against my leg to steer me over to Anthony Cork. His wire-rimmed glasses sat askew on his nose, and he clutched the mug so tightly it looked like the china might shatter.

The museum's assistant curator looked utterly devastated.

My old HR instincts activated instantly. I'd seen this before, usually in conference rooms after layoffs or in the aftermath of a brutal corporate restructuring. Anthony wasn't just sad. He was grieving.

Percy rode through the café on my shoulder, fluffy orange tail occasionally swishing across my face. Several people turned to watch our progress. To my great regret, the first lady of law enforcement and her animal entourage rarely went unnoticed anymore. Word would certainly reach Kellan that we were here for more than scones.

Anthony didn't notice us as he scratched in his notebook. When Percy announced our arrival with a meow, the pencil flew out of the man's hand and spun in a dizzying circle until I reached out to stop it.

"Hey, Ivy. I didn't see you there." He pushed his glasses up his nose with a trembling index finger. "Sorry, I'm a bit scattered this morning."

"Understandable, given the circumstances." I gestured to the empty chair across from him. "Mind if I join you for a moment?"

He blinked rapidly, as if the question required significant processing. "Please do. I could use the company. Being alone with my thoughts isn't going well. I've been journaling them out. That's what the online gurus recommend."

"Hope it helps. When I'm stressed, I prefer turning manure. Chopping wood is good, too. When something terrible happens, I feel compelled to move. Like my sheepdog."

His brown eyes fell to Keats. "He doesn't look happy."

"It's about the winter coat. His mood won't lift till spring, but a strenuous walk in the woods later will help."

I slid into the chair and Percy off-boarded onto a third chair that held Anthony's coat and backpack. There wasn't much room, but the cat was adept at squeezing into tight spaces. Keats sat by my side facing Anthony. The young man looked back, and then his eyes danced away. It wasn't easy meeting that eerie blue eye at close range. Hopefully, Keats would be generous with a dose of warm brown eye for the grieving man.

"I'm so sorry about Hester." I meant it. Whatever my own sentiments about the cantankerous docent, Anthony's pain was clearly genuine. "This must be incredibly difficult for you."

His eyes, magnified behind thick lenses, filled with tears. "You have no idea. I know most people didn't like Hester. She could be prickly. But she gave me a chance when no one else did. I guess she saw something in me."

That aligned with what Mandy had said earlier. "Hester was your mentor?"

"More than that. She was—" Anthony's voice cracked, and he took a sip of coffee to compose himself. "When I started my job, Iris didn't have much time. She was always rushing between the salon and the museum, fitting me in between haircuts and highlight appointments. But Hester? She sat with me for hours. Taught me proper archival techniques, how to catalog items, the importance of provenance and keeping a paper trail. Her passion for local history captured me, and I didn't even grow up around here."

Keats sat like a statue, and I rested my fingers on his head. His ears were nearly back in neutral position, but his hackles felt ready to spring to alert again. The dog was attentive but far from relaxed.

"Sounds like Hester made quite an impact on you." I deployed my best active-listening technique. Years of mediating workplace disputes had taught me when to probe and when to let someone talk.

"Actually, Hester changed my life." Anthony set down his cup, and it clattered slightly against the wood-veneer tabletop. Then he ran a hand through his curls, leaving frizz behind. "When we met, I had an education in museum curation and zero experience. Every position I applied for wanted five years in the field. How was I supposed to get experience if no one would hire me? Classic catch-22."

I nodded sympathetically. Countless job seekers had made the same complaint during my HR days. The experience paradox was real and frustrating.

"Hester broke that cycle for you," I prompted.

"Yeah. She convinced Iris to take a chance on me, even if it was only part-time. And then she spent every spare moment training me. She asked my opinion about exhibit layouts and artifact placement. And she really valued my tech skills. Computers scared Hester." He thought for a moment. "If not for that, maybe she would have seen me as the kid who stocked supplies and swept the floor. Like Iris does."

There was an edge to his tone when he mentioned my sister. Not quite resentment, but definitely hurt.

"Iris has said only positive things about you, Anthony. She's just been stretched thin with two businesses and the extra pressure of working directly with the mayor's office."

Anthony leaned forward, his glasses sliding down again. "Hester said Iris spread herself too thin. That the museum deserved her full attention, especially during the expansion. Instead, Iris was always fighting fires while we tried to hold things together."

It was hard not to leap to my sister's defense, but I knew Anthony was suffering. This was about more than Hester. I bet he'd never had someone in his life who made him feel special before. That was a good explanation for his intense emotions. Perhaps Hester had become a second mother to him.

Percy decided Anthony would benefit more from fluff than journaling and insinuated himself onto the man's lap. His fingers left the coffee cup and sank into orange fur.

"I hope you don't mind," I said. "Percy is very social."

"He's a beautiful cat." Anthony scratched behind Percy's ears, earning a rumbling purr. "Outside the museum, Hester would have loved him. She adored cats and had three of her own. All rescues. She showed me photos and talked about their antics."

Now I blinked at him, surprised. Hester had seemed so rigid, so focused on rules and protocol. The idea of her cooing over rescue cats didn't quite compute. But people were never as easily categorized as a museum collection. My HR career taught me that the most difficult colleague might be a devoted parent and the office grump might volunteer at a soup kitchen. Everyone contained multitudes.

"I didn't know she loved cats," I said. "What else didn't people know about Hester?"

His expression grew wistful. "She had an infectious laugh. It seemed to catch her by surprise, like she'd forgotten she was capable. Sometimes it burst out of her when she uncovered a fascinating detail in an old document or made a connection between artifacts."

"That's wonderful. I love it when people have such passion for their work."

"It was a shame she couldn't make a living at it. Her years at the law firm weren't happy, but she'd finally come into her own." Anthony absently touched his backpack and then pulled the extra chair closer. "That's what made last night so tragic. I should have been there. I should have skipped that stupid Christmas party and stayed to help her close the museum."

"You couldn't have known."

"But I did know she'd be alone after the reception. And I went to the party, anyway." His sigh ruffled the pages of his notebook. "I don't get invited to many, but I have a friend who works at the art gallery in Dorset Hills. We went to school together, and he's really integrated into the Dog Town community." He took his hand off Percy to rub his face and thought better of it when loose fur tickled his nose. "Now my social media feed is full of photos of me chugging eggnog, while Hester was fighting off an intruder. I wanted to take the posts down because they're a reminder I chose a party over the person who believed in me. If I'd been there, I could have saved her."

Survivor guilt. I'd seen and experienced it often. "Anthony, Iris wanted you to enjoy time with friends, and I'm sure Hester did, too. This isn't your fault."

"Doesn't make it hurt less."

"No, but punishing yourself won't help Hester or honor her memory." I drummed my fingertips on the table. "You know what *would* honor it? Helping Hester's cats. Finding a home for three won't be easy."

"I'll take them." His answer came swiftly, and he leaned forward. "It would be a privilege to have the cats she loved so much."

Percy gave a roaring purr of approval, but I spoke over it. "That's a wonderful offer, but three cats would be an enormous responsibility, not to mention expense. Let's talk about it more when the dust settles."

"Well, someone needs to look after them, and I won't let Hester down again."

His tone became sulky as I deflated his good intentions. At the moment, however, he only had a part-time job, and one big vet bill could put him over the edge. The Rescue Mafia could likely find a more suitable home for Hester's feline trio.

Percy returned to the spare chair and began pawing at the backpack's zipper. "Percy, stop. Are you trying to show Anthony how much trouble even one cat can be?"

Anthony just shrugged. "It's fine. He probably smells the tuna sandwich I picked up here for my lunch. I can't imagine eating it, though. My appetite's completely gone."

Percy continued pawing insistently at the canvas. I tried to grab him again, but he evaded me with the liquid grace only cats possess.

"Percy Bysshe Shelley, that's enough." I used his full name, which generally only worked if it came from Jilly. He seemed to view her as an authority figure and me as a littermate.

Anthony gently pulled the backpack onto his lap, leaving the seat mostly free for Percy. Nonetheless, the cat moved into my lap, tail lashing.

"Rude," I said. "He has a one-track mind when it comes to tuna."

"No worries. Cats are gonna cat, right?"

Keats mumbled beside me, and I looked down. Once again, his ears flattened and his hackles came up. I glanced around to see what might have provoked him.

"Did you happen to notice Powell Nobbs come in earlier, Anthony?"

"I did, yeah. He pushed ahead of me in line and tossed a twenty-dollar bill at the cashier for coffee and a scone. Didn't wait for change."

"Powell didn't see you?"

The unruly curls swished. "Nope. I'm basically the invisible man. If it weren't for your pets, I bet you wouldn't have noticed me, either."

"Don't be so sure. I've already had plenty of coffee to fuel my powers of observation. But it's too bad I missed Powell. I saw him at Mandy's store earlier and wanted to have a word."

Anthony smiled. "Maybe he didn't want to have a word with you. Because he rubbed a patch on the window to peek out before leaving in a hurry."

I smiled too. "I get that a lot."

He wrapped both hands around his coffee cup, shoulders hunching. It made him look smaller and younger. "What happens now? To the museum, I mean. With Hester gone and Iris under suspicion."

"Iris isn't seriously under suspicion," I said. "The rumor mill's made her a convenient scapegoat till the police sort through the rest."

"I know Iris would never do something like that." He paused, then added carefully, "Though she did argue with Hester sometimes. Like yesterday. I heard some of it."

"Me too. About security for the Millbrook sleigh, right?"

"Among other things. Hester had concerns about how the expansion was being managed." He shifted in his seat, clearly uncomfortable. "I don't want to say more. Feels disloyal to both of them."

I appreciated his discretion, even though it frustrated my investigative instincts. "The police will figure it out. Chief Harper is very thorough."

Anthony nodded, but his expression remained troubled. "I just keep thinking... who would do this? Who hated Hester enough to kill her?"

It was the question everyone was asking. "I don't know. Despite her kindness to you, Hester could be polarizing."

"People didn't understand her, that's all. They thought she was difficult for the sake of being difficult, but she was protecting the town's heritage." His voice grew heated. "She stood up to people like the Langmans, who just wanted to strip-mine the town's past for profit."

"The Langmans can be polarizing, too." I hadn't met a true fan of the sisters yet. At least Hester had Anthony.

He flung himself back in his seat. "They were here earlier and went out the back door. Lucky for them, because I might have said something I shouldn't have. Heddy and Kaye are vultures who've been circling that sleigh for years. Hester told me they've offered the Millbrooks ridiculous amounts of money for it. When that didn't work, they tried to convince Iris not to display it, claiming it was too valuable for a public exhibit. They just wanted to eliminate the competition."

"Competition?"

"Hester said they have a buyer lined up. Some collector who's obsessed with Victorian Christmas decor. The Langmans were desperate to acquire it before this mystery buyer went elsewhere." Anthony picked up his pencil and spun it. "Hester felt like she was the only thing standing between the Langmans and a huge payday. Now she's gone, and the sleigh is missing. You do the math."

It was an interesting theory and one that aligned with the sisters' usual motives, but while Keats had declared them guilty of something, I wasn't convinced it was murder. Not yet, anyway.

"Let's leave the math to the cops," I said. "The chief's a whiz at numbers and puzzles of all kinds. My brother, too."

"Will they see it through? Unlike Iris, Hester doesn't have anyone to advocate for her. Well, only me, and I'm a nobody. Seems like police usually go after the low-hanging fruit while the real criminals walk free."

"Not in Clover Grove, Anthony. I know that happens in some places, and I'm as cynical as you are. But here, the police are genuinely committed to finding the truth. They won't rest till the right person is detained, I promise you."

"I hope so." Anthony finally took another sip of his coffee and grimaced. "This has gone cold. Story of my day."

I glanced at my own empty hands and realized I'd never actually ordered anything. The scone mission had been derailed by seeing Anthony. Not that I minded. My pets had clearly found the conversation necessary. Maybe my job here was simply to help Anthony move past his grief and support Iris as she got back on her feet.

"Can I buy you a refill? I need a coffee myself."

He shook his head. "Better pass, but thanks. It was nice of you to listen to me ramble. I think I'm in shock."

I leaned forward, summoning my inner HR leader. She was still in there, and I appreciated being able to call on her. "Anthony, I know this seems impossible right now, but Hester's death doesn't have to be the end of everything she built. You could carry on her work. Her legacy."

He barked out a bitter laugh. "Me? Like I said, I'm a nobody."

"I don't believe that. Hester had other staff and didn't bond with them the way she did with you. She decided you were somebody and trusted you with knowledge of her collection. That means something."

"It means she had terrible judgment. I didn't keep her safe when she needed me. I didn't keep our most valuable exhibit safe."

He was resistant, but it made me dig deeper. Even though Keats was pressing on my boot with one paw and grumbling. The dog wanted to get going. "If Hester saw potential in you, you need to start seeing it in yourself. What would she want you to do now?"

His eyes welled up again behind his glasses. "Preserve the collection. Make sure her life's work wasn't for nothing."

"Then do that. Honor her by being the curator she trained you to be."

"What about Iris?"

"If you step up and prove your value, my sister will recognize it. Especially now, when she needs all the help she can get."

Anthony sat quietly for a moment, turning his cup in slow circles. "You really think I could?"

"Hester thought you could. That's what matters. Don't you owe it to her to try?"

A small, sad smile formed on his thin face. "You sound like her. She was always pushing me to have more confidence, to stop apologizing for taking up space."

"Smart woman."

"The smartest." He straightened in his chair, trying to shrug off the defeated slump. "Thank you, Ivy. I needed to hear that today. I've been drowning in guilt and what-ifs."

"Totally normal response to trauma. But at some point, you

need to wade back to shore and keep living. Hester would want that."

Percy chose his moment to step onto the table and strut across to Anthony, making another run at the tuna sandwich in his backpack.

Laughing, Anthony swished the pack away from the cat and dropped it on the floor. "No dice, pal."

"Percy!" I grabbed the cat around his middle and pulled him back. "He's usually better behaved than this."

"Really? Seems pretty on-brand to me." Anthony's smile seemed genuine, and he looked attractive, if you liked the scrawny, studious type. "It's fine. Cats are curious creatures. That's what makes them good detectives, right? Along with Keats?"

"They certainly think so." I tucked Percy firmly under one arm, where he squirmed in frustration. "Speaking of investigating, did you happen to notice which way Powell Nobbs went?"

Anthony's smile faded. "Toward town square, I think. I wondered if he'd run into Isaac Gherkin, who was already picketing when I walked here. If the Langmans didn't kill Hester, one of those guys probably did. They hated her just for doing her job."

"Make sure you tell the chief about your suspicions when you give your statement."

"I talked to your brother last night, but I'm going back soon. Now I can tell him Powell Nobbs had a limp today. And scratches on his hands that weren't there yesterday. It was like he fell into a rosebush. Or holly, given the time of year." His eyes narrowed behind his glasses. "Doesn't that sound suspicious?"

It did, given that Hester's hands had shown defensive wounds. Had she left marks on her attacker, too?

I pushed my chair back and stood up. "Just one last piece of advice, Anthony. Leave speculation to the police and focus on your work."

His eyebrows rose over his glasses, and he grinned. "Like *you* do?"

I started to grin back and stopped. "You don't want to see the things I've seen. Stick to artifacts and culture. Isn't that enough for now?"

He raked his curls again, leaving even more frizz behind. "I guess. It's all about the museum now. And cats, if the police will let me have Hester's." Watching me stuff Percy under my arm like a football, he continued, "Thanks, Ivy. I feel like I have a purpose again, something to focus on besides guilt." He rose as well, shrugging on his coat and slinging his backpack over one shoulder. "I should head to the police station to give my formal statement. Maybe then they'll let me into the museum to pick up some things. We have a grant proposal due tomorrow, and I'd like to see it through."

Keats scrambled to his feet and pressed against my leg. He was ready to move, to pursue the next lead. My working dog hated sitting still when there was a job to be done.

I waved to Anthony as he left and then ordered a coffee and two blueberry scones. One for me and one for Kellan.

It was a statement of faith in our relationship. We would come to an agreement about the pony long before his scone went stale.

And if the snowmobile militia continued to impede my progress, a scone would be a lovely treat for my perpetually hungry goats.

CHAPTER NINE

I left the Berry Good Café with a head full of questions about Powell Nobbs. The wealthy benefactor's nervous energy, his limp, and the scratches Anthony mentioned all added up to something, although I didn't know what. At the reception yesterday, Powell didn't seem like the type to fall into a patch of holly, but the wintry weather made anything possible. Maybe I'd run into him again in the town square while searching for Isaac Gherkin and be able to cross them both off in one go. No matter what, I planned to be hiking through deep snow by noon to find that pony. Edna and Gertie might very well have commandeered a tank by then. They claimed to have the right connections.

Keats turned away from the town square and trotted along the slushy sidewalk in the opposite direction. Clearly, our priorities had diverged.

"What's going on, buddy?" I asked before lifting Percy to my shoulder. "I want to catch Isaac before he moves on to the next protest. There's no lack of causes in Clover Grove."

Keats mumbled something insistent and directed his muzzle across the street, where some of my favorite stores beckoned. Either he'd developed an interest in Christmas shopping or he'd sniffed out someone on his naughty list.

"If you're just angling for treats from Mabel, I'm going to be disappointed." The dog's ears flicked forward, neither confirming nor denying. "Fine, but let's make it quick."

A visit to Mabel's Miniature Mutts was hardly a punishment. The store was a frequent destination on my circuits through town and I wondered how I'd missed my friend's new signature wreaths. Keats gave me an assertive poke in the calf to knock visions of miniatures out of my head. This wasn't entirely a social call. Mabel must know something.

The dog circled to lead me across the street, mumbling orders to stay alert. People were driving too fast for the conditions, and it would lead to collisions. That would divert police resources from where they were really needed today.

On the store's door hung a wreath covered with tiny ceramic teapots, teacups, creamers and sugar bowls. Mabel Halliday was a hardcore fan of loose-leaf tea. This had her name all over it.

I'd been collecting her whimsical creations for a couple of years, starting with a border collie and expanding to account for nearly every animal I'd met in my adventures, including a kangaroo, a penguin and more predictable livestock. Only Elaine, the emu, had eluded Mabel thus far, and I expected her kiln would triumph, eventually.

Keats tried to prod me inside, but I couldn't pass the window display without paying my respects. Ignoring Mabel's showcase would be like turning down Mandy's coconut cream pie. Each woman was a master of her craft. The window held a village of tiny ceramic buildings nestled in cotton-ball snow, complete with working streetlights no taller than my index finger. Miniature people ice-skated on a mirror pond, children slid down a slope on toboggans, and a red train engine circled the perimeter, towing railway cars filled with gifts wrapped in actual ribbon.

"Storybook Christmas," I murmured. "It's almost enough to make me forget what happened last night." Percy's tail swished across my face like a fluffy windshield wiper designed to dispel fantasy. "If only I could step into that perfect little world and go skating."

Keats mumbled a reproof. At home, spread out on the sideboard, was a scene from a snow globe that featured ceramic replicas of the three of us. Here in the real world, we had work to do. Flesh-and-blood Ivy, Keats and Percy had a pony to find, a murder to solve and a sister to absolve. The dog added a pant-laugh to suggest he wouldn't have it any other way. Snow globes were for sissies.

The bell over the door jingled as we entered, and the scent of a spicy tea blend tickled my nose. Shelves and tables held a mishmash of ornaments, ranging from models of Clover Grove's landmarks to elves, angels and multiple versions of Santa. When I met Mabel soon after my return from Boston, the place had mainly featured tiny dogs. She was expanding her wares at a furious rate, and the store typically topped the charts on the tourist must-see list.

"Ivy!" Mabel Halliday came out of the back room, wiping clay dust from her hands onto an apron. She was a petite woman in her fifties with short, highlighted hair. Half-moon reading glasses hung from a beaded chain around her neck, and paint stained her fingertips. "I knew you couldn't resist checking out my latest, and perhaps greatest, invention. Wreath charms."

I laughed. "Am I that predictable?"

"Predictably my favorite client. It was just a matter of time before you followed the trail to the gingerbread house." She paused. "Wait, does that make me the witch in my analogy?"

"Hardly. You're one of the good guys, Mabel. Not to mention a creative genius."

After smiling down at Keats, she reached out to scratch Percy's jowls. "Hello, handsome feline. I've got a catnip mouse for you in the back if you promise not to knock anything off my shelves."

Percy turned on his finest purr, despite being indifferent to catnip and typical cat pastimes. He jumped onto the counter and then to the floor, perhaps to allay Mabel's worries.

"Tell me about your new product," I said, moving away from the windows and deeper into the store. "It was all I could do not to wreath-nap one."

Mabel beamed with pride. "The wreath charms are the hit of this holiday season. I've been doing themed hobby sets, like garden tools, books, and various crafts. It's finicky work, but I love seeing the look on someone's face when it's just right. Orders are coming in fast."

"Can you make me a chef-themed set for Jilly? And how about a prepper set for Edna?"

"Prepper?" Her brow furrowed at the unusual request. "Yes! Ceramic tins of beans. Knitting needles and wool. Camouflage gloves."

"Perfect. How about a parachute? A sword? An ATV?"

She laughed. "I'm game to try anything. And before you ask, there's already a farm in the kiln. Consider it an early Christmas gift. It's the least I can do when you've directed so much business my way."

"I'll happily accept, although your work sells itself. Guests can't keep their mitts off my tiny town."

Mabel walked around the counter and bent over. "I have something else for you. Two days ago, I felt inspired to create something new for your village." Straightening, she slid a box across the counter to me. "Do you have one of these in your barn yet?"

Lifting the lid, I moved the tissue carefully aside and gasped. Lying on a bed of cotton snow was a perfect replica of a reddish-brown pony. It had a flowing cream mane and tail and wore a painted red harness studded with silver bells.

"Oh, Mabel, she's perfect! How did you know?"

She smoothed her hair behind her ears. "I *didn't* know. Just had a hunch. Is the pony bay or chestnut?"

"No idea. We haven't actually met." I traced a fingertip over the harness. "Kellan wouldn't let me search for her in the storm last night. I do know she's missing a bell or two."

Mabel's smile flickered out. "Does the pony have something to do with what happened to Hester?"

The news of the murder would have spread throughout Clover Grove and well beyond by now. Apparently, no one had mentioned the hoofprints. Mabel's inspiration to create a pony was just a strange coincidence.

"What have you heard so far, Mabel? I'm sure Justine's been spreading lies."

Her smile ignited again, turning into a mischievous grin. "She's wearing a sling and threatening to charge your brother with assault."

I rolled my eyes. "I heard Justine alternated between going limp and fighting Asher like a wildcat. There are plenty of witnesses."

"Our Tattler is doing what she does best," Mabel said. "Offering unintended comic relief in a sad situation." She waited a beat for me to speak and then added, "I heard you were the one to find Hester."

"Percy and Keats did that, actually." I kept my voice neutral and my facts sparse, as I'd learned in HR. It was best to leave room for others to fill the silence. "I followed with Jilly and Edna."

"Poor Hester." Mabel sighed heavily. "She may not have been pleasant, but no one deserves to die like that."

Keats set off on a tour of the small store, while Percy vanished into the back room. "Did you know Hester well?" I asked.

"Well enough." Mabel plucked ceramic Christmas trees from a box and lined them up like soldiers on the counter. "She came in here now and then looking for Victorian-era pieces or items with historical significance. Never bought a thing. Said my work was 'too whimsical.'"

I winced. "Sounds like Hester."

"She wasn't wrong, though. My goal isn't to create museum-quality replicas. I want to make things that bring people joy." Mabel's finger pressed the pointy top of a tree. "Hester had a way of making someone feel small. Like your passions didn't measure up to her standards."

Keats came back and mumbled something that sounded vaguely sympathetic. It wasn't like him to bolster egos mid-investigation. He wanted Mabel to keep talking.

"Did she have that effect on everyone?" I asked.

"Not everyone." Mabel pulled out another box of trees, this collection slightly smaller, and began lining them up in front of the first set. "Some gave as good as they got. The Langman sisters loved getting into it with Hester. Last year they had a shoving match at a historical reenactment in Thistledown. Your friend Thelma Tilrow wedged them apart with her cane."

"Thelma is amazing." My librarian friend had faced down a murderer to save Keats once. A dustup between Hester and the Langmans wouldn't have fazed her in the slightest. "Anyone else?"

Mabel glanced out at the street and then nodded. "Years ago, Hester had words with Constance Freely from the historical society. Hester was outraged at the way Constance handled an eighteenth-century ledger. Made quite a scene at a town council meeting. Connie never spoke to her again."

I filed the name away, though I doubted Constance Freely, who used a walker now, had the physical capability to overpower Hester. Few octogenarians embraced Edna's aging warrior mentality.

Mabel's movements as she set up ever-smaller trees kept me mesmerized until Percy meowed from a shelf by the window. He'd picked his way through a maze of ornaments without knocking over a single one. I presumed he'd found something of interest, but it seemed like he was announcing another customer.

The store's bell chimed again, and Aline Tupling walked inside, her cheeks pink from the cold. She wore a green coat, with her hair tucked under a pink knitted hat decorated with snowflakes. Clutched in one mitten was her toy drive coin box, and it jingled as she pressed it to her chest.

"Good morning, ladies," Aline said. "Although it's actually dreadful. Poor Hester is gone, the tree lighting ceremony is postponed, and the Millbrook family is reconsidering their holiday reception. All the funds raised for the toy drive, the gifts I've been collecting for weeks... What's the point if the children never get them?"

I felt for Aline, a model citizen. She organized community events, volunteered at the library, and promoted our town markets far and wide. This was probably the highlight of her year.

"That won't happen, Aline," Mabel said. "We'll call for volunteers and distribute the toys ourselves, if necessary."

Aline's furrowed brow relaxed slightly. "Really, Mabel?"

"Of course. That's what we do in Clover Grove. Band together in times of need." She pointed to a stool. "Sit down for a moment and catch your breath. Let me get you some tea."

After a grumbled protest, Aline sank onto the stool. "No tea, thank you. I can't just sit around after what happened. It's a tragedy." Her eyes rose to meet mine. "Ivy, I heard you were there."

"Briefly. Until the chief sent me home. I didn't know Hester well. Did you?"

Aline nodded. "We worked together on several community projects. Hester was difficult but dedicated. I respected that."

"Aline was one of the few to get along with Hester," Mabel told me as she set up yet another row of ceramic Christmas trees, this one smaller still. "She's Clover Grove's sweetheart."

"Hardly." Aline set her coin box on the counter and pulled off her mittens. "But fundraising relies on the ability to bite one's tongue. The toy drive is my easiest and most joyful project. At least it was until today." Her voice wavered, and tears filled her eyes. "I could just cry."

Mabel slid a box of tissues across the counter. "Don't worry too much, Aline. Hester is gone, but other things can change quickly around here. Especially with Ivy and her pets on the case."

Pulling out a handful of tissues, Aline chafed at her nose and stared at me. "*Are* you on the case, Ivy? Because the children of Clover Grove are depending on you."

Keats only got one "ha" out before I touched his head and cut him off with a "Quiet."

Mabel answered for me. "Ivy will do what she can, I'm sure, but it's not fair to put the welfare of the town's kids on her shoulders. Remember, she has to contend with the chief."

"Don't forget my brother," I added. "Last night, we tried to go after a runaway pony, and Asher stopped me with a gang of thugs on snowmobiles."

The fist with tissues drifted down, and Aline leaned forward. "A pony? Tell us more."

"There's not much to tell. The police outfoxed me before I could follow the trail, and it's buried now." I opened my left hand to reveal the ornament Mabel made. "Isn't this pretty?"

"So pretty." Aline reached out, and I let her take the miniature. "Reminds me of my Shetland pony, Peppermint. She was my best friend when I was a child." Dropping the tissues in her lap, she ran her fingers over the pony's smooth curves. "I suppose that sounds sad."

"Not to me." I pointed from Keats to Percy. "These are the best of my besties and only my brother considers me a child. Do you know anyone who owns a pony like your Peppermint?"

"I wish." Her blue eyes gleamed. "If I did, I'd bring that pony to town square and let small children take a ride. Can you imagine?"

"Maybe we can make that happen," I said. "I'm going to find

this runaway while the police figure out what happened to Hester. The chief's following several strong leads."

Aline set the pony on the counter and picked up the crumpled tissues. "I know you have faith in him, dear, but I can't share your optimism. There are so many people who might have wanted Hester—" Her already pink cheeks flushed bright red. "I'm sorry. My mouth got away from me. I'm just so distressed about what's happening to our town. And at Christmas, too."

Mabel picked up the pony figurine and waggled it at the weary woman. "Aline, when the problems of the world seem too big, you need to size them down. That's why my passion is making miniatures. It helps me, and I truly think it helps others."

"It definitely does, Mabel," I said. "Although I never really thought about it like that. My ceramic collection is comforting, and now I see you baked that right in with the clay. Everything's perfect and peaceful in my Christmas village."

Aline stared at the Shetland pony. "I'd love to collect figurines, too, but every spare dollar I have goes into fundraising. I grew up with little, you see. After my father's business went under, we had to sell Peppermint, and it broke my heart. I want to spare others some of that pain where I can."

I reached into my pocket, pulled out my credit card and handed it to Mabel. "I'll buy that pony for Aline. If you have time when the holiday rush ends, Mabel, you could make me another."

"Ivy, you're so kind," Aline said. "But you should keep it."

Stepping closer, I handed her the figurine and folded her fingers around it. "I have lots of Mabel's animals and dozens of fur-real ones in my pastures. Please enjoy little Miss Peppermint. Was your pony as sweet as her name?"

At last, Aline laughed. "Only if you expect a little bite with your candy. Peppermint was clever and spirited, and she loved company. If she didn't get enough attention, she'd go looking for it.

People underestimate Shetland ponies because they're small, you see, but they're full of personality."

"A big horse in small packaging," I said.

"Exactly." Aline held the pony up to her eyes. "My original Peppermint was easily bored and got into mischief. She opened latches and took herself around the neighborhood. And so stubborn! When she decided she didn't want to do something, you couldn't budge her with a forklift. But except for the odd nip, she was always sweet with me."

"Everyone is sweet with you, Aline." Mabel held out her hand, palm up, to take the pony. "And you deserve it. I think your secret admirer stays hidden because he knows he can't measure up."

Aline's cheeks flushed anew. "Mabel Halliday, you hush."

Keats pressed his paw on my foot, and I took the hint to follow the story. "Secret admirer? Sounds intriguing, Aline."

"It's nothing, really." Her flustered expression suggested otherwise. "Just some harmless notes."

"Letters," Mabel corrected, setting the pony back in its box. "Handwritten in elegant cursive on expensive stationery, before being sealed with red wax and hand-delivered by night to your door. It's very romantic."

My curiosity was fully engaged. "Hand-delivered? Not mailed?"

Aline nodded. "They come through the mail slot, and I find them on the mat. One was sitting there this morning, in fact. There were no footprints. I suppose the snow covered them."

"Or your admirer doesn't leave prints." Mabel picked up a ceramic angel and fluttered it. "Maybe he's celestial."

"Doubtful. I'm sure this fellow leaves as big a mess behind as my last gentleman friend."

Mabel reached for a skein of red ribbon. "That friend was no angel, Aline. I doubt he'd know fine stationery and sealing wax if he saw them."

"Probably not," Aline admitted. "I was relieved when he moved down the range."

"What did your new letter say?" Mabel asked.

"Just that a Christmas surprise is coming my way." Bewilderment crossed Aline's face. "It's nice to feel noticed, I suppose, but I'm too old to get caught up in such nonsense."

"Maybe the surprise is a huge donation for the toy drive," Mabel said. "That would show he really understands what's important to you."

Keats' paw came up in a point, and I pressed a little. "I'm sure what's important to you is *meeting* this admirer, Aline. In a small community like ours, it's hard to keep a secret. How long has this been going on?"

"Six months, give or take. I don't think about it too much."

"Close to a year," Mabel said. "The letters are brief. He just commends Aline on her recent work, wishes her well and signs off as 'An Admirer.'"

Something about the situation didn't sit right with me. Anonymous letters, secretive deliveries, promises of surprises... It sounded less like romance and more like something I should mention to Kellan. "Have you told the police about the letters?"

I kept my tone casual, but Aline reared back, alarmed. "Why would I, Ivy? They're perfectly respectful and harmless."

"Wouldn't it be more respectful and harmless if they arrived in daylight?" I touched Keats' head before continuing. "Forgive me for sounding like the first lady of law enforcement, Aline. Being suspicious comes with the territory."

"Please don't bring it up with Kellan. I'd be so embarrassed. All this writer does is compliment my community projects. There's nothing strange in these letters. Nothing that gives him away."

"I can't help wondering if he's married," Mabel said, deftly tying the box with ribbon. "He doesn't want to be traced."

"That would explain a lot," I agreed. "I don't like that he's just walking up to your door at night, Aline. It's trespassing."

Mabel looked up from her ribbon and smirked at me. "You've never trespassed for a worthy cause?"

I laughed. "Touché, Mabel. I've stepped over a few lines when animal welfare is at stake. But not to love-bomb someone."

"Ivy, you're being paranoid," Mabel said. "When you've been married as long as I have, you'll appreciate a little mystery. Aline's had her share of admirers, and I'm glad she's enjoying her golden years. This man will step out of the shadows when he's worked up the courage to let her know."

I wasn't ready to give up. "Do you have any idea who it might be?"

Aline gave a half-hearted shrug. "I've been trying to puzzle it out, but there aren't many likely suspects." She glanced at Mabel. "Just one, I suppose."

"Isaac Gherkin," Mabel said. "I'm sure of it. When I see you two chatting at the farmer's market, he seems positively entranced, Aline."

"Isaac Gherkin?" I couldn't keep the surprise out of my voice. The gruff homesteader didn't strike me as a romantic. Then again, people were full of surprises.

"He's not as surly as people think." Aline sounded slightly defensive. "I've had some lovely conversations with Isaac about sustainable farming practices, and heritage seeds and poultry. He's very passionate about his beliefs, that's all."

"So passionate that Hester Belcher threw a cup of coffee at him?" I asked.

Aline swallowed hard. "The coffee incident was unfortunate, but I understand Isaac's perspective. Clover Grove is changing so fast, and he feels left behind. With all the new development downtown, including the museum expansion, it's hard for people who remember what the town used to be."

"Actually, I understand that, too. But if you already chat to Isaac, why would he need to keep this a secret, Aline?"

She knitted her fingers together and thought about it. "Haven't you ever wanted to hold on to something imaginary just because it's nice the way it is? Making things real can ruin it."

I remembered all my years of loving Kellan from a distance. Back then, I was far too cowardly to reach out and risk rejection. "I hear you, Aline. And it sounds like you're comfortable with the secret admirer situation."

She took the box Mabel slid over and nodded. "Isaac is just shy and socially awkward. Keeping things at arm's length probably makes him comfortable. Whether or not he's my mysterious correspondent, I wish him well. There's no need to put him under scrutiny."

Percy chose that moment to jump onto the counter, and head-butt Aline's hand, demanding attention. She obliged, scratching behind his ears.

"I think he's harmless, too," Mabel said. "Enjoy this while it lasts, Aline. Once he comes out from behind the red wax, Isaac isn't likely to be your Prince Charming."

"That ship has long since sailed, I'm afraid." Aline welcomed Percy onto her lap. "Back in my younger years, I was very shy myself and far too timid to stand up to my father when men showed an interest. At least I can make my own decisions now."

"Yes, you can," I said. "And if anything makes you uneasy about this, promise me you'll contact the police."

"Don't worry about me, Ivy. Worry about Hester." Aline set Percy back on the counter and got up off the stool. "Call me a foolish old woman, but I truly believe the spirit of Christmas will set things right. This season brings out the best in people, heals conflicts, and creates peace where there was discord."

Unfortunately, experience had shown me people were just as

capable of misdeeds during the holidays as any other time of year. Maybe more so.

Just for the moment, I suspended my disbelief. Standing in Mabel's beautiful store surrounded by twinkling lights and festive creations, I watched the snow sift down onto the street outside and smiled. I could almost believe in Aline's vision.

Keats delivered a ha-ha-ha right on cue. It sounded cynical.

"I hope you're right, Aline," I said. "Clover Grove could use some peace right now."

"It will come." Aline pulled on her mittens, tucked the box under her arm and then jangled her coin box. "You'll see. The tree lighting will happen, and gifts will land in children's hands. Let's have faith."

Sometimes, I was challenged in the faith department, but it didn't stop me from trying.

Aline left without waiting for my response, and I gestured to the rows of Christmas trees. "I'll take a set of those, Mabel. They remind me of my mom and sisters. People call us nesting dolls because we look so similar."

By the time she'd packed them up, the store was full of clients, and it was easy to slip out and head for town square.

"Onward, boys," I said. "Let's see if Aline's grumpy home-steader has a heart of gold."

CHAPTER TEN

C lover Grove's town square was oddly quiet for a morning so close to the holidays. Normally, people cut through on their way to any local destination so they could admire the fir that dominated the center of the square. It was the tallest and fullest tree I could remember, and I hoped it would get the moment of glory it deserved. With the sun barely penetrating the clouds, little of the snow from last night had melted, and long boughs drooped under its weight. I wondered if Mayor Martingale, probably already inside and at her desk, felt equally weary. Meryl and I didn't agree on everything, but I appreciated how hard she worked to revitalize a once-struggling town. For every win, there was a murder, it seemed. Our reputation was in a permanent state of crisis.

Keats gave my calf a sharp poke and herded me around the tree. On the side facing city hall, Isaac Gherkin stood alone in the cold. The placard in his hand said "TREE MURDERERS" in shaky red capital letters. Below that, in smaller script, it read, "This majestic fir lived 40 years. You'll exploit it for 10 days."

I admired Isaac's commitment to his cause. The temperature hovered around twenty degrees, and he wore only a heavy flannel coat over a wool sweater. His head was bare, and gray hair stuck out in tufts. Combined with an equally unruly salt and pepper beard, he had the air of an eccentric prophet crying out in the wilderness. It wasn't far from the truth, I supposed. Isaac poured a lot of energy into protesting the Clover Grove "machine" and had little left for the niceties.

Reaching down, my gloved fingertips touched Keats' head. I'd chugged the last of my coffee at Mabel's store and put the scones into the bag with the ceramic Christmas trees. I'd learned from experience that it was always better to have one hand free to tap into the pets' energy. Right now, Keats' hackles prickled over his jacket and Percy, positioned on my shoulder again, had puffed, too.

Isaac wasn't getting a free pass just for standing on the moral high ground.

"All right, we're going in," I muttered. Closing the gap between us, I called out, "Good morning, Mr. Gherkin." I thought about adding "Merry Christmas" and decided not to poke the bear.

Not yet, anyway.

Isaac turned away from the building, and recognition flickered across his weathered face. "Is it, though? A good morning in Clover Grove?"

"Guess I've had better, now that you mention it."

He jabbed a finger at my shopping bag. There were holes in his wool gloves that exposed reddened skin. "Didn't stop you from indulging in the consumerism that runs rampant around here."

I regretted not having dropped the bag in the truck on my way here. I'd made myself an easy mark. "Someone's gotta support local businesses," I said. "Bought a gift for my mother. Did you know she repurposes thrift store clothes to make new designs?"

"Don't know, don't care. I have bigger issues on my mind." His placard tipped toward the tree. "Specifically, this monument to waste. I suppose you've come to defend the tree killers?"

"That wasn't on my radar, Mr. Gherkin. I actually understand your concern. I really do."

"Do you?" He lowered his sign to block his chest, like armor. "You run an extravagant inn. I bet there's a real tree in every room. Blood money from plant corpses."

"We have one tree cut from Gertie Rhodes' land. She donates a few to friends every year and plants three for every tree she harvests." This wasn't an argument I was going to win, but I figured a little sparring might build rapport. Or at least keep me warm. "Isn't that better for the environment than buying a plastic tree manufactured overseas and shipped here in vehicles run on diesel?"

He rolled his eyes. "I've heard it all before. Principles of convenience."

"More like principles with practical application. A modern compromise."

"There's no such thing, Galloway. You're just as shallow and self-centered as everyone else in town."

That stung a bit, but I let it go. For all his bluster, Isaac seemed sad to me. His hazel eyes were bloodshot, perhaps from exposure to the elements, and the corner of his mouth twitched repeatedly. Anxiety, most likely. I saw a similar expression in the mirror some mornings.

"I'm not perfect, but I do my part around here," I said. "Have you heard about my black-label fertilizer? It's pay-what-you-can, and the local produce was outstanding this year."

Again with the eye roll. "Woo-hoo. You donate dung. Easy to come by for a hobby farmer."

"I could list off a few more things, but that's not why I came over to see you."

He rested the placard on his shoulder. "Could you get to the point, then? I'm busy."

"Busy protesting to an empty square? You have an audience of three." I pointed from the dog to the cat. "Meet Keats and Percy. We have the best seats in the house."

"The principle stands whether or not anyone's watching. That's what makes it a principle." His voice was gravelly, probably from shouting environmental rhetoric for years. "I doubt you left the seductions of holiday shopping to debate environmental ethics with me."

Keats poked the side pocket of my overalls, perhaps reminding me of my phone and a shorter route to rapport. Pulling out the device, I swiped quickly until I found the photo I needed and then turned the screen to show Isaac. "Do you remember this?"

He bent and squinted slightly. "I don't believe in cell phones. Did you know they emit—"

"It's okay," I interrupted. "Quick recap. This is a photo of a Lincoln Longwool sheep. Heritage breed and a real beauty. Poor girl got herself stuck in a fence last spring. I was driving past and clipped the wire to set her free. You came out and yelled at me while I was repairing the fence."

The placard slipped off his shoulder as he slumped. "Thought you were poaching Patsy."

"So, you're saying I look hardy enough to tuck a two-hundred-pound sheep under my arm and run?"

"You're in the news all the time for doing strange things."

He wasn't wrong, and there was even a precedent for sheep rustling. Hopefully, he didn't know that because this was my power play. "I released your girl and didn't even get a thanks. In fact, you pulled a shotgun."

The placard hit the pavement, and the corner of the cardboard crumpled. "Felt bad about that. I was just worried about Patsy. Best ewe in my flock." He scuffed the slush at his feet. "Figured you'd ask for money, and I don't have much."

"Money! I'm a rescuer, not a wrangler for hire."

He hoisted the placard again. "You want a medal or something?"

Keats gave a quick ha-ha-ha that made the old man's eyes widen.

"No medal required. A little courtesy would be nice."

"I don't have much of that either." The placard was back in position between us, and his armor restored. "Not going to waste it on people who can't get to the point."

Percy lost patience with the cat-and-mouse game. His claws dug into my coat briefly and then he launched, landing lightly on Isaac's shoulder. The placard hit the ground again, denting another corner.

Stepping forward, I tried to grab my cat, succeeding only in getting him to switch shoulders across Isaac's face. "I'm so sorry. He's a force of nature."

Isaac sneezed, but he didn't shake Percy off. After a moment, a glove came up to rub Percy's side. "It's okay. I don't mind cats."

Percy purred, loud and proud, having accomplished what I couldn't. He'd softened the crusty activist.

"I think he likes you, Mr. Gherkin."

"It's a fan club of one. Percy gets the medal."

I smiled. "After losing a medal yesterday. He knocked a replica skull off a shelf at the museum reception. Hester Belcher was furious and wanted us expelled."

"Classic Hester." Isaac's expression hardened again. "Can't trust anyone who doesn't like animals."

"Fully agree. But from what I heard, Hester *did* like cats. Just not in the museum."

He shrugged and Percy rose and fell with the movement. "Hester was a piece of work. Threw a cup of coffee at my head, you know. In front of the mayor. Called me an ecological terrorist for protesting the museum expansion." Isaac looked chastened or even hurt. "All I was doing was exercising my right of free speech."

"I heard about that. I hope the coffee was cold."

One worn glove ran over the front of his jacket, as if he could still feel it. "Warm enough. People laughed, too." His sigh sent a gust of steam into the air. "I'm proud to defend my principles, but no one enjoys public ridicule."

Keats nudged my hand, and I took the cue to dive in. "I hear you, and I've been there. But this morning people are saying—"

"I know what they're saying," he interrupted. "That I had something to do with what happened to Hester. As revenge for the coffee grenade." His hand stilled in Percy's fur. "I didn't. I had no use for the museum or Hester, but I'm not a violent man."

My head tipped. "You pulled a gun on me after I rescued Patsy, remember."

"And I didn't shoot. Just like I didn't shoot Hester. If that's how she died." He stared at me. "Your brother wouldn't say. We had a long chat this morning, and I gave him my alibi. Then he told me not to talk to you."

Of course, he did. Squelching me was Asher's favorite pastime. "I'm glad you didn't take him too seriously. Since you're talking to me."

"Not by choice. But you did rescue Patsy, and I appreciate it. So, I'll share my alibi with you, too. Last evening, I went to Thistle-down Tree Farm to protest its clear-cutting. Got into a shoving match with a customer who probably broke a finger on my jaw." Isaac rubbed the side of his face, where a bruise was blooming out of the beard. "They can track the guy down and corroborate my statement. Your brother was confident I was telling the truth."

Maybe so, but Asher's confidence didn't rate as highly with me as that of my dog. Keats' fixed stare in the man's direction said he was still on the fence. There was something Isaac hadn't told us. I needed to keep him talking.

"I'm glad you'll be easily cleared, Mr. Gherkin. Any idea who else might have wanted to harm Hester?"

He raised the placard, probably trying to call an end to our discussion. "We've established she wasn't well-liked."

"My sister Iris said Hester wasn't so bad. She loved her job, for starters. Hester was deeply passionate about history and preservation. Hardly a crime."

"No, but it made her plenty of enemies." Isaac pulled up his sign and resumed stroking Percy. "Hester wasn't any worse than most people in this town. At least she stood for something, even if I disagreed with what it was."

"High praise coming from you."

A ghost of a smile crossed his face. "The only truly good person around here is Aline Tupling. Utterly selfless, always helping those in need. She doesn't get wrapped up in preservation, or progress or politics. She just cares about people. Kids, especially."

Keats' paw rose at the note of warmth in Isaac's voice. I took the dog's hint and followed the trail. "Aline is wonderful. Just half an hour ago, we were talking about how we could distribute gifts to children if the tree lighting ceremony is cancelled." Isaac didn't respond, so I added, "Hard to believe a woman like Aline is still single. If you're single yourself, maybe you could—"

"Galloway, skip the matchmaking and stick to sheep rescue." Isaac's face seemed to flush, but his complexion was likely permanently ruddy. "Some people are meant to be alone. I'm one of them."

"Are you sure about that? Maybe you wouldn't pull guns on people if you—"

"Just stop." He turned, positioning the placard between us. "I live a simple life on my homestead. Back to the earth. Minimal impact. No entanglements." His eyes peered over the cardboard. "It's probably more selfish than selfless. A woman like Aline deserves better than a hermit who argues with fenceposts."

Isaac might fit the profile of Aline's secret admirer. He felt unworthy and preferred to appreciate her from a distance. Still, it was hard to imagine him penning elegant letters and stamping them with sealing wax. Not if the words scrawled on his sign were any indication of his handwriting.

"You don't give yourself enough credit, Isaac. Aline spoke well of you earlier. I bet if you helped with the toy drive, you'd find—"

"How about you focus on something more interesting than my personal life? Don't you have hobbies? Other than getting under your brother's feet?"

I ignored that, with effort. "You know I have a farm full of hobbies. And I'm looking to add something new. Maybe you could help."

"Aha, so you *were* rustling my sheep."

Percy gave Isaac a headbutt to show me the man was just teasing. It emboldened me to switch on my professional-grade HR smile. "Sheep, I've got. I'm looking to acquire a Shetland pony. Heard there was a stray in the area. Have you seen it?"

His wiry eyebrows shot up, giving me the confirmation I needed. "Saw one last night, actually. Pretty little chestnut with a blonde mane and red harness. At least, I think so. It was snowing and past dark."

Excitement percolated in my chest. "Where was she?"

"Side road off County Route 5, close to Reid Brisco's place. Trotting as if she had a purpose. I went after her, but she was too quick. Thought about calling it in, but I was..."

"On your way to do something illegal," I pointed out, helpfully. "Presuming the tree farm was on private property."

"Something like that." He shrugged, sending Percy on another little ride. "Figured the pony belonged to someone local and would find her way home."

"I don't know anyone by the name of Reid Brisco. Is he new in town?"

Isaac nodded. "Moved here about four months ago. Bought the old Hutchinson place on forty acres of prime land. Woodworker, I think. Single dad with a little girl."

"I'm surprised I haven't heard about him. An eligible man is big news in Clover Grove."

He rolled his eyes again. "Put your matchmaker away. No one knows what happened to Brisco's wife. It's a legit mystery."

In a town where gossip traveled faster than electricity, a missing wife should have been a headline. It was exactly the type of story Justine Schalow liked to run.

"How can no one know about a missing wife?"

"I didn't say she was missing. Brisco probably knows where she is. Or isn't. Some folks say she died, others say she left. Either way, he doesn't want to talk about it. Couple of busybodies tried at the market and he shut them down fast. Little girl didn't seem to know anything, either."

"Huh." I stared up at the tree. Snow slid off some boughs, and they sprang up. "It's hard to keep a secret like that around here."

"More power to Brisco." Isaac's mouth set in a hard line. "A man's entitled to his privacy. If he pays his bills, takes care of his daughter and leaves his neighbors' sheep alone, that should be enough."

Maybe it should be, but it wasn't. Not for me, and not for my pets, who'd puffed a little while Isaac was speaking of Reid Brisco. It made me worry more about the pony. Had she innocently trotted into some strange stunt by a mysterious man? It was possible he'd walked the pony down through the fields and killed Hester to get the sleigh and sell it. Stranger things had happened around here.

I fully intended to wring more information out of Isaac, but a movement at the entrance of the municipal building caught my eye. A security officer in uniform emerged and scanned the square.

Isaac noticed, too. "That's my cue to go. Mayor Martingale doesn't hassle me too much about stating my piece out here, but she gets tetchy around the holidays. I don't want her coming down to bend my ear about civic responsibility and Christmas spirit."

It was my cue to leave, too. Meryl had a habit of enlisting me—more specifically, my genius pets—to help solve crimes when a public event hung in the balance. That made Kellan the filling in what he called a "renegade sandwich." Like many politicians, Meryl had principles of convenience and didn't hesitate to bend the law or exploit my weakness for animals to meet her ends. She declared it was for the greater good, but it could cost me my rings one day.

"Let's beat it," I said, turning to leave the square. "Thanks for telling me about the pony. I'll drop by to meet the mysterious Reid Brisco."

"Just leave my name out of it, okay? I don't want anything to do with him. Or anyone else for that matter." Once we were on the street, Isaac smiled for the first time. He clearly didn't boycott the dentist because his teeth were in good shape. "Especially you."

I smiled back. "Bet ewe will change your tune if Patsy gets stuck in the fence again. *Ewe.* Get it?"

The eye roll had more humor this time. "Bet ewe think you're funnier than ewe are. Get it?"

Keats beat me to the laugh with a brisk ha-ha-ha.

"Can I ask you one more thing, Isaac?"

"No, and I preferred it when you called me Mr. Gherkin."

"I'd prefer it if you called me Ivy. And I've got to ask anyway." I pointed at his shoulder. "Can I have my cat back?"

Isaac finally laughed, and it was another pleasant surprise. "Forgot all about him. He's easier to get used to than humans. Always liked a ginger."

I snapped my fingers, and Percy reluctantly leapt from the homesteader's shoulder into my arms. "Your whole cranky façade feels like it would crumble with the right cat, Isaac. Not mine, of course, but I'll keep my eye out for a contender."

"Not interested in matchmaking of any kind," he said, walking away. Percy meowed after him, and he turned. "Mind your own business. All of you."

I shook my head. "Not our strong suit. And for what it's worth, Isaac, Aline Tupling could do a lot worse than a man who cares about principles and heritage sheep."

He backed away so fast he sat down hard in a planter filled with festive flora. The words he called after me weren't for delicate sensibilities.

On the way to the truck, I said, "I hope Isaac isn't Hester's killer because I quite like him. He feels like our kind of people. 'Sheeple' fits here, no?"

Keats gave a noncommittal rumble that sounded like a reminder to keep my wits about me. I'd given a few suspects a free pass simply because of their fondness for pets, and it had come back to bite me.

Isaac Gherkin wasn't off the hook for killing Hester yet. But if he'd put me on the right path to find the pony, I'd help my brother prove the eccentric old man really got socked in the jaw defending innocent firs at a Christmas tree farm.

"That's a quality alibi, boys," I said, letting the pets in the truck. "Let's pin this crime on someone less creative."

All things considered, I was feeling pretty good as I turned the key in the ignition. We were on the right path at last.

An incoming text quickly killed my buzz.

"Please tell me you're at home," Kellan wrote.

"Define home," I typed back. "Because I'm in Clover Grove, my hometown. And I feel totally at home here."

The response was instantaneous: "Ivy."

Just my name, three little letters, but chiefly exasperation leapt off the phone's screen. I'd have to give Kellan a little more to get a little more freedom to explore my lead.

"Got a hot tip on the runaway pony," I texted. "Checking it out soon."

This time, the response took longer. He was probably trying to figure out how to derail my train without triggering the mania known to all rescuers. I used the time to shoot a text to Jilly.

"Where?" he asked at last.

I hesitated. If I told Kellan I was heading to Reid Brisco's property based on intel from Isaac Gherkin, Asher and the snowmobile brigade would be at the other end to intercept me. But if I *didn't* tell him and something went wrong, I'd be in big trouble.

"Checking a few homesteads north of town," I typed. "Will keep you posted."

It wasn't a lie. Reid's place was one of several homesteads in that area. I'd check them all, if needed, and I'd keep Kellan posted. Eventually.

He didn't answer, so I got the truck rolling. The drive to County Route 5 would take nearly half an hour in these conditions.

The phone buzzed again as I stopped at a red light.

"Be careful," Kellan texted. "Love you."

The message made me smile. "Love you too," I replied. "See you soon."

I had no doubt whatsoever that he loved me. And I had no doubt whatsoever that he'd deployed my brother to cut me off from that pony.

This time, however, Asher didn't stand a chance.

I had my own army.

CHAPTER ELEVEN

The snowmobile showdown unfolded like something out of an old Western movie, except instead of tumbleweeds and dusty streets, we had snowdrifts and a county road lined with evergreens sagging under fresh powder.

Our ragtag militia of rescuers had assembled about half a mile from Reid Brisco's property. Edna sat astride a massive Arctic Cat that looked like it could survive a nuclear winter, with her taupe perm entirely concealed by a helmet. Gertie Rhodes straddled her own machine, long braid hanging to her waist and poncho billowing from under her ski jacket. In front of our line of soldiers sat Cori Hogan. The tiny trainer looked like a doll on her snowmobile, but I knew she could handle it like a pro. Lifting her left hand in a heavy black glove, she gave a backward wave toward our opposition. The middle finger was wrapped in neon orange tape. I couldn't really hear the titter of laughter among the rest of our crew, but I felt it. Cori probably did, too, because she revved her engine with her right hand.

Across the road, a mirror image lineup glinted in the weak afternoon sun. Three police snowmobiles parked slightly ahead of what I'd dubbed Asher's Army. My brother was in the center, and his white teeth flashed a smug grin through the half-open visor. Giving a proper wave, he shouted, "Hi, honey!"

The call was meant for Jilly, of course, but Cori responded with a double orange salute.

Jilly, perched in front of me on Edna's behemoth, grumbled, "I married a traitor."

"You married a cop," I said. "Same difference when it comes to animal rescue, though."

Percy shifted in the backpack I'd strapped on my shoulders. He probably would have preferred a front-row seat, but this was safer. A loud meow declared he was eager to get going. It wasn't his first snowmobile rodeo.

"This is insane," Jilly said. "We're literally facing off against the police. At what point in our friendship did storm-the-castle become our go-to strategy?"

"About the time we rescued Keats, and it only got worse from there. Beats fishing for gators, though, doesn't it?"

Her shudder told me I'd succeeded in shifting her focus from lawbreaking to survival. Perspective made all the difference in situations like this.

Edna's helmet twisted in a smooth, robotic movement. "Visors down, girls. Things are about to get interesting."

I held out a bit longer to watch Asher confer with his troops. How many favors had he called in from neighboring cops and cop wannabes? Didn't they have better things to do with their time than keep us from finding a pony?

"We're outnumbered," I said.

"Outmatched," Jilly added.

"That leaves us with outmaneuvering," Edna finished.

Before I could ask what she meant, Cori waved another orange flare and took off like a rocket. Making a hard right, she shot toward Isaac Gherkin's property. Beside her, a black and white creature raced through the snow. It was Clem, her dog.

Then, a second border collie joined him, their strides falling into sync.

"Keats!" My heart stuttered. "Where are you going?"

My dog had a deep respect for Cori, but I didn't expect him to desert me at a time of need.

"It's part of the plan," Edna said. "The dogs will navigate a path meant for lighter loads and tip a few thugs along the way."

"Not my thug, I hope," Jilly mumbled.

"Relax, Jillian. Your squire is a natural athlete with expert driving skills. Shame he weighed himself down with ego and a badge."

The rest of our party followed Cori in a thundering cascade of motors and flying snow. Asher's militia gave chase, reminding me of border collies pursuing sheep. I suspected they'd find my friends very hard to herd.

"Why aren't we following them, Edna?" I asked, dropping my visor.

She didn't wait for me to catch up mentally. Instead, she gunned the motor, gave a battle cry worthy of an apocalyptic warrior and executed a sharp turn that nearly unseated Jilly and me. Then, she blasted through the bumpy field toward Reid Brisco's farm.

Cori and crew had decoyed my brother's army and given us a window to explore.

Right now, my only window on the world was a visor. I screamed into the helmet, creating a private abyss of terror that no one else could hear. The snowmobile caught air over a hidden rise, and my stomach relocated to my throat. Percy's yowl cut through my headgear. He loved adventure much more when he controlled the action.

When we skidded to a stop in front of a fence line, my scream transformed into something entirely different.

"Oh, my goodness," I panted, flipping up the visor. "There she is."

The cutest pony in the world stood just yards away in the pasture. She was chestnut perfection, with a flaxen mane and tail worthy of a shampoo commercial. Her compact body spoke of Shetland heritage, and her dark eyes held what looked like a spark of mischief. Beside her stood an old slope-backed white mare who exuded grandmotherly patience, and a brown cow with a pronounced limp who ignored us completely.

Before we could dismount, a blur of pink and blonde exploded from a well-maintained barn.

"Hey!" A little girl in a puffy coat and sparkly boots raced over to us, arms pumping. "Did you come to see my new pony? Well, she's not mine yet, but Santa might say yes if I'm really good. I'm being SO good. I promised to eat broccoli every day for a year."

The child reached us, breathless and beaming. She was around six years old, with fine blonde hair under a knitted hat decorated with reindeer. Her cheeks were flushed pink from the cold and excitement.

This must be Reid's daughter. She certainly seemed healthy and happy, despite her absentee mom.

Climbing off the snowmobile, I moved toward her on unsteady legs. "I'm Ivy. What's your name?"

"I'm Keely. And this is Peppermint the pony. She showed up last night." Keely's mittens gestured wildly in the pony's direction. "Just walked right up to the barn like she owned the place. Daddy says she ran away from home, but I think maybe she's magic. Do you think she could be magic? She ate four carrots and two apples, and Gretchen, our old mare, likes her. Gretchen doesn't even like our cow."

Pulling off my helmet, I grinned. The little girl's enthusiasm was infectious, and it did seem somewhat magical that she'd chosen the same name as Aline Tupling had given her own pony six decades ago. "I think any pony smart enough to find her way here might have some magic in her. Maybe she's part unicorn."

"Yes!" Keely bounced on her toes. "That's what I told Daddy. Look at her mane. It's like princess hair, but for ponies."

Jilly dismounted more gracefully than I did, removing her helmet to reveal golden curls and a wide smile. "Hi Keely, I'm Jilly, and the pony is beautiful. Why did you name her Peppermint?"

"Because she's spunky." Keely made complicated gestures with her mittens to convey a lively personality. "Peppermints aren't sweet like real candy. They've got spark, you know? And she's got spark. This morning she opened the latch on the feed bin even though Daddy said it was pony-proof. Everything's easy when you're smart."

Edna remained on the snowmobile, ready to retreat at the first sign of our pursuers. Her visor was up, and her sharp eyes scanned the fields like a military commander. "You're right, kid. Intelligence is the best skeleton key."

"Skeleton?" Keely tipped her head curiously. "Like bones?"

"Bones? What's going on?" The gruff question came from the direction of the barn, and I turned to see a man walking our way. Reid Brisco was tall and broad-shouldered, with brown hair that curled slightly at his collar and a classic jawline. He wore a heavy canvas jacket over jeans and battered work boots, and an expression that blended irritation and suspicion. "Why are you talking to my daughter about skeletons?"

"Never too early to discuss anatomy," Edna said. "I'm a retired nurse, young man, and people wait too long to cover the basics. Do you want her to learn online?"

He scowled at her. "I don't take parenting advice from strangers on snowmobiles. Why are you here?"

"Daddy, don't be grumpy," Keely said. "They came to see Peppermint." She pointed at Jilly. "Maybe you could marry this lady. She looks like an angel."

Jilly laughed. "I'm definitely not an angel, Keely. And my husband won't like it if I marry your dad."

Keely laughed, too, and pointed a mitten at me. "How about you? You're pretty, too."

"Also taken," I said. "But this lady is free."

I used both hands to showcase Edna for the sheer enjoyment of watching Reid Brisco's startled reaction.

Edna saw it and cackled. "You should be so lucky, Brisco. But I'm taken, too."

"You are?" Jilly's voice overlapped with mine.

Her helmet bobbed. "I married my cause. We won't have time for romance after the apoc—"

"Never mind," I cut her off. Despite having four nephews, my skills with young kids were sketchy at best. I didn't visit often when they were young. But I knew my sister Daisy wouldn't have wanted them to hear about a potential apocalypse at Keely's age.

"I'm not in the market anyway," Reid said. "Keely, why don't you go inside and draw some pictures while I talk to the ladies?"

"Not till I show them my pony." Keely grabbed my gloved hand with sweet confidence and pulled me to the fence. "I asked Santa for one last year and now it's happened."

Reid looked from his daughter to the pony and frowned. "Honey, this pony has another home. Someone will be missing her right now."

Leaning on the fence, I watched the pony. "She looks well fed and groomed. Any idea how she got here, Mr. Brisco?"

"Mr. Brisco," Keely repeated, giggling. "That's funny. She's older than you, Daddy."

I was *not* older than Reid Brisco, who had a good scattering of silver in his hair. Clearly, I wasn't as pretty as the kid said.

He ignored the comment and answered me. "I'm guessing the pony got disoriented in the storm. I'll ask around later and see if anyone knows where she belongs."

Keely pouted. "Peppermint belongs here. Look how happy she is."

The pony did look happy. She sidled up beside the mare, and their tails swished in unison.

"Still, we can't keep what's not ours," he said. "Imagine how upset you'd be if Gretchen got lost in a snowstorm."

I trained my trusty HR microscope on Reid. He seemed surly and suspicious of us, but his voice softened with Keely.

Protective single father. Noted.

"We can help track down the pony's owner," I said. "I'm Ivy Galloway from Runaway Farm, and these are my friends Jilly and Edna. We get pulled into animal rescue all the time."

"What brought you today?" he asked. "No one knows the pony is here."

I kept my word to leave Isaac Gherkin out of the conversation. "My dog found the trail of a small equine and we took our cue from him." I glanced around, hoping Keats might charge in to back my claim, but he was still enjoying the call of the wild. "I was worried about her."

"Livestock wander." Reid was nonchalant. "Especially in weather like this, gates get left open, latches fail. Snow covers their usual trails."

"True. Mind if I take a closer look at her?"

Reid hesitated, then shrugged. "Whatever."

I climbed over the fence awkwardly, and my boots landed in snow that nearly reached my knees. The pony watched me approach with alert, intelligent eyes. Her ears pricked with interest rather than alarm.

"Hey, girl," I said, pulling off my glove and offering each equine a sugar cube from my pocket. Then I picked up the lead rope that trailed from the pony's halter and examined it.

Just as I expected, the rope was frayed at the end, as if she'd pulled herself free. What I didn't expect were bedraggled red ribbons twisted around the rope at intervals. Two jingle bells were attached to her halter, with gaps where others had gone missing.

Her nose, soft as velvet, pressed into my palm. Then she whinnied.

An answer came as a strident meow. Percy had been so quiet I forgot he was there.

Keely squealed with delight. "You have a CAT? In a BACKPACK?"

"I do." Walking back to the fence, I slipped off the pack and unzipped it. Percy stepped onto the top rung with the regal bearing of a monarch greeting his subjects. Aside from his puffy yellow parka, that is. "Percy, meet our new friend, Keely Brisco."

"He's so fluffy." Keely skipped closer, bursting with energy. When she reached up to Percy, however, her touch was gentle. She had good instincts—or good training—around animals. "And his parka is perfect. Percy, are you magic too?"

"Some people think so," Jilly said. "He's definitely good at finding things."

The cat strutted back and forth, purring loudly. He specialized in seniors but didn't hold back from charming children as well. When Jilly and I had kids of our own, he'd make a good uncle. I wasn't so sure about Keats. The dog was impatient, selective, and nipped with abandon. We'd have to work it out, because I would never give up my pets.

Jilly climbed over to join me in the pasture, possibly sensing I'd time-traveled into motherhood. Patting my shoulder, she checked out the lead rope and halter, and sighed.

"The pony's in good condition," I said. "Well-fed, healthy hooves, good muscle tone." I rubbed the velvet nose gently again. "No signs of neglect."

"Can we ride her?" Keely directed the question to Jilly and me. "Daddy says she's too small for grown-ups, but I'm not a grown-up. Neither is Percy, so maybe we could try it together."

"Keely." Reid's voice had a note of warning. "These ladies are busy. They'll be leaving soon, and so will we."

I turned to smile at Keely, remembering how it felt to be her age. How desperately I'd wanted to learn to ride horses, when we couldn't even afford to keep a cat or dog. My mother had made all my early rescues vanish.

"It's possible, Keely," I said. "Shetland ponies are sturdy. They were originally bred to haul carts full of coal and are stronger than they look. But we should test it another time, since Peppermint had a hard night. She's probably very tired."

"She didn't seem tired when she was breaking into the food bin," Keely said. "Maybe just a short ride?"

"Ivy's right," Reid said. "Peppermint had a hard night. Let her rest."

Jilly climbed back over the fence with a grace I didn't have. "Keely, why don't you tell me more about your cow? What's her name?"

"Clementine," Keely said, taking Jilly's hand. "She hurt her leg before we got her, but Daddy says she's part of our family now, and we take care of family even when they limp." Keely launched into an elaborate story about the cow, and Jilly listened with genuine interest, slowly easing the child away from where I stood with the pony.

Reid and I were on opposite sides of the fence, and it was time to dive into a difficult discussion. "Do you have any idea what happened to Peppermint last night?" I asked. "Judging by the hoof-prints we found, she had a strange adventure."

"How would I know about that?" He sounded defensive already. "I was here looking after my daughter in a heavy snowstorm."

"I believe Peppermint was at the Clover Grove Museum, where there was an incident."

"An incident." Reid's tone flattened, and he scanned for Keely. "Is that the local code word for murder?"

Even reclusive homesteaders stayed connected, it seemed. "That's right. A pony of about this size left tracks at the scene. There was a jingle bell matching the ones on her harness."

Reid's Adam's apple bobbed. "Are you saying someone used this pony to commit murder?"

"I know the pony was present, but not her role." I reached out to stroke Peppermint's neck, and she leaned into the touch. "Maybe she saw something that would help us figure out what happened."

"Ponies can't testify in court." His tone was sarcastic now.

"Obviously. But animals can lead people to answers. It's happened to me a few times." I presumed he'd heard some of our stories, but he didn't let on. "That's why I need to borrow Peppermint for a few hours to investigate."

"No."

The single word hit me like a hard-packed snowball. "No?"

"That's what I said." Reid straightened, and I noticed he was even taller than Asher. Six foot four, at least. "That pony came onto my property injured and stressed. I'm not letting you drag her back to a crime scene."

"Injured?" My voice spiked, and Jilly gave me a warning look. "What and where?"

He flicked a finger at Peppermint's flank. "Superficial scrapes, mostly. Probably from pushing through brush and fences. She needs to take it easy, not be subjected to whatever amateur investigation you're running."

The amateur comment stung, probably because it was accurate. "I understand your concern, but all I want to do is retrace her steps. This pony might be the key to clearing an innocent person's name."

"Let the police handle it. If they ask to borrow the pony, I won't say no."

"The police are currently on a joyride through the countryside. They tried to block me from coming here, and we decoyed them."

Reid blinked. "You what?"

"Long story." I glanced toward Keely, who was clutching Percy in both arms and entertaining Jilly with animated chatter. "Reid, I know you want to protect the pony, but I'm very good with animals. My hobby farm is full of rescues, and I promise this pony would be treated like royalty."

"She's being treated like royalty here. And unless you can show me evidence that you're her legal owner, she's staying."

Edna waved from the snowmobile and called, "Ivy, we've got ten minutes tops before your brother's militia regroups. Make it quick."

Reid stared at me. "Your brother's militia?"

"Just a bunch of dudes on snowmobiles." I put my boot on the bottom rung of the fence. "My brother's a cop, though. And married to Jilly."

"Sounds complicated." Reid turned away, clearly ending the conversation. "Thanks for checking on the pony, but I'll stick with my plan to ask around and find the owner."

He started walking toward the barn, and I scrambled over the fence to follow. Opportunity was slipping through my fingers like sand. "Wait. Please."

Something in my voice made Reid stop, although he didn't turn. "What?"

"It's about my sister. Iris is the museum curator, and authorities are looking for someone convenient to blame for Hester Belcher's murder." I took a deep breath and tossed a snowball of my own. "Do you know what it's like to feel desperate to protect family?"

Reid's broad shoulders tensed, and I knew I'd struck a nerve. He spun quickly to stare at Keely.

She noticed, and her voice rang out. "Daddy! Can Percy come inside? I want to show him my crayons."

"Not right now, sweetheart," he called.

Keely came over with Jilly. "But I need him."

Reid rolled his eyes. "You need *all* the animals, apparently."

"Remember the big cat at the museum?" she asked. "I touched its fur, and the gargoyle grabbed me."

"Gargoyle?" Jilly asked. "I didn't see any gargoyles at the museum yesterday."

Keely made a face. "The mean old lady. She hurt my arm and told me not to touch anything ever again."

"*Keely*." Reid sounded alarmed. "You knew better than to pat the cougar."

"But Hester shouldn't have grabbed her," I said. "She did the same to my brother and me twenty years ago. Remember the cop I mentioned?"

A mottled flush crept over Reid's plaid scarf and up his neck. "Can you go, please?"

"Just let me borrow the pony. I'll bring her back safe and sound."

He glared with hazel eyes about the same shade as Isaac's, although neither man would likely enjoy the comparison. "I don't see a trailer. Which means you'd need to walk her past this so-called militia on snowmobiles."

"Don't worry your pretty head about that," Edna said. "We have tactics, young man."

Reid glanced at the pony who'd complicated his quiet life. "She'll be locked in the barn with the mare and cow when I leave."

My heart registered a mumble that I shouldn't have been able to hear. Keats was standing in the doorway of a long, low building attached to the barn. His eerie blue eye pinned me, and his white forepaw came up.

"What's that dog doing?" Reid asked, following my gaze.

"Finding things." I was already moving toward Keats. "He's got a nose for—"

"Stop right there. That building is off-limits." Reid circled and pushed me back with the force of his energy alone. "That's my workshop. Dangerous tools, unstable projects. Not safe for people or pets."

"I heard you were a woodworker." I wondered what he was hiding in his shop. "We'd love to pick up a few gifts."

"This isn't a retail site. And I need you to leave now."

"Daddy, don't be mean." Keely came to his side, Percy still cradled in her arms. "I like them. Especially the angel lady. She's so nice, and she cares about cows."

"You can come and visit our cows," Jilly said. "We also have sheep and goats and a dancing alpaca." She gently freed Percy from Keely's grip. "Your dad's right that we should get going."

"But I like you." Keely pouted again. "You're all awesome."

Edna leaned back on the snowmobile and smirked. "It's true, kid. I inspire awe in everyone I meet."

Jilly and I laughed, defusing some of the tension. Edna's arrogance was both her greatest weapon and her most endearing quality.

Reid didn't smile, but his shoulders relaxed slightly. "I'm sure you do, ma'am."

Jilly tucked Percy into his backpack and slid it over my shoulders. Leaning in close, she whispered, "Don't even think about stealing that pony, Ivy. Reid knows where we live."

"I'm thinking about stealing the kid," I whispered back. "She's good with animals, and we could totally bypass the baby phase."

"I heard that," Reid said dryly.

"As intended." I laughed. Thanks for letting us see Peppermint. If you change your mind—"

His glove sliced through the air. "I won't."

Pulling a slightly crumpled business card from my pocket, I held it out. "In case you need to reach me. About borrowing the pony. Or visiting the alpaca."

Keely snatched the card and threw her arms around Jilly's waist. "Can I come and dance with the alpaca?"

"Of course." My best friend hugged Keely back. "Alvina prefers men, though."

"Daddy can do it, then."

Reid shook his head. "Not a chance."

Keats rounded us up, and we climbed onto the snowmobile behind Edna. My phone vibrated in my pocket, but I let it go. No doubt Kellan had heard from Asher about the "Code Ivy." He could lecture me later. Right now, I had planning to do. There was a pony to liberate, a workshop to investigate, and a newcomer to background-check.

Reid Brisco thought he could keep his secrets locked away with dangerous tools and unstable projects.

Clearly, he knew nothing about me or my pets.

CHAPTER TWELVE

E dna grabbed my elbow to keep me from colliding with a display of handmade beeswax candles. "You're about as stealthy as a toddler," she whispered. "I can't believe people rave about your sneakery."

"Complain about it, you mean." I ducked behind a faux Christmas tree made entirely of candles. "Guess I won't win any awards for surveillance."

"Maybe you should have stuck with HR." Edna slid out of the beeswax booth and moved with furtive ease to the next stall. "Some people are just better behind desks."

Jilly followed, earning a solid B for espionage, despite high-heeled boots on a slick surface. "Go easy, Edna. If you make Ivy self-conscious, she'll knock over—"

I knocked over a six-foot cardboard cutout of a wheel of cheese. Luckily, it fell toward me and concealed me from our target.

The cheese vendor propped the sign upright and offered me a generous square of gouda on a toothpick. I accepted it and grabbed another square, mumbling my thanks around a double mouthful. I always tried to live as if each bite of cheese might be my last.

"Dagnabit, Ivy, no snacking on the job," Edna said. "Gouda is a well-documented choking hazard. I won't blow my cover doing the Heimlich."

"I can sample *and* stalk, Edna. A decade of executive multitasking trained me for this."

Jilly giggled and caught an elbow in the midriff from our tutor. Nothing in our corporate experience had trained us to tail an antiques dealer through a Christmas market. We were both excellent observers in a boardroom setting. Combining that skill with physical maneuvers was the hard part.

Still, I had a pretty good sense of when Heddy Langman was about to turn around and ducked into a stall selling pine wreaths to avoid being seen. I reached out to steady myself and got a glove full of needles.

The kind-eyed woman running the booth smiled as she extricated me. "Hiding from a Langman sister?"

"Is it *that* obvious?" I asked.

"You're not the first, and I know the signs. At least it's only Heddy tonight. Usually, both are here casing out old treasures. My friend accidentally sold them a valuable family heirloom for five bucks two days ago. She didn't know it was a Tiffany lamp appraised at five grand. All sales are final here, and the Langmans dined out on steak afterwards."

Edna beckoned from the other side of the aisle. "Ivy, are you here to fraternize or learn something?"

Bidding the wreath vendor goodbye, I darted over to join my friends behind a tall pile of squash and turnips. "I *did* learn something. The Langmans tricked someone into selling a family treasure for next to nothing this week."

Edna shooed the produce vendor out of his own stall and pushed us down. Since our earlier mission, she'd transformed from snowmobile warrior to secret operative and was wearing black from head to foot. "So, the Langmans bilked someone. Hardly news."

"What's Heddy doing?" Jilly asked, afraid to straighten up.

"Digging for precious stones in a pile of old Christmas lights," Edna said. "You two stay here. I'll circle Heddy and flank her position. Should have brought walkies."

Jilly laughed. "Sounds like a military operation."

"Everything in life is a military operation, Jillian. The sooner you accept that, the more likely you'll be to survive the end times." She snapped her fingers. "Keats, Percy... You're with me."

The dog decided Edna was the better source of entertainment and left with her. Meanwhile, Percy slunk from stall to stall on his own reconnaissance mission. The cat was born to spy, despite his bright attire and fluffy packaging.

"I'd like to make a squash soup, but I guess shopping is out of the question," Jilly said, running her hand over gourds.

"Not necessarily. You could bowl Heddy down with acorn squash. Seeing everything as a weapon is part of the exercise."

She laughed again, clearly enjoying our mission. The Christmas Market was one of our favorite destinations during the holiday season. Its popularity had grown to the point where it covered several blocks of prime Main Street real estate. Traffic closed down for five evenings, and people came out in droves to enjoy the festivities and support local vendors. Mayor Martingale had threatened to cancel after the museum murder but gave in to public pressure. Kellan responded by bringing in extra officers from other towns and positioning them on every corner to control the flow of foot traffic. Security was easier to guarantee here than it was in town square with people packed in like sardines to stare at the tree. Giving citizens the Christmas they craved while keeping them alive was a difficult balance.

If you could ignore the uniforms, the scene was cozy and festive. White lights twinkled in the bare branches of oak trees, and dozens of booths offered everything from handcrafted jewelry to baked goods. The scent of roasted chestnuts mingled with spices and wood smoke from a firepit where families gathered to warm their hands.

Carols drifted from speakers mounted on lampposts, and children's voices clamored for treats.

The familiar jingle of coins a few yards away told me Aline Tupling hadn't given up on the toy drive. Meanwhile, raspy shouts in the distance confirmed Isaac Gherkin was doing his bit to steal joy from consumers. All was as calm and bright as it could be, considering.

Jilly peeked over the produce and nudged me. "Heddy's on the move."

Still squatting, I poked my head out from behind the tablecloth and saw familiar khakis and a black puffer jacket weaving between booths. Heddy moved with purpose, stopping occasionally to examine merchandise with a critical eye.

A few yards behind her, a white tail tuft rose briefly. Keats had his blue eye on the prize.

"Where's Edna?" I asked.

"Probably rappelling from the rooftops." Jilly grabbed my hand and pulled me upright. "Come on, Heddy's crossing to the next block with the most popular artists. Maybe we'll get last-minute gift ideas. Or first-minute, in your case."

I was behind in my shopping, as usual, and had expected to pick up a few items here, along with a heaping helping of gossip from Clover Grove's never-reliable grapevine. I also wanted to ask around about the pony, since Reid Brisco hadn't cooperated.

Our plan to drop some cash fell by the wayside when we saw Heddy and tailed her. The junior Langman had a penchant for verbal slips, and there was a chance she'd reveal something of interest about Hester or the stolen sleigh during discussions with vendors. So far, we hadn't gotten close enough to hear anything at all. Maybe she wasn't as hungry for valuables after landing the Tiffany lamp, and possibly the Founder's sleigh. But she was still here. Like a great white shark, Heddy had to keep on swimming or cease to exist.

The crowd was denser on the next block, proving I wasn't the only one behind on my Christmas shopping. Here, there were booths with knitted and crocheted goods, stained glass, paintings and intricate objects made of metal. Mabel Halliday and Teri Mason had stalls, despite their brick-and-mortar stores, and I hoped we'd have time to say hello.

Keats turned a blue eye back as if to remind me we were still on the job. He was much closer to Heddy now. So close that he could be kicked if she turned too quickly. She must be onto a hot lead that the dog also wanted to follow.

We pushed through a cluster of people admiring beautiful quilts and emerged near a booth displaying wine racks, cutting boards and old-fashioned toys, all made of wood.

I couldn't see the vendor, but I suspected we shared a fondness for Peppermint.

Heddy Langman's hands landed on her hips. Her fingers were bare again, despite the chilly temps. Was she a cold-blooded reptile? And if so, shouldn't she be dormant in a mudhole by now? "Brumation," I murmured.

"What?" Jilly asked.

"Heddy should be brumating. That's what it's called when reptiles like gators go dormant in winter."

"Good to know. Although I'd love to go even half a day without a gator reference. How about that for a Christmas present?"

I snickered, earning myself another glare from a blue eye. If the dog were closer, I'd get a nip.

"Tacky," Heddy announced to no one in particular. "Absolutely tacky. I cannot believe anyone would stoop to something so taste-less. The police should show you the door."

"There is no door." The voice belonged to Reid Brisco, as I'd suspected. He was behind a table in the booth, and I couldn't see him. "It's an outdoor market, and you can keep moving along, ma'am."

Raising a hand to shoulder level, Heddy snapped her fingers. "Everyone needs to know what you've done here. It's a travesty."

"They're just collectibles, lady. Nothing to get hot under the parka about."

Jilly and I abandoned the spy exercise and moved forward together.

"What's going on?" I asked.

Heddy's arm came down, but her fingers still snapped. "They've got your cat, Ivy. Save him."

Percy was indeed behind the table, cradled in Keely Brisco's arms. The little girl hugged him tight while her blue eyes moved from her father to Heddy and back.

"The cat doesn't want to be saved," I said. "He looks quite happy with Keely. She has a way with animals."

"You know these people?" Heddy's fingers kept on snapping, like a mouthy gator who didn't realize it was supposed to be brumating.

"We do," Jilly said. "Well enough to trust our Percy with them. The same can't be said of you. Not after you stole Gertie's Fleecy."

The snapping stopped. "For the last time, I did not steal that cat. I found her."

"In Gertie's house," I said. "Along with other valuables."

Jilly turned to me. "Why didn't the police arrest her? And is it too late?"

In the distance, I saw my favorite officer of the law leaning against a lamppost with his arms crossed. He didn't hide his surveillance of us.

I pointed Kellan out to Jilly. He was giving us some rope, and I didn't want to hang myself too soon.

"Heddy, why are you picking on Reid Brisco?" I asked. "That's not how we treat newcomers in Clover Grove."

"Since when? He claims to be a skilled woodworker, and I call foul." She swept her arm in a flamboyant gesture worthy of a game show host. "Look at those. Absolutely atrocious."

On a second table sat several hand-painted replicas of the Founder's sleigh in various sizes. One was small enough to hang on a tree. Another was big enough for a child to ride.

"Wow, they look a lot like the real thing," Jilly said. "You're very talented, Reid."

"Talented?" Heddy's voice rose even more. "This is the work of a rank amateur. And given what happened last night, some might even say it's suspicious."

"Suspicious?" Reid asked. "How?"

"You modeled those after something," Heddy said. "Perhaps you have the original."

"That's ridiculous." Reid picked up one of the sleighs. "This isn't the work of a day. It's taken months. I saw a photo of the Millbrook family sleigh in the tourist booth right after we moved here and then designed these from memory."

"Sounds convenient," Heddy said. "You're an unknown in town, Mr. Brisco. A man without a history. How can we be sure you weren't at the museum last night to steal that priceless sleigh?"

Tears filled Keely's eyes and then spilled over, landing on Percy's fur. He gave a long, low yowl that boded ill for Heddy's scalp if she continued. Keats circled and nudged my fingertips to take more action.

"That's enough, Heddy," I said. "There's a child present in case you hadn't noticed."

"Mind your own business, Ivy Galloway. You're another one who seems to turn up wherever there's drama."

"You mean wherever you're creating drama," I said. "There's a difference. Tonight, we're here to build up local artisans, whereas you want to tear them down."

"I'm simply pointing out that this stranger is profiting from a tragedy. Less than a day after the original sleigh was stolen, here he is selling copies. Don't you find that distasteful?"

Edna stepped out from behind a rack of gaudy clothing in the next booth. "Heddy, you attend every funeral in town and hand out business cards. *That's* distasteful."

"My sister and I help to find good homes for the belongings of the bereaved. It's practically a public service."

I picked up Reid's smallest sleigh and admired the craftsmanship. "Beautiful work, Reid. We'll hang this one on our tree at Runaway Inn."

"We'll take a dozen to hand out to our guests," Jilly said. "If you'd like to deliver them, Keely can meet Alvina and the other animals."

Heddy's fingers started snapping again. "Don't encourage this charlatan. He'll probably steal your candlesticks."

"The ones you cased out when you let yourself into the inn that day?" I asked.

"What's your point, Ivy?" She snapped her fingers right in my face and regretted it when Keats dove at her cuffs. Her squeal turned Keely's sadness to shock and then something like relief.

"It feels like you're deflecting attention from your own suspicious behavior," I said. "Yesterday, you and Kaye made no secret of coveting the Millbrook sleigh."

She hopped away from Keats. "Bulletproof alibi, remember? I'm simply helping the police identify the guilty party for the good of the town."

I pointed to Kellan, still leaning against the lamppost. "Does it look like he needs help?"

Heddy glanced at Kellan and scowled. "It looks like he's taking a night off. He was never lazy before you came home, Ivy."

That earned her another nip. A fabric ripper, judging by her tone. No one was permitted to give Kellan a hard time except Keats. The chief was a valuable sheep in the dog's prize herd.

Edna looped her arm through Heddy's and pulled. "Let's take a little walk while you still can. I left my first aid kit at home."

The junior Langman resisted. "I don't want to go anywhere with you."

"You have choices," Edna said. "Buy me some chestnuts or call the chief over to rescue you."

Heddy gave up the fight, and they vanished into the crowd.

After a brief and awkward silence, Reid said, "Thank you. You didn't have to do that."

"Actually, I did." I pulled cash out of my pocket. "No child should have to watch her parent being bullied. I've been there."

"Don't worry about Heddy Langman," Jilly said. "She's blameshifting. It's her favorite strategy."

"If her alibi was bulletproof, she probably wouldn't be hassling you when she could case out the consignment booths," I added.

Reid let out a long breath and wrapped an arm around Keely. "I really did make the sleighs months ago. My only crime is selling them now."

Jilly's smile was kind. "It might have been better to wait till the original was recovered. Heddy won't be the only one who gives you a hard time."

"I don't have the luxury of missing the Christmas rush," he said. "I spent good money on materials and was counting on the income. The past few years have been..." He paused and looked down at Keely before finishing, "Difficult."

I wanted to know more about that but couldn't expect Reid to crack his heart open about his difficulties in front of his daughter. No matter what broke up his family, he was just a homesteader trying to make a living.

Percy squirmed until Keely set him down on the table. He strolled around the polished wood offerings with his usual nonchalance. Keats had settled at my feet with his ears in a neutral position. The pets' calm demeanor made me doubt

Reid Brisco had anything to do with the museum crime. But there was still a question waiting to be asked, and I had to do it before someone else came along. Particularly someone chiefly.

"Reid, did you ever have words with Hester Belcher?"

"Words?" He looked down at the replica sleighs. "I only met her that once."

"Right. The time Keely patted the cougar."

The little girl reached out to do the same to Percy, and he came back to enjoy the attention. "Percy's softer than the cougar," she said. "I didn't really like touching it and I was sorry I did. The lady made Daddy mad."

Reid picked up a chamois and started polishing a cutting board. "I wasn't mad, honey. It's a father's job to protect his kids. So, I apologized for breaking the rules. Then I asked the lady not to grab you again. Or any kids, for that matter."

Keats mumbled a commentary to me, but I already knew there was more to the exchange than Reid was offering. At the very least, he'd raised his voice at Hester. On the other hand, it couldn't be too far off the truth or Keely would react. The kid wore her heart on her puffy pink sleeve.

"Was anyone in the taxidermy gallery with you?" I asked.

He glanced up from his buffing. "Yes, and I'd be happy to provide details to the snowmobile army. Can we drop this for the moment?"

"Sure. Why don't we talk about the pony instead?"

I figured he'd shut me down, but he was so grateful to put the topic of Hester aside that he nodded. "I asked around, and so far, no one seems to know where she belongs. It's strange. A well-kept Shetland should have an owner within a reasonable walking distance for a pony."

"She's magic, like I told you." Keely rubbed her eyes. Either she had orange fluff in them or she was exhausted from an exciting day.

"Maybe Peppermint doesn't belong to anyone because Santa came early and left her for us."

Reid squeezed her shoulder. "Peppermint belongs to someone, honey."

"But what if her owner is mean to her, and she needs us?" Keely's lower lip trembled.

I signaled for Keats to go over to her. He wasn't a fan of small humans, but he might as well start training before more of them arrived in his life. "The truth usually comes out, Keely," I said. Keats looked back at me pleadingly and then shoved his ears under the girl's mitten. "In my experience, animals end up exactly where they're supposed to be."

Keats gave her another nudge that warmed my heart. The canine who'd fight to the death for me was facing one of his biggest challenges: an unhappy child. His courage in being kind made me love him even more, and he mumbled something that sounded like, "Don't get used to it."

The dog caught a break when the first notes of "Silent Night" drifted through the market and Keely looked up, entranced. The crowd in the street quieted as a small group of carollers appeared, moving between the booths carrying lanterns with flickering candles inside. Their voices blended in exquisite harmony, transforming the pre-holiday bustle into something sacred.

In the lead was my sister Iris, her crystal-clear soprano rising over the other voices. All the carollers wore matching red cloaks with faux fur accents that had doubtless whirred right out of my mother's sewing machine.

I'd forgotten Iris was scheduled to perform tonight. Seeing her fulfill that commitment despite the murder and the whispers that followed impressed me. It took courage.

The slow procession stopped in front of Reid's booth, where a small crowd gathered, drawn by Iris' voice and the flickering candlelight.

Keely stood transfixed, Percy and Keats forgotten. Her eyes were wide with wonder as she watched my sister sing.

When the song ended, Iris caught my gaze and smiled. Then her eyes fell on Keely, flanked by my pets. Keats mumbled something that my sister seemed to register. Stepping forward, she bent and said, "Would you like to hear another carol? We take requests."

Nodding, Keely said, "The First Noel, please."

Iris straightened, turned to her colleagues and then launched into the carol. She beckoned to the rest of us, and we joined in.

Even Reid mouthed a few words, although I could tell he was faking it. There was no faking the light in his eyes, however, when Keely walked over and held Iris' hand while they sang.

When the carol ended, Keely hugged Iris before running back to her dad, and I introduced Iris to both of them. They fell into pleasant conversation, but Keats was having none of that. Instead, he prodded me, and I took my orders.

"Reid, sorry to interrupt, but—"

"You can't borrow the pony," he interrupted right back.

My sister gave him an earnest smile. "I know we just met, but it would mean the world to me if you'd let Ivy borrow that pony, Reid."

"I don't see how it can help," he said.

Iris handed him the lantern to free both hands and then adjusted the hat over her dark hair. "Some things you take on faith. Ivy's connection with animals is one of them. I know my sister, and if she thinks the pony is important, it will be."

"Peppermint is half unicorn," Keely told Iris.

"Is that right?" Iris' smile expanded. "Then there's no mystery about this at all. Let Ivy take the unicorn-pony for a walk and you'll see some magic."

He set the lantern on the table and then picked it back up when he noticed Keely's interest. "Fine. Tomorrow morning at nine-thirty. Four hours max."

"Wise decision, young man," Edna said, rejoining us. "You never want to force a rescuer's hand."

Reid didn't have time to answer because the people who'd followed the carollers stayed to buy his wares.

Keats herded Jilly, Edna and me away before Reid could change his mind.

"That was smooth," Jilly said. "Using Iris as bait."

"Not me. Keats was the mastermind. Iris is a puppet, like the rest of us."

The dog gave a pant-laugh and trotted ahead into the crowd.

I nearly screamed when a hand shot out of a booth. Someone pulled my glove up and spun me in a little pirouette until I stood facing my beloved.

"Nice ambush, Chief," Edna said. "We obviously studied under the same spymaster."

Kellan shrugged. "I've got a log of every interaction since you ladies arrived." He held up his phone. "On video."

Edna put her hands on her hips. She looked even trimmer without her camouflage jumpsuit. "Don't you have crooks to catch? Leave an old lady in peace."

"It's the younger lady I'm concerned about." He signaled for the others to go ahead. "Your field work today wasn't too bad until about an hour ago, Ivy. How was the gouda?"

"Tasty," I said. "So was your scone. I decided to eat it before it got stale."

Kellan gestured around him. "I won't starve here. I'll even buy you a hot chocolate if you fill me in on your day."

I walked to the lamppost he'd vacated and leaned against it. Suddenly, I was exhausted. Nailing down an appointment with the pony had changed everything.

Staring up at the twinkle lights, I combed through my mental logs and shared my observations. About Powell Nobbs with his limp and scratches. About the slippery Langmans and their suspiciously perfect security footage. About Isaac Gherkin's grudge against Hester and his esteem for Aline Tupling. And even about Reid Brisco's tense exchange in the taxidermy exhibit. Turning back to the woodworker's booth, I shrugged. "I hope it wasn't Reid because I have a crush on his kid."

Kellan laughed. "She is a cutie. Can we order one just like her?"

"Maybe a couple, with a decent gap between them. No twins, no matter how sweet."

"Agreed." Kellan tipped his head. "I can't rule Reid out, or anyone else for that matter. The museum's security feeds were all disabled."

"All of them? That's deliberate."

He nodded. "Someone understands technology. That probably rules out the Langmans."

"Not so sure about that. They showed me their security footage and it looked too good to be true."

"Seems authentic to me, if conveniently timed," he said. "We're looking into it."

"How about Powell Nobbs? Does he have an alibi?"

Kellan's frown gave him away. "Said he weathered the storm at home after falling into his planter. Explains the scratches and limp, but there's no hard proof."

"He tried hard to avoid me this morning. Succeeded, too."

"That is sketchy." Kellan gave me a fond smile. "Can't imagine why people wouldn't want to chitchat with you today."

"Right? I'm a town favorite." I stared up at him. "Any sign of the murder weapon?"

"Not yet. Surprised your dynamic duo hasn't found it."

"Maybe that's the pony's job. Was it a knife?"

He shook his head. "Some kind of tool. Results aren't back yet."

"Huh. Like something you'd find in a woodworker's shop?"

"Or many other places. If I'm correct, this tool is as common as gossip around here." His smile grew impish. "Speaking of intel, would you care to disclose when you're planning to break into Reid's barn? It could help me with staffing tonight."

"I admit I thought about visiting the pony. Lucky for both of us, Reid said I can take Peppermint out in the morning. I'll see if I can get the pony to walk herself home. I hope Asher doesn't find reinforcements because the snowmobiles might spook her."

Kellan dropped his arm over my shoulder, a rare on-duty PDA. "I'll call them off. As a thanks for being so honest."

I relaxed against his chest. "I wasn't, entirely."

"Oh?" He leaned back to meet my eyes. "Which part was a lie?"

Fumbling in my purse, I pulled out a grease-stained paper bag. "I didn't eat your scone."

CHAPTER THIRTEEN

Jilly and I rolled down the farm's lane the next morning 15 minutes early. I wanted nothing to keep me from getting to that pony on time in case Reid Brisco slammed the barn door in my face. His mild thaw at the Christmas market couldn't be taken for granted. This man wasn't full of sunshine, and most of his good weather likely went to his daughter and livestock. I couldn't argue with his priorities.

Edna and Gertie were meeting us at the Brisco property with snowmobiles in tow. The horse trailer rolled behind my truck, already modified to suit Peppermint should the need arise. I'd packed sugar cubes, carrots, lead ropes and other sundries. Edna had come over at dawn to clunk around in the back of the pickup, adding and subtracting equipment to make sure the load was balanced.

"You're sure you want to do this without the Mafia?" Jilly said, as we turned onto the highway. "Usually, you welcome more boots on the ground."

"Figured it would be easier to get the pony to trust me and focus on the mission without Cori running around barking orders. Our core team can manage. The less time we spend flailing in the snow, the better."

"You got that right." She anchored Keats with both hands on her nylon snow pants as he grumbled complaints. He preferred to navigate with paws on the dash but couldn't get a proper grip. Percy had given up and retreated to the back seat to curl up on a blanket. "I don't relish the walk, but at least it's sunny."

"Peppermint will pick the easiest route, I'm sure. She may be sturdy, but she's not very big."

"I hope you're right. You can always use a lead rope to drag me."

I was grinning when my phone pinged. "Can you check that? Maybe it's Reid trying to cancel. We're going anyway. He basically promised, and I'm holding him to it."

Her phone pinged as she fumbled for mine. "Probably Edna. Maybe traffic is snarled."

My phone pinged again.

Hers, too.

And... repeat.

I lost count at five double pings, but it didn't matter. I knew what we were up against.

Jilly set both phones in the console between the seats without checking them. Then she flung herself back, causing Keats to slide into the door. He scrabbled upright with a frustrated rumble.

The phones kept pinging, and I kept driving, as if we weren't drowning in ignored notifications. "Not this time, Jilly. They cannot derail this mission."

"I don't think they want to derail it. They've probably forgotten it's happening."

That made me grip the wheel tighter. "How can they forget something so important to me?"

She patted my arm. "Because they're thinking about something important to *them*. Which is ultimately important to you, too. Am I right?"

My lips tried to move into a pout, but I resisted. Rescuers didn't pout. They kept driving toward the animal in need, even when their family activated the homing device.

"Asher hasn't forgotten our mission," I said. "He stirred his coffee super hard this morning. Sometimes sibling aggression tinkles rather than roars."

"Heard the clinking down the hall. Your brother's just tired. He only got a short nap and a shower."

I pressed down on the gas, determined to ignore the summons. "He's not just tired, he's mad because Kellan told him to disband the snowmobile army and let us take the pony home."

"That, too. Hearing my snow pants swish really seemed to set him off."

I couldn't help laughing. "He'll have eyes on us, guaranteed. Maybe a drone army will buzz along every step of the way."

She waited until I stopped at a red light. "Ivy, you know we have to go the other way." Flipping her phone, she confirmed the usual destination. "To Daisy's house."

"Nope. I refuse. It'll make us an hour late for Reid. More, if Mom's on a roll."

Bracing the dog with both hands, she shrugged. "Okay. Your decision."

Keats turned to stare at me, first with his blue eye, and then the warm brown one. He mumbled something that sounded both cheeky and resigned.

"You too, buddy? I was sure you'd take my side."

"It's not a matter of sides," Jilly said. "But you know what I always say about family meetings."

I eased the truck onto a side road to look for a place to turn around. "Yeah. 'Be grateful you have a family to complain about.'"

"Something like that. I know Butter Tart 911s are an inconvenience, but—"

"Understatement of the year. Somehow, I always end up on the hot seat when it's never my problem."

"Always and never?" she said. "Sounds like the absolutes they told us in corporate communication seminars not to use. Along with 'everyone,' 'no one' and 'none.'"

Jilly was too smart by half. It was annoying and awesome at the same time. "Whatever."

"'Whatever' was on the naughty list, too. *Sometimes* you end up on the hot seat, and *sometimes* it really is your problem. Either way, we need to go and find out."

Pulling into a double driveway, I backed the trailer around without ending up in a ditch. "Fine. But I maintain there's a time for sweeping statements." Our phones started a fresh round of pinging. "Nuance is completely wasted on my family."

She picked up her phone and planted two thumbs-up emojis in the text box. One for each of us. "I'll let Edna and Gertie know what's happening. Then I'll tell Reid we're running late. He'll understand."

"He won't." The pout fought to take over my face again. "Bet he cancels."

"Bet he won't." She hit send and waited. "Incoming message, and... it's fine. Reid says, 'Family first.'"

I turned back onto the main road and sped up as much as I could with the trailer. "Let's keep this short and sweet. Don't let my mother throw any of her spanners in the works."

"Dahlia has a lot of spanners, doesn't she? Must get them as a perk at thrift stores for buying so much red fabric."

My best friend pulled off the unexpected, and I laughed.

We were quiet for the rest of the drive, both of us probably running scenarios. Family meetings were tough for me, but they were tough for Jilly, too. She was the only in-law who attended regularly, probably because she was my best friend before she was Asher's wife. She walked a precarious tightrope, supporting negotiations between us as she once had warring executives. Sometimes I wondered if the family could enjoy holidays together if not for Jilly. Hopefully, it would be easier for the next generation. One thing all the Galloways agreed upon was the need to break old patterns. Intergenerational trauma was no joke.

"It's about Iris," I muttered as we got out of the truck and walked towards Daisy's house. "Gotta be."

Jilly was too busy looking around to answer. Daisy's house was always pristine, both inside and out. The walkway had been cleared down to bare pavement, with the snow piled in mathematically precise mounds on either side. The wreath on the front door was perfectly centered. Even the icicles hanging from the eaves looked uniform. Did she get on a ladder and trim them?

My eldest sister had been a clean freak since childhood, but after becoming a mom to two sets of twin boys, she'd elevated it to an art form. It was probably her way of imposing order on utter chaos. The trait also made her a great asset at the inn. I reminded myself to check the icicles at home for signs of intervention.

We didn't bother knocking. Butter Tart 911 calls overrode standard etiquette.

Keats and Percy parted ways with us in the front hall and raced off in search of the boys' ferrets. Jilly draped her coat over a pile on the bench, but I kept mine on in protest. A zipped parka conveyed a "keep it short" message.

"At least unzip it," Jilly whispered. "You'll need room in there for box breathing."

Deep breaths came with a freight of vinegar at Daisy's house. When we walked into the kitchen, she was spritzing the countertop and buffing it vigorously with a chamois. The rest of the family were in their usual places, trying not to touch anything but coffee cups. Her drive for hygiene was in the red zone today. It always got worse around holidays.

And murder.

If Daisy could cleanse crime out of existence with vinegar spray, the world would be a better place.

No one was speaking when we walked in, and the silence continued as Jilly took a seat with Iris, Violet and Poppy at the kitchen table. Mom sat on her stool at the counter, and Asher leaned against the stainless steel fridge.

My standard position was floater. I needed to be ready to dodge the guilt grenades that always came my way.

Okay, sometimes.

Usually.

So frequently it was hard to remember a time I left without being pressured to give up what I very much wanted to do. Or to agree to something I didn't want to do.

Sometimes, I agreed just to end the meeting. Sometimes, I even planned to do what they asked. Usually, I twisted the request into something I actually wanted to do that served the same end. Which is why Asher called me his twistiest sister, or Twisty for short.

It would never come to twisty if they just let me go about my business as Keats, Percy and I saw fit. *Never.* I was standing by that absolute.

"It's about time you got here," Mom said, without so much as a 'good morning.' Or a 'thanks for changing your plans.' The first guilt grenade was in the air, and I dodged it.

"We were on the road, Mom. Pulling a horse trailer. On the way to rescue a pony."

Asher crossed his arms. "That pony looked happy in Reid Brisco's pasture yesterday. She's already rescued."

"That's not her home, Asher," Jilly said. "Someone is missing Peppermint right now."

He pushed himself off the fridge and crossed to the coffeepot. "If she were missed, the owner would have called Animal Services by now. Or posted on the town's social media group."

"We don't know the full story," I said, watching him pour coffee into a mug and then add cream. "The pony was in good condition. What if the owner is stuck in a snowdrift or desperately ill and can't reach the phone?"

His fingers hovered over the spoons long enough to tell me he hadn't thought of that. "We've made some calls," he said. "People are on the lookout. We'll find out where she came from soon."

He stirred the coffee quietly, clearly satisfied with himself.

"Fit ponies like Peppermint can cover ten miles a day," I said. "Hill country is a big place."

His spoon clinked against the china. "Just let Animal Services handle it, Ivy."

I leaned against the counter. "That's not going to happen. I'm walking that pony home."

He turned around, clinking harder. "So, you'll just stroll around in deep snow till Jilly faints?"

Jilly glared at him. "Faints? Do I seem like a frail flower to you?"

The spoon stopped. "Of course not. You're in great shape, honey. But what if you fall into a gully? It's rocky out there."

"The pony will show us the easiest way," I said.

The clinking started again. "Like you know ponies so well."

"I've done my research. And besides, all animals pick the easiest, safest route when given the chance. I have faith in Peppermint." Soft ears arrived under my fingertips. "And Keats, of course. He's an expert navigator, as you know. Managed to lead you and your snowbros astray."

Asher kept stirring while giving an elaborate eye roll. "The landscape is buried. All scent trails are gone."

"How about you leave the pony to me while you follow other leads? There are at least half a dozen waiting for you." I waited until his eyes rolled back to their usual piercing blue stare. "Kellan endorsed this mission, Asher."

"Just to get you out from underfoot. We were cleaning up after you all day yesterday. I'd take a statement, you'd take an unofficial statement and... repeat."

"I was just going about my day. It's not my fault people love chatting to me."

Keats punctuated my comment with a pant-laugh. Most people tried to leave in a hurry when they saw us coming, but he doghandled their cuffs into cooperating.

"Darlings," Mom said. "Don't be like this. We're all working together toward the same goal."

"I'm working on getting Peppermint home, with Jilly, Edna and Gertie," I said. "We don't need more help."

"Not *that* goal." Mom pursed her scarlet lips. "Our actual goal is exonerating Iris."

Asher's spoon clattered even more. "You mean the police are working toward solving the museum case, Mom."

"Of course, Asher darling. You and Kellan work so hard. That's why you need extra hands sometimes." Mom applied a lipstick print to the white china mug before adding. "And paws."

My brother tapped the spoon against the rim of the cup. "The police do not need Ivy and her pets getting slush all over a critical investigation."

"As the senior Galloway here, I say you do." Mom shifted the cup and added another waxy half-circle. "Time is of the essence."

"As the only cop here, I say back off." He tapped the mug once more for emphasis.

That clink was the last straw for Daisy. She snatched the spoon out of his hand and then swooped in to collect Mom's mug. "Stop punishing my china while you debate. Someone tell Ivy what's going on."

Daisy rarely cracked, but when she did, everyone listened. That was an absolute.

My brother started to speak, but Mom shushed him and took over. "Iris is going to jail. That's what is going on."

"Jail? What do you mean?" I asked.

"There's nothing unclear about jail, Ivy." She smoothed her silk blouse under a jacket and skirt that didn't quite match but complemented each other. The outfit, entirely in crimson, was perfect for a holiday gathering but extravagant for a coffee klatch in Daisy's kitchen. "It's tragic. Catastrophic."

If Mom had dressed up to melt down, we were in serious trouble.

Iris' appearance was a more accurate reflection of her state of mind. Her hair was pulled back in a messy knot, her jeans were only a step above my worst overalls, and her pink T-shirt was very likely a pajama top.

The coffee mug she cupped between her hands wobbled, and she set it down before Daisy could swoop in.

Jilly plucked Percy off the floor and offered him to Iris. "Tell us what happened."

My sister hugged the cat, who instantly went limp, paws kneading the air. He'd become an excellent emotional support cat. "Kellan called this morning," she said. "The police have finished checking my alibi." She rested her cheek on Percy's head. "It's not good."

"Not good *how*?" I asked.

"The hardware store clerk doesn't remember me, although I tried to make polite conversation. I paid in cash, so there's no credit card record. There are no security cameras in the parking lot, and the one inside the store malfunctioned." She looked at me over the cat. "I can't prove I was there when I said I was."

"You bought supplies," Poppy said. "You must have a receipt."

"I tossed it in the trashcan on the way out, but it wasn't found."

Mom chimed in. "The clerk is a teenage boy with the attention span of a gnat."

"Am I really that forgettable?" Iris asked. "I think I was just some old lady to him."

"Old!" Mom was horrified. "You can't be old. You're my second-born child."

Poppy smirked. "There are too many of us, and we look so much alike. People called me Ivy so often I dyed my hair blue again."

"You should try that, Ivy," Asher said. "It'll make it easier for the police to find you."

Jilly shook her head. "Never mind, Asher. Help us solve this problem instead. Have the police tried everything?"

"Short of torturing the kid, yeah," Asher said.

"Torture him then," Mom said.

"Mom!"

The word came out of six mouths, with a Dahlia on top from Jilly.

"Relax, darlings. I didn't mean waterboarding. Just take the boy's phone away until his brain goes back to normal, and he remembers customers."

Daisy spritzed the already clean counter. "I think kids' neurons are permanently damaged by electronic devices."

"They can rewire again with enough time," I said. "Plenty of academic articles say so."

"We don't have enough time for that." Iris rocked Percy and sighed. "The mayor wants Kellan to detain a suspect in Hester's death today so the tree lighting can happen. I'm the Christmas scapegoat."

"Kellan isn't going to scapegoat you for politics, Iris." Turning to Asher, I added, "Is he?"

"It's not about scapegoating," he said. "We're under a lot of pressure from the mayor to—" he raised his fingers in air quotes— "'save Christmas.' People are up in arms about losing the highlight of the holiday." He shrugged. "Iris had the motivation and means."

"There's no physical evidence linking Iris to the crime," Jilly said. "Is there?"

"Just circumstantial," Asher answered. "People overheard Iris arguing with Hester. Some said it sounded threatening."

"Threatening!" Iris straightened in her chair, still clutching Percy. "It was a professional difference of opinion. I told her we needed to have a chat in the new year to work out the issues she raised. That's all."

Asher stared at the floor to avoid looking at Iris. "Someone said you lost it. And that Hester looked scared."

"That's ridiculous," Iris said. "It was the other way around. I was scared of Hester, like everyone else. Obviously, I should have spoken to her in private. Doing it then and there proved how tired I was."

"Exhausted," Mom said. "You've done so much for this town, darling, and this is the thanks you get? I should speak to Meryl myself."

"*Don't!*"

The same chorus of voices offered the word.

I walked over to pour a cup of coffee I'd regret later, during a long hike through snowy fields. "Remember, I witnessed that confrontation, too. Iris did not 'lose it.'"

"Your standards are different from other people's," Asher said. "You've seen a lot of people lose it big."

"True, but Iris didn't even raise her voice." Sipping my coffee, I turned back. "It was a minor dispute."

"That Hester may have seen as major, since the museum was her reason for getting up every day," he countered. "All I can tell you is a couple of independent witnesses said Hester looked scared during this discussion. We need an alibi on record. Quickly."

"That's where you come in, Ivy," Mom said. "Do your thing."

"My thing? I'm taking the pony home today. That's my thing. And I'd like to get on with it."

She slid off her stool and clicked toward me on red stilettos. "Ivy Rose Galloway, your sister's reputation is more important than this pony. Go over to that hardware store with your brilliant dog and cat and find evidence she was there."

Looking down at my dog for confirmation, I shook my head. "He doesn't want to go."

"Keats Galloway, you will do as I ask." Mom wagged a ruby fingernail too close to his face. He was fond of my mother, but her hose would pay if she kept up the disrespect. "Go and clear your Aunt Iris."

The dog backed behind me and poked my leg. It was time to leave before either of us did something I'd regret.

"Sorry, Mom," I said. "I need to put the pony first."

"Above your own sister?" Her voice got shrill. "That's not how you solve cases."

I slid away from her and passed my cup to Daisy. "Any cases we help solve start with animals. The rest is accidental. I mostly stumble around and occasionally get lucky."

That didn't begin to describe what happened, but it would have to do, because the clock was ticking.

"You're being too modest, Ivy," Violet said. "You see things other people miss."

"Because she's trespassing and stumbling around where she shouldn't be," Asher said.

Poppy shrugged. "Details."

I walked to the front hall and turned back in the doorway. "It's not like I haven't done anything. Since Asher stopped me from helping the pony, I spoke to a lot of people yesterday. There are plenty of good scapegoats available to Meryl."

"Ivy, come back here," Mom said. "What if they arrest Iris and we have an empty seat at Christmas dinner?"

Jilly pushed her chair back and got up. "Dahlia, it won't happen."

"You don't know that, Jillian."

"Oh, I do." Jilly slipped past Mom's grasping hands. "There

won't be a Christmas dinner without Iris. My kitchen will be closed for business until she's available. I suppose you could have the meal catered."

"Never." Asher grabbed his wife's sleeve as she passed and stooped to kiss her cheek, proving there was a time for absolutes after all.

"Why are you leaving? Girls, we're not done here." Mom spun on the spot, hysteria rising. "Asher, you know Meryl Martingale won't rest till she has someone in leg irons."

"Leg irons?" Iris sounded horrified.

"We hardly ever use leg irons," Asher said. "Only when perps get violent."

Mom stopped whirling to rebuke him. "My daughter is not a perp. I detest that word."

He gave me a smirk. "One daughter's a perp. Twisty's broken the law a dozen times."

"More," I said. "Sometimes with you."

"Cops are allowed to bend the law in certain instances. We're the exception to the rule."

I let Jilly pass in front of me to collect her coat. "Let's talk about Champagne Alley."

"Let's not," Mom said. She wasn't above reproach when it came to that story. Asher and Kellan had been drag-racing on the back country trails since before they were old enough to drive legally, and she'd known about it. "Your nephews are eavesdropping through the basement door."

"I doubt that very much," Asher said. Pushing himself off the fridge, he tiptoed across the kitchen floor and slapped the door with an open palm.

Four voices yelped, "Ow."

Daisy cracked open the door and spritzed vinegar mist through it. "Eavesdroppers never prosper."

Mom continued to harangue me about Galloway family priorities while I tied my bootlaces. "Can you stop, please?" I said. "Maybe I'll get a lead from the pony today." I made a show of checking my phone. "We're supposed to pick her up in three minutes."

Dahlia fixed me with a look that had never been as terrifying as she hoped. "Then hurry. Your sister's life is on the line."

"That's a bit dramatic," Iris called from the kitchen table. "Just let her leave, Mom. I trust Ivy, Jilly and the pets to do what they can to help."

"They'd better. We cannot have the Galloway name in the gutter."

I wanted to point out that the Galloway name had survived far worse, including allegations against nearly everyone in this room, including—and especially—Mom herself. It was Iris' first time in the spotlight, as I recalled, which explained why she looked so scared.

"Don't worry too much, Iris," I said, opening the door to let the pets out. "I'll do everything I can."

Asher stepped forward. "Ivy, I need you to promise me you'll coordinate with the police. Don't go rogue on this."

Mom spoke for me. "She'll do what she needs to do, Asher. Meanwhile, you find Meryl another scapegoat."

Jilly pushed me out the door, followed, and then closed it firmly. With anyone else, I'd call it a slam.

At the bottom of the steps, she looped her arm through mine. "Well, that was fun. Like always. Or is it never? There's a case to be made for absolutes here."

"Everyone in my family is nuts," I said. "No one escaped the gene."

"Too harsh, my friend." Jilly turned and looked back. "Do you think Daisy trims those icicles?"

CHAPTER FOURTEEN

Peppermint looked like she'd won the lottery when I showed up at Reid Brisco's barn with a pocketful of treats and a plan. The flaxen pony frolicked, sending up sprays of snow that caught the morning sun like glitter. Then she trotted over to me and nuzzled my hand with a velvety nose. It felt like an invitation.

"Okay, let's get this party started," I said, attaching the lead rope and heading out the gate Reid held open. "We'll stay in touch."

He nodded before shutting the gate behind us. "It's going to be stormy around here if that pony isn't back when Keely gets home from school."

"I hope Peppermint gets to stay here, too," I said. "But we need to close the open loop. I don't understand how she hasn't been reported missing. Word spreads fast in our community."

"Tell me about it. Last night, the Langmans started an online smear campaign about my replica sleighs. I'd be surprised if I sold another."

Jilly patted Reid's arm, and he didn't resist. "When the Founder's sleigh is recovered, yours will sell out in minutes. It'll be the year's hottest gift."

"No sign of it yet?" He pulled off his toque and rubbed his hair. There was more gray in it than I'd thought.

"Not yet," I said. "But the police are working day and night."

Edna cleared her throat conspicuously. "As should we. No problem was ever solved yammering beside a pasture."

"True," Reid said, backing away.

"False," I said. "I've learned more in and around pastures than almost anyplace else."

Raising a camo glove, Edna pointed up the lane. "Let's deploy."

The pony tugged on the lead, so I waved goodbye to Reid and set off. "Gertie's in position?" I asked Edna.

"Locked and loaded. She'll shadow us on the roads with the truck and trailer, in case we need an extraction." Edna jerked a thumb toward her backpack, where I suspected she'd stashed everything from energy bars to emergency flares. "We're covered for twenty-four hours in the wilderness. Thirty-six if you girls keep your cravings in check."

"Thirty-six hours?" Jilly's voice soared an octave. "Asher will lose it."

I laughed. "He'll rent a chopper and leap out of the skies to rescue his lady."

"We always prepare, Jillian," Edna said. "Hope for the best, plan for disaster. That's my personal philosophy."

"It'll be fine." I turned to the pony and touched her shoulder, marveling over her thick coat. "Okay, Peppermint. We're going to follow your lead. Take us wherever you want to go. Home, or anyplace else you think we should see. No pressure. This is your show."

The pony walked out into the first open field and immediately got down to roll in the powdery snow. For a moment, I worried that playing might be the only item on her agenda. She got up, shook snow all over us, and then pranced in a circle, tossing her cream-colored mane.

"At this rate, I'll be home in my recliner by lunch," Edna said. "With nothing to show for the effort."

"Give her a moment." I glanced at Keats and found him watching the pony. "If the most impatient dog on the planet can give her a moment, you can, too."

That moment stretched out as Peppermint stared around the field, perhaps considering her options. Then, just as I was questioning my investigative approach, she marched forward, settling quickly into a steady rhythm.

I worried she'd head back to the museum, but she went straight across the field and into the next. I rested my right hand on her neck as we walked. If she noticed, she didn't object.

Jilly stayed on my left side, carrying Percy in his backpack. The cat didn't mind snow at all, but it would be hard going for a feline, and he might need his energy later. He wore his smart yellow bomber to retain his body heat until he could run around.

Edna was here, there and everywhere, in a state of constant vigilance.

And Keats fell behind the pony, moving in gentle arcs. While Peppermint led our party, the dog was playing a support role. Despite nearly a foot of snow on the ground, he seemed to have some idea about where we were going. Maybe he tapped into the pony's vibe.

"I bet Peppermint could be trained as a therapy animal," I said. "She doesn't seem like the type to hang around a field all day. Maybe she has big ambitions, like Clippers." The miniature horse I loved so much spent his days volunteering with my grandmother, while his donkey bestie hung out at home with my grandfather. "If she stays here, Keely would probably love working with her."

Edna tapped her hat. "Head in the game, Ivy. It's a beautiful day, but that never stopped a killer."

I stared at her. "Someone's a Debbie Downer."

"It's my job to remind you there's a murderer at large and we're a clear shot in an open field."

I pointed to Keats, whose mouth hung open in a happy pant. "Warnings are *his* job. Yours is to keep us upright and moving forward. Mine is to keep the pony confident and happy so she'll want to work with us."

"And my job?" Jilly asked.

"To stop me from doing anything crazy," I told her, grinning.

"That only worked when we were corporate drones. Now, my advice usually spurs you to do the opposite."

I gave her a gentle shove. "If not for you, I'd be in jail. Would you postpone holiday dinners for me, too?"

"Doubtful. Unlike Iris, you court trouble." She grinned and kept walking. "I'm glad Peppermint seems to have a destination in mind. And that the destination isn't the museum."

"Me too." It was a perfect winter morning, with the sun high in a cloudless sky. The temperature had climbed enough to make the walk pleasant rather than punishing. "This is actually nice. Fresh air, sunshine, good company. Almost makes up for the lack of coffee."

"Check your backpack," Jilly said. "Edna's not the only one who prepares."

I dropped the lead rope and pulled the pack around. Inside was a thermos. "Jilly Blackwood-Galloway, you're a star."

"Save the praise. By this point, the coffee's tepid at best."

I poured a cup and then offered it around.

Edna waved it away with a scowl. "This isn't a pleasure cruise, soldier. You've left that pony free to bolt while you caffeinate."

"She won't bolt. We're Peppermint's herd, at least for today. Besides, Keats can handle her."

He mumbled confirmation. A single Shetland pony had nothing on a testy pig or Drama Llama. To this day, the only creature that gave my dog a workout was Elaine, the emu.

Peppermint proved she didn't need policing. She maintained her steady pace, occasionally pausing for a sniff or to adjust her trajectory by a few degrees. Keats stayed close to her, and I noticed the way the dog's ears moved forward when the pony shifted direction. They were communicating in a language I couldn't quite parse but recognized as teamwork.

We cut across fields that grew corn and hay in warmer months but lay dormant now under a blanket of white. The landscape was so quiet that it was almost possible to forget a murder had brought us here.

"How long have we been walking?" Jilly asked at last.

I checked my phone. "Just over an hour. It passed quickly."

"The next hour won't," said our camo-clad ray of sunshine. "Woods ahead."

My inner peace fled at the sight of the tree line. Hill country was more forest than field, and I spent too much time stumbling around in the woods searching for animals. There were bogs and swamps that could swallow a person faster than you could say "search and rescue."

"Great," I said. "Bushwhacking."

Edna picked up her pace, relishing the challenge. "The woods are perfectly safe if you know what you're doing."

"Do we know what we're doing?" Jilly asked.

"Absolutely," Edna called back. "We've got a pony, a genius dog, and a cat with questionable decision-making skills. What could go wrong?"

Percy seemed to recognize his cue and yowled to get out. Falling behind Jilly, I released him from the backpack. Within moments, a streak of orange fluff vanished into the trees.

The pony didn't alter her pace. She walked straight onto a trail and entered the woods with placid confidence. Had she taken this walk before?

Only a couple of inches of snow had penetrated the coniferous tree canopy, leaving the forest floor relatively clear.

Keats charged ahead of Peppermint to join his feline colleague on the trail. A few yards away, the cat's fluffy paws flashed in an elaborate Kung-fu sequence.

"Uh-oh," Jilly said. "Is he litterboxing?"

It was a verb, now.

The cat was most definitely alerting us to something of concern. Keats' paw rose in a point, too.

"Aha," Edna said, reaching them first. "Hoofprints. Boot prints from a man under six feet. Somewhere in the neighborhood of two hundred pounds."

"You can tell all that from a print?" Jilly asked. "Or do you have an app for that?"

Edna knelt and used her phone. "Both, Jillian. It's nice to have digital confirmation of what I already know." She stood and swept her arm forward and back. "They came, and they went."

"But where?" Jilly asked. "Does your app tell you that, too?"

Flicking her finger over the screen, Edna shrugged. "I can make an educated guess. Gertie's less than a mile away, at Crow's Corner. It only has a gas station and convenience store, but maybe Peppermint's owner lives there."

"Okay, but it looks like the guy walked out the way we came in." I stared at the boot prints. "His trail looks a little fresher. Maybe they parted ways."

"He probably found the road and walked home in the storm," Edna said. "That's what I'd do."

"Then Peppermint must have decided to go to Reid Brisco's instead."

Percy swept the snow again, churning up needles and making me worry that Peppermint's owner had fallen somewhere. We'd have to comb the entire area if this trail came to a dead end.

Poor choice of words. Luckily, I hadn't said them aloud.

"Hope the guy's not dead in a ditch," Edna offered rather cheerfully.

"Edna, no need to go there," Jilly said.

Our prepper friend smirked. "We all went there thanks to the cat. Unlike you, I find the prospect of death by snowdrift rather comforting. There are worse ways to go than hypothermia. We've seen plenty of them."

"Let's keep going," I said. "And remember, Percy's litterbox move isn't always about death. He does it whenever Justine Schalow's around. It just signals something foul."

Either way, the spring left our step as we plodded on. With a visible trail, Percy and Keats could take the lead, with Edna close behind. I followed with Peppermint, and Jilly brought up the rear.

Time became elastic in the way it does when you're concentrating on every footstep. It felt like forever but was probably only half an hour when Peppermint's ears pricked forward and her pace quickened.

In the distance, Keats barked to announce a discovery.

"We're here," I said. "Wherever that is."

Ahead, through the trees, I could make out a structure. As we got closer, it resolved into a dilapidated hunting shack that looked like it had been forgotten by time and anyone who'd ever used it. The roof sagged on one side, a pane in the window was broken, and the entire building tilted slightly to the left, like it was considering just giving up and falling over.

"Is this where the wicked witch lives?" Jilly whispered.

"Possibly. Or we might find a wolf in a dress."

"Why do fairytales have to be so terrifying?" she asked. "I refuse to read them to my kids."

"They're cautionary tales about life's perils," Edna said. "Someone should do a zombie picture book. Modern toddlers need to understand what they're up against."

I laughed, and Edna grinned, too. She was yanking our chain to help us relax. There didn't seem to be any cause for worry. My pets were calm and curious and looked back only once before parting to circle the building.

Peppermint wasn't scared either. She walked right up to the door of the hunting shack and then turned to look back expectantly. Meanwhile, Percy peered down at us from the saggy roof, his green eyes catching a ray of sun through the heavy tree cover.

I scratched the pony's withers, and she leaned into my hand. "Good girl. Thank you."

Edna bent to examine the latch on the door. "Brand new padlock. Someone visited recently."

"Can you open it?" I asked.

"Can an osprey fish?" She didn't wait for an answer, which was good, because I didn't have one. Pulling a small tool from her pocket, she picked the lock in under a minute. Then she opened the door and stepped back. "After you, Nancy Drew."

Keats was back and took that as permission to head inside as lead scout. Then I moved into the doorway.

The single room was very dim. There were only two small windows, and the trees outside blocked most of the sun. However, even in the shadows, I could see someone had decorated the place in a peculiar fashion. For a hunting shack and anywhere else.

Edna leaned over my right shoulder, and Jilly my left. Peppermint forced her fuzzy head under my forearm near my waist. Percy slipped between my legs and began his reconnaissance.

Taking a deep breath, I turned on my phone light.

We gasped in unison.

Someone had hung garlands along the walls and around the window frames. Paper hearts of various sizes dangled from the ceiling on lengths of ribbon, spinning slowly in the draft. In one corner, old-fashioned ornaments outshone a scrawny Christmas tree.

And at the center of this festive explosion sat the Founder's sleigh.

"Dagnabit, girls!" Edna's voice was loud in my ear. "This is where our reputation turns around. Hello, hometown heroes."

"Peppermint found it," I said. "She gets the kudos."

The antique sleigh seemed undamaged. Its curved runners and ornate details were exactly as I remembered from the museum. Pinecones were piled onto the velvet seat, while unlit fairy lights with a battery pack twisted around the entire sleigh.

"Okay, this is weird," Jilly said, taking the first picture. "Is it a shrine of some kind?"

Edna pressed a high-powered flashlight into my hand, and I flicked the beam around the room. In the corner opposite the tree, long-stemmed red roses drooped in a vase. "Hearts and red roses. Do you think someone stole the sleigh as a romantic gesture?"

Edna slid past me to explore and pointed to a stack of wooden crates that served as a table. On top sat tall candles in silver holders, two champagne glasses and another frozen rosebud.

"Touch nothing," Jilly said, as I followed. "It's all evidence."

The open crate below held a box of stationery, the kind with weight and texture that spoke of quality. Next to it sat half a stick of red sealing wax and a rubber stamp bearing a symbol that reminded me vaguely of Wilma.

"Aline's secret admirer. He must have been planning to pop the question." I shone the light at the glasses. "Unused. It hasn't happened yet."

"It *can't* happen now," Jilly said. "Aline knows the sleigh's been stolen. She'd never say yes."

Edna shrugged. "Plenty of women pine for convicts. When someone's locked away for life, it's a safe relationship."

Jilly and I stared at each other and let that go.

"This must be the work of Isaac Gherkin," I said. "He didn't hide his admiration of Aline."

"Isaac always seemed sane," Edna said. "Within a margin of error. We all get a little close to the line sometimes."

"It's too much," Jilly said. "Way too much."

Edna puckered in distaste. "You mean tacky. No one would want to remember this as the site of their betrothal."

"All in the eye of the beholder," I said. "Or nose, in my case. Kellan proposed on my manure pile, remember. I wouldn't have it any other way."

Keats mumbled a reminder to focus. Our time here was limited. Soon, the shack would be overrun by the police.

"Stealing a priceless antique seems like a huge gesture for someone who won't even talk to Aline in person," Jilly said.

I nodded. "It's a tragic story. Lonely, alienated homesteader steals antique to woo lady who collects coins for charity. Maybe Isaac wanted to sell it so Aline could do good works with the proceeds."

"He'd have to be more than marginally insane." Edna started pacing. "I spoke to him often enough to doubt he's that far gone."

"People can hide these things well until they crack." I snapped photos of everything. "Maybe Isaac thought he needed to do something grand to prove himself worthy of Aline. And then it went terribly wrong. Presuming he killed Hester to get the sleigh."

Keats continued his own investigation, nose to the ground as he circled the room. He paused at the sleigh, gave it a thorough sniffing, then moved to the walls. Meanwhile, Percy claimed the high ground on a rickety shelf and surveyed the scene with typical feline superiority.

Edna stopped pacing and crossed her arms. "The big question is whether the sleigh thief killed Hester intentionally or by accident. Maybe she caught him red-handed and things spiraled."

"The other question is how Peppermint played into all of this," I said. "It seemed like he'd hooked her up to pull the sleigh." I turned and walked over to the pony, who was still in the doorway, watching us. "At least he was good to you, sweetheart."

Jilly was also photographing everything to document the strange scene. "Do you want to call Kellan?"

"Yeah, it'll be nice to give him some good news for a change."

Before I could, however, Percy called me over. At least, that's how I interpreted his unique meow. He'd moved to the edge of the shelf and was trying to reach the top of the window frame. I presumed the fluttering garland had attracted his attention, but he seemed more determined than playful.

Finally, when I tried and failed to reach the upper frame, the cat hurled himself at it. He landed with a light thud alongside a small red velvet box that snapped open, facing the dirty floor.

"Percy, no," Jilly said. "Do not touch that box."

Percy deftly flipped the box. Telling the cat not to do anything just made him more resolute.

When the box turned, it revealed a diamond ring.

A ring that was likely supposed to adorn Aline Tupling's hand while she shook her coin box.

Edna bent over for a closer look. "A carat and a half," she said, as if she appraised diamonds all the time. "Big, but not ostentatious. The setting is old-fashioned. Tasteful, unlike the décor."

"Confirms the proposal theory." I took a good look, too. "I'm surprised Isaac would go with a traditional ring. Environmentalists usually denounce mined diamonds."

"Maybe it was a family heirloom," Jilly said.

"Or Isaac has principles of convenience. Like he accused me of having."

I left the ring box where it landed on the floor, although it seemed disrespectful of something that held so much sentimental value.

Jilly gave me another chance to call Kellan, and I nodded for her to go ahead. After tapping on her phone, she said, "Kellan? We discovered the Millbrook sleigh. And so much more. You'll want to come right away."

"The pony found it," I called out. "Kudos to Peppermint." Keats mumbled a complaint, and I added, "Plus Keats and Percy. That goes without saying."

Jilly walked Kellan through our location, the contents of the hunting shack, and the condition of everything we'd found. When she mentioned the ring box on the window frame, there was a long pause. "It just fell," she said. "After Percy shot himself out of a cannon."

I grinned at her. "Welcome to my life of excuses."

My own phone buzzed. Checking the screen, I sent "Private Caller" to voicemail.

The phone rang again.

And again.

Private Caller was not easily deterred. Had my family sprung for burner phones?

Jilly waved at me. "Kellan says you should answer."

"Tell him he can't make me answer my own phone," I said. "What do you think, Keats?"

The dog stood beside me, and his mouth dropped open. The ha-ha-ha sounded a bit like "hurry."

Sighing, I answered on the fourth ring. "Ivy Galloway, at your service."

"Good. Because I need to see you. Immediately."

I straightened as if she could see me already. "Mayor?"

CHAPTER FIFTEEN

I t wasn't the first time I'd led livestock into a public institution, and it probably wouldn't be the last. Peppermint followed Jilly, Edna and me through the double front doors at City Hall with Keats providing encouragement from behind. The rubber-backed mats covering most of the lobby made the place at least moderately hoof-friendly.

That was about as friendly as City Hall got for me. Normally, I was only there when I was in trouble. Or stirring up trouble. Either way, I'd found taking animals along had advantages. Mayor Martingale was an occasional friend and a frequent adversary when it came to public safety. In the latter category, a donkey or lamb could tip the scales in my balance. Despite being the leader of a homesteading community, she was wary of animals. She was also decidedly interested in optics and stylish attire.

"Ivy Galloway, are you serious about this rodeo?" she said by way of greeting.

"Serious as a heart attack." I turned to Jilly and got a face full of fluff, since Percy was parked on my shoulder. "Did I get that expression right?"

"Technically yes, although it's in questionable taste," my best friend said. "I told you Meryl wouldn't welcome the pony."

"I couldn't leave Peppermint in the trailer. She deserves to be treated like a queen."

Mayor Martingale stood on the opposite side of the security turnstile, arms crossed over a scarlet suit that would make my mother apoplectic. The two women were sartorial rivals, and Mom had unofficially trademarked smart business wear in all shades of red. They were the same age and nearly the same size. Meryl had flashy blonde highlights and money, whereas Mom had skills and ingenuity. I wondered if they'd up the ante to ballgowns at Christmas dinner this year.

"We banned livestock from City Hall for good reason," the mayor said. "I already make a big concession with the dog and the cat."

I shrugged with extra oomph to let Percy's rise and fall make the statement. "If I had to guess, it's the dog and the cat we're here about. You want Keats and Percy to do you a favor. I'm here as their wrangler."

"And I'm here as Ivy's wrangler," Edna said. "Do you want to negotiate across a turnstile, Meryl? We're fine to shout if you are."

"It's a conversation, not a negotiation," she said.

Which meant I didn't get a say in whatever she wanted me to do. I planned to fight every step of the way. Points scored today might come in handy down the road, when there was more wiggle room.

The pony couldn't get through the turnstile, which left Meryl to join us in the lobby, where a slow but steady stream of people passed. There were temporary booths along one wall, including one normally occupied by Aline Tupling. Her coin box sat on a trestle table alongside a pile of toys people had dropped off. The coffee cup and gloves on the white tablecloth made me wonder if Kellan had already collected Aline to talk about what we'd found in the woods.

Given her gentle temperament, Aline was likely to be distraught over the actions of her secret admirer. I doubted she'd be jingling that box around town again today.

The metallic click of the turnstile brought me back to the moment. Meryl snapped polished fingertips to get us to follow her around a large arrangement of poinsettias, where we were shielded from most of the indoor foot traffic. Jilly and I swished after her in our snow pants and bulky parkas. I was already sweltering, and the negotiation hadn't started.

"Do we have to stand here?" I asked. "Poinsettias are toxic."

She rolled her eyes. "Are you planning to eat them?"

Peppermint reached out for a nibble, and I shortened her lead rope. "If your clandestine meeting kills my pony, it will kill the spirit of cooperation, too," I said.

"How clandestine is it when anyone walking by outside can see us? Besides, it's not your pony. Chief Harper prefers to keep it that way."

I glared at her. "Maybe so, but I doubt he wants Peppermint dead in your lobby. This equine deserves a hero's welcome."

A man cleared his throat behind the wall of poinsettias. "Mayor? What's happening back there? Are you okay?" An old man in a municipal uniform poked his head around red leaves. "I just went out to check on the preservationist hooligan."

"And came back to find even more hooligans," Edna said. "How are you doing, Habbie?"

Haben Burl had been an accountant before joining the mayor's internal security team as a retiree. He was probably 10 years Edna's junior and still fit from years of running a farm on the side.

"Edna." He scanned her winter-weight fatigues. "Been through battle?"

"Every day, old man. Wouldn't have it any other way." She beamed at him. "Meanwhile, you're in the hallowed halls harassing homesteaders."

Haben shrugged. "Beats pony detail. Is a Shetland the best a warrior can do?"

A red sleeve rose. "Stop squabbling, you two. Haben, can you clear Aline Tupling's table? She had to leave early."

When he was gone, Meryl directed her cool gaze my way. "I presume you know why Aline left."

"We do." Edna answered for me. "And you're welcome, Meryl."

The mayor's red lips pursed as she resisted the urge to get sucked into Edna's personal rodeo. "I'll thank you when the job is done. No one is under arrest. The tree in the square is unlit. And tomorrow is Christmas Eve."

Reaching down, I found Keats' ears where I needed them. "When you say 'job,' are you talking about police work? Because *my* job is managing Runaway Inn."

Meryl's pucker turned into a smirk. "That's the least of your jobs, isn't it? Jilly and Daisy do the heavy lifting while you're doing your other job."

"Rescuing? You're right, Mayor. That's exactly what we were doing when we tracked down this wonderful girl." I rested my free hand on the pony's neck. "Peppermint, please meet Mayor Martingale."

Meryl's pucker formed again. "I only wish I had time to be interested in a pony, Ivy. All my energy goes into making sure the people of Clover Grove are safe and happy." She gestured to the square outside. "Are they safe and happy? Is their tree lit?"

I focused on my fingers and the warm fur under them. "It will be soon. I'm sure you've heard from Chief Harper. You two chat so often. If I were the suspicious type, I'd be worried."

Edna guffawed. "Poor Larry. Maybe he deserves a taste of his own medicine."

There were rumors Larry Martingale had stepped out on Meryl before she entered the political arena. If so, they'd survived the marital strife admirably. When they stayed at the inn, they seemed perfectly content.

Meryl shot a chilling glance at Edna and then passed it along to me. "No one is under arrest. Until that's the case, we can't gather en masse to celebrate. It's not Christmas without the tree lighting. You know that."

"There was no tree in the square until Jilly and I spearheaded the Culture Revival Project," I said. "People managed to celebrate the holiday for forty years without it."

"Reinstating the town tree was one of my more successful moves as mayor," she continued, as if I hadn't spoken. "We need it to offset everything else that happens around here. Sometimes, small things like a communal tree are all that stand between us and civil unrest."

I shrugged again. "Hit the lights, then. We just handed the police a suspect on a silver platter. In fact, we should have been there for the handoff instead of leaving Gertie Rhodes alone in the bush to pass the torch."

"She wasn't alone," Edna said. "She had Minnie. And your brother arrived quickly on his souped-up snowmobile bought with taxpayer dollars. Won't deny I'm jealous of it."

"Let's get the conversation on track," Jilly said, lowering her voice. "Mayor, we're standing down. Isaac Gherkin is obviously behind what happened to Hester Belcher."

She shook her head. "Isaac's not our man. I've known him a very long time."

"Since when has knowing someone for ages meant they're innocent?" Edna asked. "Most people degrade, unfortunately. Gertie and I are exceptions, but it takes constant work."

"I like Isaac, too," I told the mayor. "But it's not the first time love has pushed someone over the edge in Clover Grove. Remember when—"

Jilly touched my arm to keep me from delving into the town's sordid past. "The police will get to the bottom of this. Obviously, what we found today places someone at the scene of the crime."

"It gets my sister off the hot seat," I added. "Iris certainly didn't grab the Founder's sleigh and run off to stage a weird proposal in the woods."

Meryl splayed her hands and pressed down. "Hush. This is the type of story that has legs."

"Yeah, skinny legs. I bet Justine Schalow is plodding through the snow to get the scoop." The pony shifted under my hand, and I realized she was probably getting warm. It wasn't fair to Peppermint to prolong this discussion. "Circling back to jobs, Mayor, we exceeded expectations. Made sure the pony was safe. Got her to flush out a good lead. Exonerated my sister. Now, we'd like to return Peppermint to her home and then get ready to host you and your family for the holiday."

"Isaac Gherkin has a solid alibi," she said. "Someone came forward with video evidence of the quarrel at the Thistledown Tree Farm. There's no way he made it back to the museum in time for what happened." When I didn't speak, she added, "Unfortunately, Iris' alibi hasn't been confirmed." Meryl's finger spun in a circle. "You and your rodeo had better keep rolling."

"The chief said the opposite. What were his exact words, Jilly?"

"'Go home,'" she said. "'Do not pass City Hall.'"

I nodded. "That's what I heard, too. He didn't want us to come here."

Red sleeves crossed again. "Yet you did. Usually, you're up to your armpits in alligators until a case is solved."

"Mayor, Jilly put a moratorium on gator mentions. Better find another metaphor."

Keats slipped behind me and gave me a poke to close the distance between us. Peppermint clopped forward over the mat, too, and then reached out to nuzzle Meryl's skirt.

The mayor stepped back, and we stepped forward. It turned into a little dance until she was against the window.

Edna pressed the issue for me. "Meryl, I'm bored. Tell Ivy her sister's in the clear so we can leave."

The mayor's back was literally against the glass, and Peppermint moved to create a sturdy barrier in front of her.

Meryl shook her highlighted bob and slid away from the pony's head. "I can't clear Iris. Isaac may be guilty of a doomed crush, but he didn't kill Hester and I'm sure of it." She escaped from behind Peppermint. "You need to take your dog and pony show and do more."

Lifting her tail, the pony delivered manure directly onto the mayor's red suede pumps. The load wasn't large, but it was soft, probably because of recent changes in Peppermint's diet.

"There's something you *can* clear, Meryl," Edna said. "It's a sign to choose more practical footwear before you're too disabled to outrun what's coming. And I don't mean the next election."

Color rose in the mayor's cheeks. "Clean this up right now."

"Pass." Raising her hand above the poinsettias, Edna called, "Habbie, you're needed here. Stat."

Coming around the plants, he muttered something spicy. "Stand still, Your Worship. I'll call the custodial staff and get those shoes cleaned up pronto."

Meryl shook her head. "Never mind, Haben. I'll sacrifice them to the cause." Stepping out of her red pumps, she went back through the turnstile. At the bottom of the stairs, she turned, and her nylons slipped on the hardwood. Like any adroit politician, she got her balance and stuck the landing. "Ivy, why are you still here? I can feel your dog staring at me."

She was mistaken. Keats was stalking across the lobby to the Clover Grove information kiosk situated beside Aline's table. A man with his back to us hung his overcoat on a coat rack and then set a fedora on top. Before he turned, Peppermint jerked her lead rope out of my hand and trotted across the mats toward the man.

Lifting Percy off my shoulder, I handed him to Jilly and ran after the pony, hoping to reach Peppermint before she knocked the old man over. She moved at a good clip, whereas snow boots hampered me. "Peppermint, wait!"

She beat me to the man and nudged him aside rather rudely to get to his coat on the rack. Grabbing the pocket with her teeth, Peppermint twisted her head until the fabric tore. Objects scattered on the floor with thuds, splats and rattles.

"Get away from there," he said, trying unsuccessfully to shove the pony. She outweighed him by at least 200 pounds. "Stop that right now."

It was Powell Nobbs, showing up for a volunteer shift to lecture visitors about Clover Grove. He wore a navy suit over a white shirt with a striped tie and zipped galoshes over his shoes.

Bending, Powell started gathering the fallen objects. Peppermint grabbed his tie and ripped off about half of it. Keats picked up the chunk of pinstriped silk and delivered it to me with a flourish.

Meanwhile, Powell lowered himself stiffly onto his knees and collected carrots and oat treats, jamming them into the pockets of his pants. Red-green-and-white peppermints in plastic wrapping scattered as he flailed. One candy spun toward me, and I planted my boot on it before the pony could turn back.

Glancing over my shoulder, I signaled for Edna to clear out the lobby. She strode away, yelling orders, and Jilly joined me with Percy in her arms.

"Too many sweets are bad for ponies, Mr. Nobbs," I said. "Look at the load this girl left for the mayor over there, and you'll see her gut is upset." I offered him my hand, but he ignored it, continuing to scrabble for the treats. "Or maybe it was the stress of running around in a blizzard with you. Either way, she's not up to scratch."

"I don't know what you're talking about." He reached for the table to pull himself up, but it was too far away. Then he tried the coatrack and pulled it down on top of him, missing his head—and mine—by inches.

Edna brushed past me. "I can't stand to see an old man acting old," she said, hoisting him to his feet. "Besides, it's best to take a punch dead on, Powell. No flinching."

"A punch?" He smoothed his shirt, found the ragged ends of his tie and stared from Edna to me. "I'm sure no one wants to be charged with assault. Don't think I won't do it."

"No one's punching anyone," I said, looking down at the fabric in my hand. "But I fear you're going to be charged with more than assault by the time we're done here."

His posture improved, and his chin came up. "I am a pillar of this community."

If I had a buck for every time a suspect said exactly that, I'd be able to buy myself a brand new ceramic village. I wouldn't, but I could.

Touching the tie pin in the silk fragment, I said, "Your insignia is a boar's head. I noticed it earlier on the wax seal stamp you left in the hunting shack. It reminded me of my pig, Wilma."

His Adam's apple bobbed. "People haven't used seal stamps for well over a hundred years, young lady. If you spent more time at the museum, you might learn something."

"I spent too much time there this week for my liking, sir. Did you and Hester get into an argument like this before she died?"

He stooped to pick up his fedora and placed it on his head before answering, "I did not stab Hester Belcher."

"Never said she was stabbed, Mr. Nobbs. You'd only know that if you were there."

His fingers wrung the remnants of his tie. "I don't... I don't know what to say."

"The truth is always a good place to start, Powell," Edna said.

"Otherwise, things get more complicated than a pocketful of pony treats."

He sank to the floor, his legs straight out, galoshes askew. "It wasn't supposed to happen like that," he whispered.

I sat down too, crossing my legs in something approximating the lotus pose. Snow pants and boots made that even harder than usual. "Can we start with the pony, Mr. Nobbs? I need to know where she lives."

"I don't know. She was on the road near my house when I left the museum reception. It's all her fault."

"Peppermint's? How?"

"I never would have imagined borrowing the Millbrook sleigh otherwise. She's exactly like the pony that..."

His voice trailed off, and I prompted, "The pony Aline Tupling described? From her childhood?"

There was a long pause followed by a simple nod. "I thought if I brought them together—the pony, the sleigh and Miss Tupling—the magic of Christmas would do the rest."

"You're her secret admirer and you wanted to propose," I said. "We found the ring, sir."

Bleary eyes rose from his tie. "That ring belonged to my mother."

"It's safe, don't worry." I gestured to Aline's table, now empty. "I know you two had a lot in common. You're an expert in the town's history, and she took care of our community spirit."

"Such a kind and generous woman." He took his hat off again and held it over his chest. "I hoped she might think fondly of me, but I wasn't sure. It took me a full year to get the courage to state my intentions. When that little horse blocked my car, what else could I do?"

"You could have gone home, had some sherry and slept off a bad idea," Edna suggested.

I flicked my fingers at Keats, and he backed Edna off. "So, you left your car at home, packed up your decorations, and walked back to the museum with the pony?"

He nodded. "It's a long walk to the hunting shack, and I figured the pony could pull the sleigh with my pack. Then I'd figure out a way to get Miss Tupling to come out there." He went back to wringing the tie. "She loves history and tradition, and I wanted to create a memorable moment. I thought if I could borrow the sleigh for one night, I could propose and return it before anyone noticed." After a moment, he added, "It seems foolish now, but it felt romantic at the time."

"Sounds like you overdid the sherry, Powell." Edna's voice was further away now. "No woman wants to hike that far in a snowstorm to liaise with a secret admirer. Someone who might be a murderer. And in this case, actually is a murderer."

He glared at her over my shoulder. "I am *not* a murderer. All I did was let myself into the museum with my personal donor key to borrow the sleigh. The place had already been ransacked when I got there. I went out the back door and found Hester lying in the snow with the sleigh beside her. Such a terrible shock. I didn't know what to do."

"Calling 911 is normally a solid choice." Edna was even further away, but her voice carried, as always. "Grabbing the sleigh and running was a boneheaded move, Nobbs."

Powell reared back as if she'd slapped him. "You wouldn't know romance if it bit you in the fatigues, Edna. The pony came over to help that night. I knew it was a sign."

"A sign to do the wrong thing," Edna said. "A sign to be an idiot."

"Edna, stop," Jilly said. "You're asking for a different sort of bite in the fatigues. The canine variety. Just let Ivy do the talking."

"She's beating around the bush. How does she ever get anything done?"

I wished I had Cori's gloves to send my prepper friend a

message. There was a natural order to discussions like this, and Edna was derailing my train of thought. "Mr. Nobbs, it's hard to believe you just happened to find Ms. Belcher conveniently lying beside the antique you wanted to borrow."

"Death isn't overly convenient, in my experience," Edna said.

Powell swallowed hard again. "It was convenient for me that night, I admit. Hester was already gone, and the fool who killed her left the precious sleigh behind." His expression brightened. "I saved it. That's what everyone needs to remember. Someone less reputable than me may have gotten their hands on it if I hadn't taken it away."

Edna started to speak and yipped instead. Keats was tired of her interruptions.

"The valuable antique that's supposed to be kept pristine?" I asked.

"It was built to ride behind a pony and survived nicely," Powell said. "Granted, I did most of the pulling. That stupid animal went on strike. She jerked her lead rope out of my hand and tailed me all the way to the hunting shack. I got lost on my way home, and she was gone by then. Utterly useless."

He tried to kick Peppermint with one overshoe, and I held his foot down. "Don't. This pony is the hero of the story. You're the villain."

His foot flailed until he managed to kick me in the chin.

Jilly came closer with Keats. "Don't you dare kick my friend. Try that again, and you'll answer to our pets."

Powell pulled his galoshes back and rested his head on his knees. It annoyed me to see that a man in his seventies was more flexible than me. "Aline will never marry me now."

"No one likes a quitter, Nobbs." Edna was right behind me again. "Many a convict has a lady on the outside, as I was telling the girls earlier. Epistolary relationships have a lot going for them."

I leaned in and said, "Tell us where you stashed the murder weapon and we'll leave you alone, Mr. Nobbs."

His head rose and our faces were uncomfortably close. There was a glint of madness in his eyes, but it wasn't as intense as I'd witnessed in confrontations with others. "I have no idea where that is. Do your own homework."

Percy came over and swished under my chin. Patting the cat, I said, "Don't you regret this at all, Mr. Nobbs?"

Some of his bluster deflated. "I should have done things differently, and I know that now. I panicked. Figured everyone would think I killed Hester. I was there, I had a key, and I'd argued with her earlier about the taxidermy exhibit. It seemed smarter to run."

"Not that smart," Edna said. "Runners usually trip."

There was a steady thud on the floor behind me, and a pair of soiled red stilettos arrived carrying the mayor. "That's enough, Ivy. Your brother is on his way." The heels turned. "Perhaps Edna would be good enough to help Haben secure Mr. Nobbs."

"With pleasure," Edna said, offering me her hand.

I took it, and Jilly and I walked away with Meryl.

"There you go, Mayor," I said. "New silver platter. New suspect."

Her blonde hair swished. "Not convinced, I'm afraid. I think he's telling the truth about finding Hester already..."

The mayor's voice trailed off, and Edna called over, "*Dead*, Meryl. It's a simple, one-syllable word. People overcomplicate it."

Frustration percolated under my layers of winter clothing. I wanted Meryl to be convinced Powell was the killer so that she'd take Iris' name off the suspect list. But I also couldn't encourage her to go ahead with the public tree lighting when someone more important wasn't convinced.

Namely, Keats.

He sat near my feet watching Edna tie Powell's wrists and gave what amounted to a canine harrumph. We weren't done, and Iris was not in the clear. Unless Powell was a better actor than he seemed, the real killer was still out there.

Worse, the real killer was smart enough to frame someone else.

That didn't mean Powell was home free, however. Percy was hard at work scraping invisible litter over the old man's galoshes. There was a lot of flash and flair, which meant my feline sidekick wasn't taking it too seriously. A stolen sleigh and secret letters weren't sufficient cause for the cat's trademark scalp massage.

"You'd better get going, Ivy," Meryl said. "Consider yourself deputized."

"Kellan wouldn't agree to that, Mayor. Besides, I'm out of ideas. I'll focus on getting this pony home, wherever that might be."

"Let me locate the pony's owner while you find out who left Hester—"

"Dead," Edna supplied cheerily, joining us. "Keep practicing, Meryl. You'll get the hang of the word before it comes for you, too."

"It already came for me once, and I dodged it," she said. "That gingerbread cookie, remember?"

I couldn't help but smile. "Keats and Bocelli the donkey, saved you."

Edna pointed downward. "Better get those shoes cleaned up before it comes around again. Is that how you want to go, Your Excellency?"

"She prefers 'Your Worship,'" I said.

Meryl walked across the mats and unlocked the front door. "I prefer to see all of you doing what you do best."

"And that is...?" Edna asked, pulling up the rear as we left.

"Supporting our wonderful—and terribly busy—police force. I look forward to hearing you sing with the carollers, Edna. You have such a lovely voice."

Edna swept off her hat to reveal permed curls. "Thank you, Meryl. That means—"

The door cut Edna off and literally hit her on the way out.

CHAPTER SIXTEEN

The snow was falling hard by the time I left the farm and started back down the darkened lane to deliver Peppermint to Reid Brisco. I'd dropped Jilly and Edna at home after our visit with the mayor. Jilly wanted to get dinner started, and Edna had gear to organize for tomorrow's adventure, whatever that turned out to be. We agreed to regroup to brainstorm our next steps when I got back. The day had started with my family pressuring me to clear Iris and ended with the mayor pressuring me to save Christmas for Clover Grove. I was the filling in a guilt-trip sandwich. Kellan wouldn't be happy about any of it. No one could "deputize" me to solve crimes but him, which wouldn't happen because he wanted me to be safe and follow the law.

Keats mumbled what sounded like a warning to keep my wits about me. The road conditions were deteriorating fast. Normally, our three plows were in constant motion, but maybe the drivers were on a dinner break. Couldn't begrudge them that. Winter had clearly decided it wasn't joking around.

Keeping Peppermint at Runaway Farm overnight would have been the sensible move, but I knew Keely would be heartbroken. I'd promised to bring the pony back today and didn't want to let the little girl down.

"Understood," I told the dog as he put his paws on the dashboard. "I'm just worried. Only two days till Christmas and the town's in an uproar. People are depending on us, and I feel like I'm failing."

The dog's next rumble sounded dismissive. He didn't appreciate or indulge self-doubt. Angst was nothing hard work wouldn't cure. That was the border collie way. We just had to keep rolling and trust things would sort themselves out.

Trying my luck with Percy, I rested my hand briefly in fluff. A sonorous purr told me the cat wasn't fussing over misfires. Instead, he wisely conserved his energy for the next challenge.

I focused on Christmas lights to stay anchored in the present. They were harder to find than usual, and not because of the snow. People had turned off their festive displays, likely out of respect for Hester Belcher. Maybe not Hester specifically, but for the situation in general. The inflatable snowmen, Grinches and Santas were flat tonight, and I felt the same.

Still, color gleamed through the snow in enough places to ground me. I loved the old-fashioned multicolored strings. Jilly preferred to keep things simple and tasteful with clear lights at the inn, so I needed to find my rainbows elsewhere.

Keats' paws tapped a little dance on the dash, and then he turned to stare at me with his eerie blue eye.

"What?" I said. "I'm not doing anything."

Apparently, that was the problem, because the intensity of the tapping increased. We were approaching the road that would bypass the town and get us to Reid's house faster. Keats looked ahead intently. The dog wasn't inclined to bypass anything.

"Fine, we'll go through town. No lack of Christmas lights there. The stores are staying open late, and murder takes a back burner to commerce. It's the most funderful time of the year."

The paws stopped their dance. My co-pilot was satisfied, and we cruised slowly into town. As expected, the sidewalks were busy. I rolled down the front windows, and carols blew in on a flurry of snow. Keats lifted his muzzle, angling it this way and that.

The dash dance began again. He wanted to stop somewhere.

"Really? Who have we missed? Should we visit Teri Mason and see what she knows?"

Keats stared resolutely ahead as we passed Hill Country Designs.

Not Teri, then.

"What do you have in mind, buddy? Back to the Berry Good Café? Mabel's Miniatures?" I thought for a moment. "How about the hardware store? Thirl Norland may be able to help confirm Iris' plumbing alibi."

He mumbled a negative. Wrong again.

The paws picked up speed when we reached town square and he poked his nose out the passenger window. It was an order to turn right.

Toward the museum.

"Seriously, Keats? Why? I don't even know if the police have cleared the crime scene."

They hadn't. Yellow hazard tape blew around the old building, adding a hit of color that wasn't at all grounding.

Percy got up and weighed in with an eerie meow. Two pets agreed. We were making a pit stop.

Not at the museum, for which I was exceedingly grateful.

Keats' paws kept dancing, and Percy crawled into my lap. My tuxedoed navigator commanded me to take the next left. Then a right. And another right. The streets were normally wide enough here for a truck and trailer, but with the snowdrifts on either side, it was a bit of a squeeze. I didn't want to jostle the pony more than necessary. She'd had a big day.

"Can I get a hint, boys? If we're stopping, parking is going to be a challenge."

The dog directed me to pull into the empty yard at the town's only private school. Happily, it was also privately cleared of snow, and the entire lot was free. I backed in behind the double dumpsters and got out.

"That's what I want for Christmas," I said. "More dumpsters. They make sleuthing life so much easier."

Keats urged me forward with a hint of teeth that pierced my overalls but not my long johns.

"I'm not leaving Peppermint, buddy."

Another nip told me I was doing just that.

I twisted and turned to get around him and failed, as usual. By the time we'd left the schoolyard's rear entrance and emerged on the next street, I understood.

"Okay, yeah. I've been here before with Iris. Last year, she dropped off a Christmas gift for Hester. One of those ceramic trees with lights. Used to be kitsch until Mabel made them hip again. Hester told Iris it wasn't her style and that she donated it to Aline Tupling."

Percy trotted ahead of us, leaving tiny paw prints in the snow. His mewing was continuous and urgent.

"Hester's cats. Of course. We should have checked in already. Asher said they were covered, but he's not a reliable source with animal care. I hope he remembers to feed his future kids." I shrugged. "At the rate we're going, we'll all have challenges in the parenting department."

Keats circled and threatened my long johns with a grumble, forcing me to pick up the pace on the slippery sidewalk.

We followed Percy down the lane beside Hester's bungalow. The house was as severe and sensible as she'd been in life. No frivolous lights or inflatables here. Just a back porch recently shoveled and heavily salted by the police and a simple fixture with one bulb.

The dog and cat waited at the bottom of the stairs. I presumed they were avoiding the salt, but Keats had gone into a point. Under the snow, there was something worth seeing. I went back down to join them.

Unfortunately, I kicked it before I saw it and fell to one knee. That's when Percy took pity on me and helped excavate a rather menacing stone ornament. I couldn't help thinking about Keely Brisco calling Hester a gargoyle. It was a big and unflattering word for a little kid, and she must have picked it up from her father.

This gargoyle was about 18 inches tall, with folded wings and a gaping mouth. For yard décor, I far preferred stone bunnies and gnomes. Historically, gargoyles were thought to fend off evil. I could see why Hester would choose one, but it clearly hadn't done the trick.

Keats sniffed at the figurine and directed his blue eye at me.

"Gotcha." I tried tipping the gargoyle, but it had frozen to the ground. Then I pulled off my glove and stuck a finger into its mouth, poking behind the fangs. The fearsome creature spat out a metal key wrapped in plastic.

Standing, I brushed snow off my pants and then returned to the porch to open the door.

Hester's kitchen was as spartan as expected. My phone light revealed two bowls—one full of kibble, the other water. The cats would not perish from hunger or thirst.

I followed my pets into the dining room and then the living room, keeping my light low.

Keats went into an entirely unnecessary point in front of the sofa, where two gray tabbies perched, hissing. The dog backed away, but Percy stayed to taunt them with mews and tail flourishes.

"Hey guys," I said. "Sorry to wake you. Just checking in. Where's the third musketeer?"

Percy followed Keats down the hall, and the two tabbies allowed me to scratch their jowls. They were friendly and well-socialized for rescues. Anthony Cork hadn't been wrong about Hester treating them well, despite her beef about pets in the museum.

Trailing after my own pets, I sighed. There wasn't a hint of Christmas anywhere that I could see. Why didn't Hester have a tree or at least a poinsettia? Maybe it was enough to be surrounded by decorations all day.

Still, the place felt bare and more than a little lonely. It smelled faintly of menthol, which I traced to a bowl of cough drops on a hall table.

Percy and Keats came out of the first bedroom and went into the second, which had been converted to a den. Two wingback chairs faced a small TV. One chair held an afghan Hester had probably knitted herself, judging by the basket of wool beside it. The other had a fleecy cat blanket covered in fur.

In between, on a round table, sat the ceramic tree Iris gave Hester last year. Despite what she'd told my sister, she'd kept it. I flipped the switch and smiled as tiny sparks of color lit up the tree. Behind it, sat a framed photo of three cats. The ginger dominating the shot was still missing in action.

Bending, I used my phone light and confirmed there was plenty of orange fur on the cat blanket. He was around.

At least, he should be.

Keats mumbled something that worried me before heading downstairs with Percy. Was the cat ill or injured? Had he escaped outside with the police coming and going?

While my pets explored, I took a peek into Hester's cupboard and opened the single drawer on her small desk. I didn't find any clues about what happened, and that didn't surprise me. Hester had made a clear demarcation between work and home. The décor was mostly mid-century modern with nary an antique in sight. Maybe her gargoyle was the threshold between old and new.

Keats and Percy weren't optimistic about solving the crime here.

They came back upstairs and went straight to the sofa, as if to confer. The tabbies offered another hiss, fed up with the intrusions.

Heading into the kitchen, I leaned against the counter and argued with myself. I knew what I had to do, but that didn't make it any easier.

I called Kellan.

"Hey," he said. "Did we leave enough food to meet your standards for feline husbandry?"

"How did you know I was here?" My brain whirled until I realized he had set up a security feed and was monitoring me. I wasn't sure where he'd hidden the cameras, so I smiled and threw a few kisses around the room.

"Thank you for that," he said. "It's the closest we're likely to get for the foreseeable future."

"You don't sound as mad as I thought you'd be."

"Annoyed, but not surprised. You mentioned Hester's cats, so it was just a matter of time till you used that as an excuse to poke around." He paused for a second. "I bet you turned on the ceramic tree."

I laughed. "You know me so well. I turned it off."

"And the cats are fine, I trust?"

"There's enough food," I said. "But not enough cats."

He was clicking on his keyboard, giving me only half his attention. "How so?"

"Hester had three cats, Kellan. The ginger is missing. I called to see if you guys had seen him."

The clicking stopped briefly and then started again. "You magically know it's a male?"

"There's nothing magical about it. Most gingers are male. Most calicos and tortoiseshells are female. If you're bored, I'll tell you more about cat genetics."

"Not that bored. Or bored at all. Solving a murder has a way of keeping my brain engaged."

"Didn't you notice the photo of the three cats? Or the orange fur on the blanket?"

A sigh wafted my way. "It wasn't my highest priority. No one mentioned a ginger cat." He clacked on the keyboard quickly. "Nope. Only two cats noted. Gray with stripes."

"Well, the ginger is MIA. Keats and Percy are concerned. I'd better call the Mafia to start a search outside."

There was a long pause at the other end and then more clacking. "Hang on. I need to check something. Huh. Interesting."

"What? Is there something you haven't told me?"

"Plenty, and for good reason. But I'll tell you this. A neighbor's security cam caught someone breaking into Hester's house on the night of the murder. The image is grainy because of the falling snow, and we haven't been able to ID the intruder yet. He or she left with a duffel bag. Carried it as if it contained something precious. We presumed it was an antique or collectible, but now I wonder."

My fingers reached down and touched Keats, and he mumbled some advice. "I need to see that security footage. They took the cat. I'm sure of it."

"Who breaks into a house to steal a cat? That's nuts."

"It's not the strangest thing you've heard." My phone pinged as I received the two clips, and he went back to his clacking as I watched them. The first showed someone in a balaclava casing out the house and then climbing in a side window empty-handed. The second clip showed the person coming up the lane, carrying a bag. "Are you kidding me? Kellan, that's Heddy Langman, and there's a cat squirming in the duffel bag."

"Heddy? What makes you think it's her?"

"Her hands are bare, and she stood there snapping her fingers before going in. It's a tic she's picked up recently. Look at how many times she does it."

"That's not enough to go on. With the balaclava, it could be anyone."

"It's Heddy. When I saw her yesterday, she had orange fur all over her scarf, and it wasn't fluffy like Percy's. Besides, you know the Langmans stole Gertie's cat. It's a pattern."

The clacking had stopped again. "This break-in happened at about the same time as Hester was attacked at the museum."

"Divide and conquer," I said. "Kaye Langman must have gone to deal with Hester on her own. They showed me the alibi footage from their store, and it looked too good to be true."

"It was true, just creatively edited. Their store is a short drive from both Hester's house and the museum. They could have set up their shots and then left, I suppose. We're having it analyzed." He fell silent for a moment. "I get that Heddy may have broken in to look for antiques, or a key to the museum. What I don't understand is stealing a cat."

"I know it's weird. They're collectors, though. Maybe they needed an orange one to round out their set. Or maybe it was payback because Hester gave them a hard time at the reception."

"If she cared enough about the cat, I suppose they might have planned to use it for leverage. The Langmans wanted Hester to return the sleigh to the owners. Heddy and Kaye had a buyer lined up, and the Millbrooks were crumbling under pressure. Only the family's commitment to the museum held them back."

"Hester cared about the cat," I said. "But I doubt she would have succumbed to blackmail without escalating the issue. She took great pride in her work. A true professional."

"I'd better swing by and talk to the sisters again. You're sure about the finger snapping?"

"You've got more evidence." I said. "Last night, you videoed our surveillance at the Christmas market, and that's where it was most obvious. I noticed she was snapping like an alligator. Nerves, I guess." I gave him a second to scroll through his phone before adding, "Did you know gators brumate? Burrow into mud in cold weather and go dormant?"

"I did not. Nor did I care to know."

"You *should* care, Chief. Facts like these will give you the advantage over the other chiefs in the region."

Somehow, I made him laugh. "Then I look forward to dropping brumation into casual conversation with my colleagues."

"There's always a way. You see how I do it."

He laughed again. "It's very casual. So casual I barely notice yet leave with a headful of strange factoids. I worry they'll come out when they shouldn't."

"Like when you're arresting someone? You're snapping on the handcuffs and launching into an explanation about how reptiles brumate?"

"Exactly. Sometimes I look these things up online to see if you're pulling my leg."

"Hardly. Brumation is serious business."

"Obviously." There was a rustle that sounded like he was putting his coat on. "I'm not sure this gives me an advantage in law enforcement, but you know what *does*?"

I zipped my coat and got ready to leave, too. "Nope. What?"

"You," he said. "Plus Keats and Percy."

"Really?" Warmth flooded my heart like rich cocoa. Praise for my sleuthing was scarce from Kellan, especially when I was somewhere I had no business being. "Merry Christmas to you, too."

A door slammed on his end, and snow crunched underfoot. "I wish it were merrier. You'd better get on the road now. Two of the snowplows are down."

"Two at once? Is that a coincidence?"

"Vandalism, unfortunately. Someone poured eggnog into the fuel tanks."

"Festive." I let the pets out Hester's back door, locked it behind us, and fed the key to the stone gargoyle.

Kellan's SUV beeped as he unlocked it. "That's not all. Inflatable figures have been slashed. Snowmen have been decapitated. Ice sculptures at the market were melted. And the entries for the town's gingerbread house competition were smashed and partially consumed."

"Wow. Seriously? Sounds like high school kids on a rampage."

He turned the key in the ignition. "Think bigger. Someone used red Christmas lights to spell out the word 'quit' on the mayor's front lawn."

"Poor Meryl. No wonder she was so relentless when we went to City Hall earlier. She really twisted my arm about helping with the investigation."

"I know." His tires spun on the ice as he gunned the car. "I'm not feeling jolly about that. Can you at least work in daylight? After the Langmans, I need to visit Powell Nobbs and Isaac Gherkin. It'll take ages with roads like this, and worrying about you won't help."

"I'll be fine." I hurried back to the schoolyard and opened the trailer to check on Peppermint. She whinnied a welcome and went back to eating hay. "I'm going straight to Reid Brisco's to drop the pony and then home."

"Ivy, it's not safe to be on the road towing a trailer in this weather."

Closing the door, I got into the truck. "How long does it take to get eggnog out of a snowplow?"

"Too long." He sounded so weary it made my heart cool again. "We've asked to borrow one from Dog Town. They're bringing it over after they've done a first pass on their roads."

I turned on the truck's engine and held my hands over the heater. "Keep me posted on the Langmans. And make sure you check under the beds."

"Under the beds?"

"For the cat, Kellan. I need to know the ginger is safe. Hester cared about him. If he's not there, we can send the Mafia to the Langman's country house."

"I'll keep the cat near the top of my list. Second only to figuring out if Kaye murdered Hester."

I let the truck roll slowly out of the schoolyard. "I could argue about your priorities."

"Please do. It'll be the best Christmas ever."

I laughed. "Any Christmas with you is the best ever."

"Even if we're arguing?"

"*Especially* if we're arguing. It's near the top of my list. Second only to making up."

"Ditto. Be careful, Ivy."

"You too," I said.

He was already gone, and for a second I felt as lonely as I suspected Hester had.

A sharp nip in the upper arm chased that thought away.

I was never alone with Keats and Percy riding shotgun.

And judging from the tapping paws on the dash, our ride was far from over.

CHAPTER SEVENTEEN

K eats mumbled, tapped and snorted at the crack in the window as I drove away from Hester's neighborhood and toward the museum.

"No, no, no," I murmured.

Yes.

The message was clear.

That's exactly where we were going.

Captain Keats left no room for argument.

Groaning, I maneuvered around the old red building and eased the truck and trailer into the back alley. Spontaneous investigation was complicated with livestock in tow, but not impossible. Far from it. Bocelli and Clippers had been double the challenge. More, since the donkey wasn't overly cooperative. Like Clippers, Peppermint enjoyed adventure, and she backed happily out of the trailer after I parked.

I still had the key Iris gave me at the reception. No one thought to ask for it back and, naturally, I didn't offer. There was always a chance I'd need to come again to dig deeper. Having a key basically made it legitimate, especially with the mayor twisting my arm to get to the bottom of what happened here.

"Let's keep this simple," I said. "Peppermint stays in the back entryway where she can't knock over priceless antiques. Boys, we'll go inside and take a good look around. Apply your noses and super-powers to the situation. Then we'll get out before anyone notices. Agreed?"

Percy was already standing at the door in the circle of light, shaking one orange paw after another. It was just for show because he didn't mind snow. Behaving like a normal cat now and then reset expectations and made his remarkable feats even more astounding.

I walked the pony around a large dumpster and then stuck the key in the lock. When the door opened, the cat and dog shot ahead of me into the darkness.

"Sorry, girl," I told Peppermint, as I moved some cartons into the doorway to block her in the mudroom. "You'll be warm and dry in here. There are rubber mats for traction. I doubt we'll be long, because the boys are onto something."

Saying the last words out loud reminded me to let Jilly know where we were.

Her response was just a long series of exclamation and question marks.

Oops. My best friend was rarely at a loss for words.

"It's fine," I texted back. "The boys just want a quick look around."

The word "quick" should slow Jilly's roll. When it came to crossing police tape, she was tempted to put my safety above best friend code and call Asher or Kellan. But she wouldn't want them to leave their work only to find us already gone.

Her next text comprised more than punctuation. "We're on our way. Stay."

Stay. That made me smile. We knew the command, but obedience wasn't our strong suit.

The dog reappeared and mumbled something more urgent. Giving the pony a pat, I allowed myself to be herded down the hall.

I was grateful for the baseboard lighting. The less I waved my phone light around, the better. We weren't far from the hustle and bustle of town square. All it would take was one call from a concerned citizen to earn me a lump of coal from Kellan in my Christmas stocking. I far preferred diamonds and other pretty stones. Despite my appreciation of overalls and work boots, I loved the jewelry Kellan chose for me. Mostly, the pieces stayed safe in my drawer, coming out to twinkle on date nights and holidays.

Keats circled and delivered a sharp nip to my calf.

"Hey! That was unnecessary. I'm moving."

He gave a short grumble that I interpreted as "mooning."

The dog wasn't wrong. When I was tired, I fell more easily into romantic musing. It felt like an emotional shield against what was more likely to happen with my beloved if he found me here. Namely, a dressing down. While I might not technically be trespassing, Kellan wouldn't agree that having a key qualified as a free pass to poke around a crime scene that hadn't yet been cleared. The sweet moment we had would sour quickly.

"Yeah, yeah. Where are we going, anyway?"

A gentle poke herded me into a dark room with a small, high window. There was no baseboard lighting, so I pressed my phone light.

We were inside the staff office, which held three desks. All had been emptied by the police, but the lamps remained. Iris' desk held a quirky one I recognized from her childhood bedroom. It had an orange glass base, and a spangled shade with a fringe. My sister's style was nothing like that tacky piece from the hippie era, but I understood why it was there. We had little growing up, and it was easy to get attached to things like that lamp. It probably reminded her of how far she'd come. I had a thrift store jewelry box that did the same for me. Now, it held precious baubles, and I treasured the box nearly as much as the actual treasure.

Keats mumbled a veiled threat about mooning, and I moved

ahead of his teeth. The next desk held a Tiffany-style lamp with a tulip design that had likely belonged to Hester Belcher. The afghan at her house also had a tulip pattern, and I guessed they were her favorite flower. And the last desk held a simple fluorescent lamp from a big-box store. Modern and understated. It must be Anthony's.

Percy cased out his options and, like my own version of Goldilocks, decided Hester's desk was just right. Hopping up, he pawed at the top drawer on the left side. Keeping my black knit gloves on, I opened it.

"Nothing, pal." I tried the other drawers. "The police were thorough. Not so much as a pencil left behind."

The cat wasn't so sure. Reaching in, he swished around with one orange paw.

Bending with my light, I took a closer look, tracing around the edges with my black fingertip.

"All I got is dust and bits of rubber eraser," I told him.

Keats mumbled to get my attention. His paw was up in a point, also toward the desk.

"You're never wrong, but there's a first time for everything."

I was about to shove the drawer closed when Percy dove inside with the skill of a professional contortionist. He scrabbled around on the wooden bottom in his classic litter box move and then got out again. Claw marks raked one corner.

"What did you find, buddy? A dead mouse?" I bent to peer into the drawer and sniffed. Nothing to get queasy over, luckily. I had eaten nothing since Edna let Jilly and me split a protein bar in the field.

Percy went back inside to add some paw flourishes.

"Okay, if you feel that strongly about it, I'll try my utility knife." Groping in the front pocket of my overalls, I pulled it out. Then, I shooed the cat from the desk drawer and slid my blade into the crack in the back corner.

"Huh. There's a little notch. If I angle the knife just right— Oh, wow."

The entire bottom panel shifted and lifted, revealing a shallow hidden compartment. Inside sat a small spiral-bound notebook with a plain black cover. It was the type you could buy at any office supply store for a few bucks.

"Interesting. Looks like Hester had a secret diary. Bet she kept tabs on every move Iris made that wasn't up to curator code. Maybe she was trying to get her fired."

Setting the notebook on the oak desktop, I swapped out my knit gloves for neoprene and opened the cover.

The first 20 pages were blank, but I wasn't fooled. Hester didn't keep a notebook in a false-bottomed drawer without good reason.

I kept flipping, and finally, the docent's neat handwriting appeared. I'd seen it on displays in my childhood, before the museum had its own printer.

There were pages and pages of notes.

Dates. Item descriptions. Dollar amounts. Initials.

A few things jumped off the page:

Oct 3: Josiah Millbrook's pewter tankard, c. 1847. Listed as "deaccessioned due to condition." Sold for $1,200. Buyer: H.L.

Nov 17: Collection of antique maps, Hill Country region, 1820s. Listed as "transferred to storage." Sold for $5,800. Buyer: H.L.

Dec 2: Victorian pocket watch, gold case. Listed as "lost in inventory audit." Sold for $2,400. Buyer: H.L.

The list started in September with small, inexpensive and possibly inconsequential items and grew with time. Page after page of museum artifacts had apparently left the museum's care and been purchased by the not-too-mysterious H.L.

Heddy Langman must have melted her wallet and then revived it in resale. For all their shady shortcomings, the Langmans sure knew how to make money. Their cats, stolen or otherwise, would never go hungry.

Unless I could help put the sisters behind bars. Then, I'd adopt the cats myself.

"I don't really understand what Hester Belcher was capturing here," I said. "Was she selling stolen museum goods to the Langmans? Maybe she had money problems, but Iris said she had a good pension and would accept only a stipend for her work as a docent."

I flipped another page. There was a starred note from three days ago that read, "Spoke to D.B. and confirmed online sales. Must speak to I.G. ASAP, or D.B. will report."

Someone with the initials D.B. knew what was going on. Hester didn't have many friends she trusted, according to Iris, and few could track something like this online.

My mental lightbulb switched on. "Aha. So, Hester and I had something in common, after all. Our local genius librarian, Dottie Bridges, knows her way around the dark web, and that's probably where these items were sold. Did Dottie go to Kellan, I wonder? Or was she waiting for me to pop in to borrow a book on Shetland ponies? I feel like a missed a step, but it's hard to be everywhere at once."

Keats stepped on my boot and mumbled. He wanted me to hurry, and he wasn't the only one. I heard shuffling and pawing near the back door. Peppermint was getting restless, and I could hardly blame her.

"Okay, we know enough. Hester suspected someone was running a black market antique ring and got Dottie to confirm her findings. She was about to tell Iris, or I.G., and never got the chance. Did the seller find out Hester knew and kill her? Did Heddy and Kaye Langman split up to jump the gun? Or did someone make a play for the sleigh and it got messy?"

My hand shook a little as I flipped another page and found Hester's last entry on the day of the museum reception.

"Next target confirmed by D.B. today. Buyer offering $10,000 for a rare, extinct ivory-billed woodpecker. One male bird currently in the taxidermy exhibit is scheduled for restoration, with a replica on order. Due diligence done. Reporting is critical. Our heritage is being sold."

There were almost as many exclamation marks under this entry as Jilly had used in her text earlier.

"Did the thief get the woodpecker?" I asked aloud. "Pretty sure I saw it in the taxidermy wing during the reception. A stunning bird that died out nearly a hundred years ago. I think this one belonged to the Millbrook family as well before they donated it to the museum."

I ran my neoprene-covered fingertips over Percy, and his fluff rose with static, making him look like his hackles were up.

Or were his hackles up for real? It was hard to be sure when he wore his yellow bomber. The cat wasn't too worried, though. I got the distinct impression he wanted to check out the woodpecker. I probably wouldn't know a replica from a taxidermic bird, but Percy would. He could easily scale to the top shelf it was on, too. It would give Kellan and team a head start on confirming Hester's last big discovery.

"If only she'd reported it earlier," I whispered. "That's why she got hot under the collar with Iris at the reception the other day. Bet Hester felt bad she hadn't noticed it sooner in all the hubbub of moving. Seeing the Langmans making brash plays for items on display must have rattled her even more. Success went to their heads. Turned Heddy into a hungry gator."

I slipped the notebook into a plastic dog poop bag and tucked it into my chest pocket. Hester would be disgusted that her discoveries were being transported to the police in such a manner, but I wanted to keep the evidence pristine. This was the work of her lifetime. If I had anything to do with it, the town would remember

Hester for preserving our town's culture. She deserved her own plaque at this institution.

"We'll take a quick look in the taxidermy exhibit and then drive straight to the police station," I said. "I want to deliver it myself."

The taxidermy exhibit would have answers. If the real woodpecker was still on display, the police might set a trap by reopening the museum and baiting the killer out. If it was already gone, they might be able to track it on the dark web. Kellan had connections to highly skilled digital analysts. That was becoming increasingly important in police work.

Keats and Percy led me out of the office and turned left. The cat moved in silence, but the dog's claws clicked softly as he dropped into a low skulk. Peppermint huffed and snorted in the back entry, letting me know she was fed up. A pony of her caliber deserved a bigger role in what was going down tonight.

The darkness swallowed Percy's bright bomber and fluff as he went into the natural history exhibit. Keats turned back, his blue eye gleaming in the low lights of the hall. I stopped for a second, holding my breath. It felt like the entire building held its breath, too.

Doubt coiled in my stomach, like the big snake I'd seen in the exhibit earlier. The last place I wanted to be was in a darkened room surrounded by dead animals. It was the opposite of festive. Right now, I should be kibitzing with Keely about Peppermint's unicorn magic.

My thumb tapped out one word to Jilly: "hurry."

Why was I so jumpy suddenly? The prospect of creeping among stuffed animals wasn't appealing, but I'd faced worse than a long-dead bear.

Something felt very wrong, and I didn't need Keats' flattened ears under my fingertips to confirm it.

"Should we leave?" My voice was barely audible, but I didn't really need words to communicate with my dog anyway.

Moving behind my legs, he pressed me through the doorway,

and once I was inside, the answer to my question was obvious in the dog's posture.

Spending some quality time at the taxidermy zoo was inevitable.

It was too late to do anything else.

Because we weren't alone in the museum anymore.

CHAPTER EIGHTEEN

The footsteps were deliberate. Measured. The visitor was cautious, which likely meant they knew someone was here. Maybe they were more afraid of being surprised by us than the other way around.

Keats' ears came up to capture the sound and then flattened again in judgement. Percy climbed swiftly onto a shelf with stuffed songbirds, his tail so puffed I was afraid he'd send a bird plunging to a second death.

I should have been scared. I *was* scared. Yet I felt resigned as well. No way out but through, I figured. My best fur friends were here with me. My best human friends were en route. And my beloved was just a call away. Locating Kellan's number on my phone, I let my thumb hover. Before I sounded the alarm, I had to be sure. It wasn't the time or place for a lecture. If I played my cards right, maybe Kellan wouldn't need to know until I was out of here and back at the farm. Ideally standing on the high ground of my manure pile.

The taxidermy room was eerie. Baseboard lighting seemed to hurt more than help here, with thin beams being absorbed by bodies and pelts. Glass eyes stared at nothing from every direction. The bear reared up on its hind legs in eternal aggression. The cougar crouched mid-pounce, frozen before a leap that would never come. A family of raccoons huddled around a fake log, their tiny paws reaching in perpetuity. Moose and deer tried to keep the mood calm and failed miserably. None of these animals would hang out together in the wild, yet here they were jammed into one large room.

I'd never been a fan of taxidermy. It felt wrong to stuff and pose creatures that had once been vital and alive. But I had to admit the craftsmanship was impressive. The animals looked so natural it seemed entirely possible they'd start moving again.

Percy stalked across the floor, nearly glowing from the golden-hued baseboard lighting. He wove between displays with the confidence of a cat who knew exactly where he was going. Keats stayed close to my left leg, his body tense and ready.

The footsteps paused.

I held my breath again.

If I were correct, the museum's new visitor had arrived by the front door and was making their way through the main gallery. Past the pretty tree and baubles, and into the next room, with the empty stand where the Millbrook sleigh had sat. Was it just one set of boots, or two? Had Heddy come alone or brought Kaye for backup? Either way, I could probably handle them until the cavalry arrived.

Percy hopped onto a display case and swished his paw vigorously around the resident animal. Tiptoeing closer, I inspected the wolverine. I doubted hill country had ever hosted wolverines, but here it was, and not too happy about it, judging by the snarl. Its mouth gaped, and its sharp teeth glinted in the faint light. My knowledge of the creature was scanty, but I knew it was ferocious and strong. Capable of killing many of the animals exhibited here without batting a glass eye.

Percy swished again and turned to make sure I got the message. Glancing down, I saw Keats had his paw up, too. What was so fascinating about this mustelid? It was an oversized ferret that looked ready to rip out my throat.

The cat swished relentlessly until I accepted I needed to touch this fearsome beast. I ran my fingers over the wolverine quickly. Even through my neoprene glove, its fur seemed dense and dry. If there was a clue, I missed it.

Percy gave a dramatic yawn, which seemed strange given our current level of stimulation. It reminded me of Hester's stone gargoyle.

Of course.

The wolverine's mouth.

I poked one finger inside, grateful for the layer of synthetic rubber between us. It helped me keep a mental distance from the operation.

While I'd never poked around in a wolverine's mouth before, I had certain expectations. Sharp teeth. A tongue. Nothing like what I found, which was hard, round and vaguely familiar.

Pinching, I pulled gently until a handle appeared, followed by a long stretch of metal, marked with dark streaks and flakes.

A screwdriver.

Flathead.

There was one in my side pocket now. It was a handy, versatile tool that could apparently double as a murder weapon if the need arose. As Kellan had predicted, it was as common as gossip in Clover Grove.

I didn't want to rattle another poop bag, so I slipped my gloves off and carefully covered the screwdriver before slipping it into my side pocket beside my own flathead. Now I had all the pieces Kellan needed to put someone away, if I could get the evidence into his hands.

The wolverine's mouth gaped in a rather nasty smirk. He'd coughed up the goods, but it was on me to find a way out of this gnarly maze.

When had the screwdriver arrived in the wolverine's mouth? The police scrutinized the place and found nothing. I had an advantage in my assistants, but there was a chance the killer came back to stash it here.

The footsteps had stopped, and the hair on my arms prickled. We were being watched.

I slipped behind the towering bear on its hind legs and motioned for Keats to stand beside me. Percy jumped onto a white-tailed deer's back and went higher, where he was less visible. There were many shelves with smaller animals and birds. One of them had the shape of a large woodpecker, but I couldn't get a good look without turning on my light.

Who was here with us? Heddy and Kaye were my first and best guesses, but I was far from certain. They were part of the scheme, no question. Eager participants. They'd falsified their alibi and split up on the night of the murder, with Heddy breaking into Hester's house. Still, I wasn't sure they were the brains behind the operation, or that Kaye could pull off the murder alone. Would a living, breathing Langman leave the Millbrook sleigh behind? That's what they coveted most. It didn't make sense.

Nothing else made sense, either. My brain seemed as paralyzed as these animals. Normally, my mental slot machine would chime merrily by now, spitting out answers and coins of evidence. Whose alibi was weak? Who had access to this wing? Who would know where to hide a weapon in the taxidermy exhibit? Who could redirect items from the museum's collection without raising immediate suspicion?

Ding-ding-ding.

Someone ticked most of those boxes, and with creativity, alibis could be fudged. Especially in this day of digital deception.

It wasn't a Langman, as much as I wished to see the sisters gone from Clover Grove. It wasn't Powell Nobbs or Isaac Gherkin, as eccentric as they might be. It most certainly wasn't Iris.

There was someone with inside access. Someone trusted. Someone who'd been around the whole time, hiding in plain sight while we chased red herrings.

Someone with whom I'd shared advice and empathy.

And someone my pets had disliked, now that I thought about it.

Keats leaned into my leg and let out a quiet "ha." Just the one. He wasn't laughing so much as gloating, I suspected. He had called this early. His nose knew, but he had to wait for me to catch up. Not that he particularly minded. For my furry geniuses, the fun came from flushing out the facts one by one.

Now, the final flesh and blood fact flushed itself into the natural history exhibit.

The newcomer was slight and fleet of foot. I barely caught a glimpse before the person slipped behind the moose. The jeans and boots showing between hooves could belong to anyone. The head of dark curls peeking over the moose's shoulder could not. That mop belonged to someone who knew this place like the back of his hand.

My thumb pressed down on Kellan's number, and I slipped the phone into the front pocket of my overalls.

"I know you're here, Ivy." The voice was familiar. Pleasant, even. The same voice had spoken fondly about Hester only yesterday. His kind words stood out in a sea of dissenters.

"Hey," I said, trying to sound equally pleasant. "I preferred our previous meeting spot. The coffee's better. How about we head over and talk there?"

"Just you and me?" he asked. "Where's your army?"

"On their way. They can join us at the café. And the pony needs to come along."

"I figured. What about the cat and dog? They here, too?"

He'd find that out soon enough, possibly the hard way. If he couldn't see them right now, all the better.

"They're around. This place is full of cool sights, sounds and smells."

"Especially this evening. Your pony pooped near the back door."

"I'll clean it up," I said.

"Don't worry about it."

What was he saying? That I wouldn't be around long enough to clean up after Peppermint?

"Mucking is my responsibility, Anthony," I said, naming my opponent for Kellan's sake. I kept my voice steady, channeling my HR training for high-conflict situations. Stay calm. Don't escalate. Find common ground. "I'm surprised you're here."

"Why? I work here."

Not anymore. On the other end of my phone, someone was firing him and preparing a holding cell with an uncomfortable cot and no pillow. Anthony Cork's curls would be frizz by morning if I had anything to say about it.

"It's past closing," I said. "Iris wouldn't want you clocking overtime during the holiday season."

"No big deal. Just wanted to tie up some loose ends."

Starting with a flathead screwdriver, I presumed. "Gotcha. Iris asked me to pick something up."

"Her alibi? I heard it's missing in action."

He was ready to play hardball. Alright, fella. Game on.

"Good one," I said. "Luckily, she's got an in with the chief. Kellan's like Santa Claus. He knows who's been naughty or nice. How's your scorecard this year, Anthony?"

"Spotty," he admitted. "Big hopes for next year."

I started moving sideways. If I kept it slow and steady while distracting him, I could navigate to the door with the boys and run. I had to protect Peppermint. The pony couldn't become collateral damage in a fight I'd picked.

"Sounds good," I said. "Too bad this year ended on a sour note. With Hester falling onto that blade."

"Falling?" He laughed quietly and mirrored my movements in

reverse. We were engaged in a strange waltz around the silent, watchful animals. "Hester never stumbled. Never fell. She was always so sure of everything. So certain she knew best."

His voice wobbled slightly on the last words.

"Hester was your mentor." My tone was compassionate. The same tone I'd used with countless employees on the verge of breaking down in my corporate office. "She taught you everything she knew about the museum."

"She smothered me." The words burst out of him. "Every decision I made, Hester questioned. Every exhibit I designed, she redesigned. 'That's not quite right, Anthony.' 'Let me show you the proper way, Anthony.' 'You have such potential if you'd only listen, Anthony.'"

"How frustrating," I said. "Hester had strong opinions."

"Very. I couldn't take a breath without checking in with her about my cadence."

I ducked behind a white-tailed buck and tried to plan. The stuffed animals formed a maze that I could use. Anthony was familiar with the layout, but my dog was a master of complex maneuvering. Keats would herd this hobby farmer out of here safely. Agility classes were never fun for me, but they'd served a purpose.

If Anthony jumped me, we could give him a good fight depending on weapon status. Had he counted on reusing the screwdriver, or did he come with the rest of the set? The flathead was out of commission, but he could stab me with a Phillips or a Robertson. What was the one with the star head? Torx. That's what I'd choose.

A screwdriver we could handle. But what if he'd upgraded to a gun? They were easy enough to find, especially for someone familiar with the black market.

Keats prodded my calf to stop my spinning thoughts. Spinning took us nowhere fast.

"I hope Iris was a kinder leader," I said. "How did she fit into all of this?"

Anthony circled a white-tailed doe before moving on to the moose calf. He was agitated, unable to stand still. "Iris didn't even see me. I was like furniture to her. She'd breeze in a couple of times a week, make sweeping changes to my work, and leave again. At least Hester noticed I existed, even if it was to criticize."

"So, you started selling artifacts." I slipped behind a laddered display of game birds. "To get out from under debt. And create an escape route."

He froze. "Debt? How did you—?"

"Just a guess from working in HR. Maybe you had scholarships but still graduated thirty grand in the hole. The weight of student debt is crushing. Feels like you'll never get ahead."

"Sounds about right."

Even when they'd done terrible things, people needed to be heard and validated.

Especially when they'd done terrible things.

"It's tough enough to make a living in the arts," I said. "Two degrees and what did your education get you? An entry-level job in a small-town museum where there was no room for growth. You could never be more than an assistant here. Not before Hester retired."

"She said she'd never retire. That she'd be carried out in a pine box. Which is basically what happened. Only without the box." His laugh was grating in the quiet room. "I did everything right. Followed the rules. Sucked up to people. Where did it get me? Buried under debt in a basement apartment, watching people like the Langman sisters make a fortune off the same artifacts I catalogued for pennies."

I crouched behind the cougar whose body was frozen in time. Its glass eyes peered in Anthony's direction. Meanwhile, Keats had circled around to flank the man from the other side. My eyes flicked up and found Percy between the antlers of a mounted moose head. How many dead moose did one museum need to make a point?

"So, you started small," I said. "Taking items that wouldn't be quickly missed. Things Iris or Hester marked for storage or restoration. You'd redirect them before they reached the inventory system."

"Easily done." His voice had a note of pride. "Hester trained me too well. I had access to the collections database and was better with technology than either of them. I knew which items were valuable on the market. A pocket watch here, some antique maps there. The Langmans were my best customers and surprisingly discreet. Word spread. My prices rose, and my debt went down. Best part? Nobody noticed.

"Until someone did. And it wasn't Hester."

"The librarian. Stupid old cow."

"Dottie Bridges is far from stupid," I said. "She's a whiz with the dark web. And when the two ladies put their heads together, they found quite a trail. Hester probably would have noticed it sooner if not for the hubbub of the move."

"Noticing was normally her superpower, which is why I felt so good about how things played out. Figured her brain was finally declining like a normal person's." He slapped the moose calf's backside. "After all, Hester should have been like this guy. Long dead."

Anthony laughed again, which encouraged me. If he enjoyed his tale, he'd keep talking. And the longer he talked, the more time Kellan had to send backup. I was surprised they weren't here already, given the police presence in town square. It was an eight-minute run for an athletic cop like my brother. What I wouldn't give to see Asher right about now. His hero complex was annoying, but he was willing to put his money—and gun—where his mouth was.

I decided to get a little bolder and then make my exit. "Anthony, what happened the night of the reception?"

"I left when everyone else did. Went to my friend's party. Took a lot of selfies. Arranged for my friend to tell anyone who asked that I had stayed till the bitter end. He owed me, you see. Sometimes debt goes my way."

"That's a good friend," I said. "And then you came back here."

"Yeah." He was moving again, near the bear where I'd started our circuit. "I wanted to collect the ivory-billed woodpecker. It's worth ten thousand dollars to the right collector. Enough to put me in the black. I was ready to leave town. New city, new job, new life."

"But Hester was still here in the museum when you arrived that night."

"Broom in hand, like a witch. She couldn't let the custodial staff clean up. Had to do it herself, making sure every garland was straight, every display exactly as she wanted it."

Anthony didn't notice Percy right over his head, perched between the moose's broad antlers. The orange cat was hard to miss unless you were a murderer caught up in your own story of being victimized.

"That's when Hester confronted you," I prompted.

"I half-expected it, given what I overheard her saying to Iris at the reception. But I hoped I could swap out the woodpeckers and go. She was waiting when I let myself in through the front door." He paused, but I didn't need to prod him again. "That's when she came at me. Said she had a notebook detailing every item missing. At first, I thought she was blowing wind, but she'd done a full forensic audit. Then the lecture began. She'd expected better of me. Invested so much in my education. I was a total letdown." One hand landed in tangled curls. "Anger would have been easier to handle than disappointment."

"That does sound hard. How did the sleigh come into play?"

"Honestly, it wasn't even on my radar. There was no way I could sell a thing like that without being noticed. But Hester got it in her head that it was my next mark. I told her to chill out, but she grabbed it and dragged it outside to get away from me. Do you know she actually shielded that thing with her own body?"

"Wow. That's dedication."

His curls bobbed in agreement. "I wanted to let her go. Part of me still respected her. But she was yelling for help. Threatening to call the police, call Iris, call everyone she could think of, only she wouldn't let go of the sleigh to grab her phone."

My heart thumped faster. We were getting close to the moment when everything changed. "You must have been worried."

"More like frustrated. I didn't want her precious sleigh. I'd been selective about what I sold and was nearly done. Why did she have to go and ruin everything?"

"Hester never backed away from a fight. Did she swing at you?"

"Verbally, the shots kept coming. Called me a thief. A disgrace. Said I'd thrown away every opportunity she'd given me." His voice was slow now, as he relived the moment. "Eventually, I cracked. Couldn't listen to one more sermon. It reminded me of my mother. Hester wasn't saying anything I didn't already know."

"Still, it must have been hard to hear." I kept my voice calm. Neutral. "Especially at Christmas. A time that brings up a lot of emotion."

"Christmas." He practically spat out the word. "Who cares about Christmas? It's for people who have families. Normal lives. Not me."

"Nor Hester," I said gently. "In a way, the artifacts here *were* her family. That's probably why she was overwrought."

"Possibly." A long pause followed. So long I thought things might turn around. "I hated that about her. So pathetic."

"I thought it was a given in your line of work. Iris has cried over rare relics."

He walked back and forth in a small clear space, pondering. "I guess I was like that at the beginning. Didn't take long to realize all this crap is worthless, aside from the meaning we give it. The more meaning, the higher the price tag. Once I detached from the old mindset, I found success."

We had different measures of success, but this wasn't a teachable moment. It was a moment for more validation.

"I see what you mean about the artificial value placed on antiques. You turned tradition on its head and cleared your debt. Now you can find your true purpose."

His agitated movements slowed, and he stared at me. I couldn't really see his eyes, but I felt the madness. "Just need to clear up a few things before I go," he said. "Starting with what's in your pocket."

The blood in my veins turned to slush, and my extremities became numb. "My pocket?"

"You were holding a screwdriver when I came in."

"I always have a screwdriver in my pocket. Any self-respecting hobby farmer does."

"I do, too. Helps me pry open locked drawers." He leaned casually against the wall. "Does yours have blood on it? Because mine does."

The air seemed to cool, and I looked for steam when I exhaled slowly. The stuffed animals practically leaned in closer to hear his confession.

"Blood? Ah. You used a screwdriver to stab Hester."

"Technically, she ran into it. At least the first time. She came at me with the sleigh and tried to whack me. I held out my hands and... Well, you know the rest."

"So, it was accidental. You didn't want it to end like that."

"I wanted a fresh start. No strings attached. Instead, I got a mess to clean up. Hester was just lying there in the snow with the sleigh beside her. I didn't know what to do. Froze for a few minutes. Literally. I couldn't feel my body."

I knew all about dissociation. Even now, it was hard to stay present. "That's when Powell Nobbs showed up."

He laughed a little. "That pony was a gift from the universe. Just trotted around the corner and came toward me. I think it was curious."

"Probably. Peppermint's a spunky girl. What did you do then?"

"My first thought was to tie the pony to the sleigh and get her to pull Hester into the woods where I could dump her." Anthony paused and then corrected himself. "*Bury* her. At least in snow. I turned to go back into the museum to find a rope and heard thumping."

"Powell was looking for the sleigh."

"He was talking out loud like he was crazy or something. 'Where is it? I need it.' I wasn't sure what he was after. I ran around the side of the building and watched him come out. He grabbed the sleigh. Stepped right over Hester like he didn't see her. Picked up the pony's lead rope and walked into the field." Anthony shook his curls in bemusement. "Dude talked about some lady. How she'd love it, no matter what, and the plan would still work. He got mad at the pony because she didn't want to come with him. There was a tussle, and noise and complaining. Finally, they were gone."

"Then you tried again to move Hester?"

Anthony's pacing resumed as agitation grew. "I couldn't just leave her there, could I? So, I tried dragging her. Only got as far as the recycle bins when I heard a truck out front. I knew you were coming back to help close. It was game over."

I'd maneuvered to the doorway at last. It wouldn't be hard to slip out and race to the back entry. I'd grab Peppermint's lead rope and run into those very fields until we were safe.

"Game over," I repeated, backing slowly into the hall.

It was as if Anthony felt the shift, because he followed. "Not quite. There's still some trash to take out. And that's you."

"Trash? How insulting, Anthony. I've been nothing but nice to you."

"Nice would be handing over the screwdriver so that I don't

have to take it by force. I shouldn't have to see violence again. I'm a very sensitive person."

"I can tell. That's what happens when we have a critical mother. Mine was no picnic, either."

"This isn't about my mother." His voice was sharp. "Why are you talking about her?"

Keats' came back and positioned himself between Anthony and me, a low rumble building in his chest.

"Sorry," I said. "You mentioned her, and I could relate to feeling like a disappointment. It's something we share."

The tension hung as thick as the flock of bats dangling on fishing line from the ceiling.

"Give me the screwdriver," he said. "Now."

"It won't help." I dropped the HR façade. "Anthony, it's over. The police know everything, and they're on their way. You can't—"

"Can't what?" He lunged toward me, and I jumped back. There was a flash of something metallic in his hand. Another screwdriver. He did carry a full set. "Can't make sure you don't testify? Can't disappear before they arrive?"

"You'd better use the front door. There's a pony blocking the back, remember?"

"I'll deal with the pony." He made jousting motions at a deer with the screwdriver. "I used these animals for target practice when the police let me come inside to get my laptop and files. I stashed the screwdriver here then. That's probably what your cat was after in my backpack. The tuna sandwich was a fabrication."

I blew out a loud sigh. "Should have listened to Percy. Instead, I bought your story about wanting to keep Hester's cats."

Anthony actually chuckled. "That was fun. If only you knew how much I hate animals. Taking out your pony and pets will bring me some well-deserved Christmas joy."

That did it. Threatening my animals woke my inner wolverine.

"You're not stabbing the pony," I said. "You'll have to go through me."

"Exactly what I had in mind."

He moved faster than I expected, darting around the displays. I stumbled backward, nearly tripping over my own feet. My boots skidded on hardwood, and my arms pinwheeled to keep my balance.

That's when Percy made his move. Orange fluff catapulted from the mounted moose like a furry missile, landing directly on my adversary's curly head with 18-claw landing gear deployed. Anthony's high-pitched scream might have been funny under different circumstances, but no one was laughing now. He flailed at the cat attached to his skull.

I didn't waste the opportunity. Re-entering the room, I swung my leg back and kicked a rock holding a badger. It wasn't a real rock, however, and the lightweight structure rose into the air and landed in front of Anthony. Still grappling with Percy, the skinny young man tripped over the badger and went down hard.

Percy released his hold at exactly the right moment and landed on the cougar's back. It was bizarre to see two snarling cats at the same time—one huge, one small but highly potent.

Keats leapt on the fallen man in a flash, his teeth finding an earlobe with skill and precision. Anthony's scream went up an octave.

"Go!" I shouted to my pets.

Percy sailed off the cougar and hit the ground running. Keats gave the earlobe a savage twist and then followed. I brought up the rear, boots pounding on the hardwood as I raced for the back entry.

Behind me, Anthony groaned and cursed. He was up and moving. I heard the thud of his pursuit.

Peppermint's anxious neigh echoed through the hallway as we approached. Almost there. Just a little farther.

The pony had knocked over the cartons, clearing the path to the mudroom. The exterior door was open, and Peppermint was outside. Percy and Keats streaked past me into the alley. I left next, slamming the door.

"Come, Peppermint," I told the pony. "We need to run."

She didn't run. Instead, she moved into position against the back door and leaned.

Now all that stood between me and a maniac was four hundred pounds of Shetland pony.

CHAPTER NINETEEN

Peppermint had made up her mind. She was blocking Anthony's exit from the museum, even if it came at a cost. And it might, given the way he was throwing his weight against the door inside. Each thump made the pony's ears flick, but only in resignation. So far, the door barely budged.

"Peppermint, come on, girl." I tugged on her lead rope. "Let's get out of here."

The pony stared straight ahead. Pure defiance wrapped in fuzzy packaging.

I pulled harder.

She pulled back, harder still.

"Keats? A little help here?"

My border collie walked past the pony and sat a few feet away. He huffed a "ha" that sounded a lot like "nope."

"Seriously? Now you're unionizing?" I looked towards the cat. "What about you, Percy? How about a hint of claw in her rump? Like spurs."

Percy walked away from me and settled in a clear spot behind the dumpster. Then he started grooming a forepaw with exaggerated nonchalance.

"Hey, buddy. This is not the time for a bath."

The cat paused mid-lick to stare at me with brilliant green eyes. It felt as if he was accusing me of being melodramatic.

Maybe so. Drama seemed totally acceptable given the situation. I was trapped in an alley with a killer who was behind a door blocked by a pony. The only text waiting for me from Jilly was gibberish. She'd probably typed it in gloves.

"Peppermint, *please*." When begging failed, I moved to her shoulder and pushed, also to no avail. She was immovable. "I know you're trying to protect us, but if we stay here, you'll get hurt. He keeps hitting that door. You'll need to yield, eventually."

The door shuddered. Anthony had apparently taken a run at it. Luckily, he was only about 140 pounds soaking wet.

Kicking away the snow to get traction on the asphalt, I pulled on the lead rope with everything I had. Peppermint's hooves didn't slide an inch. Now, I understood why Shetlands were so valuable as pit ponies for coal mining. Hardy with a low center of gravity. No one was tipping this girl.

"This is ridiculous," I said. "I've moved all kinds of livestock before."

Keats mumbled a correction. *He* had moved all kinds of livestock while I flicked my fingers and barked orders. And he wasn't moving this pony. Not now. Apparently, the animals had come to an agreement, and I wasn't part of the discussion.

When force didn't work, I tried bribes. "Look, if we leave now, I'll give you all the carrots you want. Apples. Sugar cubes." I groped in my parka pocket. "I still have that fancy peppermint you scored from Powell."

One ear twitched. For a moment, I thought I'd won.

Then Anthony thudded on the door again, sending Peppermint back into passive resistance.

"Okay, new plan." I looked at Keats. "If I *can't* move her, and you *won't* move her, then I'll need to go back in by the front door and offer myself to Anthony as a sacrifice for the taxidermy exhibit. How do you like that idea?"

A roar from the side of the building drowned out any response from the dog. Keats knew I'd never leave them. Not while I had breath in my body and a flathead screwdriver of my own. Clearly, he had also known help was very close by.

Relief drained out of me so quickly that I nearly added my weight to the pony's burdens.

The familiar roaring came from snowmobiles. With the volume, I expected Asher's militia. Only two machines hurtled around the corner, however, with the drivers on their feet and leaning perilously to one side to take the turn at high speed. A long braid lashed under one driver's helmet, and both sleds threw up a spray of powder.

Slowing, Edna flipped up her visor and let out a war whoop. Jilly sat behind her, clutching the handgrips.

Gertie coasted in gently beside Edna and brought the machine to an elegant stop near the dumpster. The engines cut out, leaving sudden silence.

There was silence on the other side of the door, too. Anthony had heard the motors through the door. Perhaps he was quietly questioning his life decisions.

Jilly clambered off the snowmobile and ran to me through deep snow. Grabbing my upper arms, she looked me up and down. "Are you hurt? Did he get you? Asher called a minute ago to say you were screaming."

"That was Anthony," I said. "Percy and Keats had a go at him."

Edna snorted. "Whiny sad-sack. They don't make killers like they used to, do they, Gertie?"

"No, they do not." Gertie strode over to us. "Full report, please. We only got scraps from the cops."

Pulling my friends away, I brought them up to speed. "Pepper-mint is blocking Anthony in the museum. He was giving his all to the door, but now he's gone quiet. Maybe he ran out the front exit."

"Doubtful," Edna said. "The area's crawling with emergency personnel. There's been a situation."

"What kind of situation? Is that why Kellan hasn't come?"

"He tried, believe me," Jilly said. "Kellan and Ash were at Powell Nobbs' house when you called. At first, you cut in and out, and he wasn't sure if it was a pocket dial. They left anyway, but the road was blocked with a truck rollover. People were injured."

"That was just the beginning," Edna said. "Kellan tried to deploy the bumbling cops from the Christmas market. The also-rans."

Jilly frowned at her. "They're good cops who happened to be closer to the museum."

"It's a ten-minute stroll," I said. "Where are they?"

Edna took over again. "There's a situation. A rumpus."

"A rumpus?"

"Or a ruckus. A brouhaha, if you prefer." She glanced at Gertie. "What's the fancy French word?"

"Mêlée?" Gertie shrugged. "Let's settle for mayhem."

Jilly snatched back the conversational baton. "It all started with a multi-car collision on Main Street. Things got out of hand."

"Out of hand *how*?"

"Tempers flared. Things were said. People were pushed. Shoppers took sides. The fight spilled into the square and—" Jilly's gloves came up and pushed the air. "They toppled the tree."

"The town's Christmas tree? Meryl's going to lose her mind."

"Already happened. We were in Gertie's van monitoring the police radio. Heard the discussions. Decided to mount a rescue using the sleds." Jilly gestured to the snowmobiles like a seasoned rider. "It was easier to get around the carnage."

"Carnage! Did anyone die?" I asked.

Jilly shook her head. "Just Christmas spirit. So far."

The police certainly had their hands full, which meant we were left to our own devices. It was one young sociopath against a hobby farmer, a chef, two senior citizens with tactical training, a dog, a cat, and an extremely stubborn pony.

I'd faced worse odds.

"The smart move would be to block him inside till the police are free," Gertie said. "What do you think, Eddie?"

I answered first. "Anthony will smash the artifacts out of spite. Hester died trying to save the town's culture. It wouldn't be right to let that happen."

Gertie flung her braid over one shoulder and shrugged. "Then we have no choice but to relocate the equine asset and detain the felon."

"You can't move Peppermint," I said. "She's four hundred pounds."

"We've moved more." Edna stomped over to the door. "Granted, a pony is awkward, especially in heavy snow. But if you're not going to do your woo-woo thing, what choice do we have, Ivy?"

"I tried asking her nicely, and she wouldn't move."

Edna rested her glove on the pony's back. "Try harder. You have reinforcements now."

The banging behind the door started again, and Anthony shouted, "Let me out of here or I'll rough this place up. And I know what's valuable." After a pause came the sound of glass breaking. "That was the Millbrooks' punch bowl. Next, I'll smash the original chandelier from city hall. It's here in a box, and I have a hammer."

I ran to Peppermint and bent over. "You've done such a good job protecting us, my friend, but we need to open the door. Don't worry. We've got this covered."

"We do?" Jilly asked, as something else shattered behind the door.

"We do," Edna answered. "I will turn that brat over my knee when we get him out."

Peppermint's rigid posture softened, and she knickered.

"That's right," I said. "Stand down and let the preppers take over. They're trained in combat."

The pony's ears swiveled, but she still didn't move.

"Keats," Edna called. "You're up."

My dog, who'd been on strike since we escaped from the museum, sprang into action. He trotted to Peppermint's head to stare at her briefly and then moved to her hindquarters. It took only the slightest nudge to get the pony moving, and he herded her away from the door.

"Are you kidding me, Keats?" I said. "*Now,* you listen?"

He gave a quick pant-laugh as he hustled the pony out of harm's way. Then he came back and herded Jilly and me to stand with the pony by the dumpster. Percy meowed from the metal rim above us.

"Fall back with Minnie, old friend," Edna said.

Gertie backed up and dropped to one knee in the snow. "Ready."

"Come on out, Cork," Edna called. "The party's waiting."

No response.

Anthony had given up on the door.

"He's getting more stuff to smash," I said.

Edna shook her head and whispered, "He's right there. Listening. I can feel it."

She moved closer, raised her fist and then thumped the door hard.

"Ow!" Anthony yelped and then retaliated by shattering something else.

"Looks like we're doing this the hard way." Edna glanced back at Gertie. "Cover me."

Gertie crept forward. "Go."

Flinging back the door, Edna grabbed Anthony by the hood of his parka and yanked him out into the snow. "On your knees."

He didn't drop as ordered. Instead, he stared around, wild-eyed and panting, his dark curls chaotic from Percy's massage. His bare hands were at his side, and I saw a glint against his jeans.

"Edna, he's got a screwdriver," I called.

Anthony dodged around her, then Gertie, and came straight at me through the snow. His face was a snarling mask of fury.

Keats leapt forward, but the pony blocked him. She pranced sideways, body-checking Anthony hard enough to knock him off balance. He stumbled, recovered, and tried to dart around her.

Peppermint wheeled and body-checked him again.

Screeching in rage, Anthony swung at her with the screwdriver and missed.

The pony reared up on her hind legs. Anthony stepped back quickly, shielding his face with one bare hand.

He dodged left. She cut him off.

He went right. She was already there.

Finally, Anthony bent over like a quarterback, feinted and made a desperate lunge toward me. Peppermint spun quickly and grabbed a mouthful of curly hair with her teeth. The same hair Percy had raked not long ago. The man would be lucky to have any functional follicles left when the night was over.

Keats and Percy were ready to deploy again, but Peppermint was in the way.

"Drop the weapon or lose your right eye," Gertie called. "I'll shoot it out from behind. Done it before."

Anthony's fingers opened, and the screwdriver fell into the snow. He was still bent and his knees wobbled.

"Peppermint, let go," I said. "He's surrendered."

The pony released Anthony's hair and stepped back, snorting. Crumpling into the snow, the young man clutched his head and moaned.

Gertie moved in with the gun. "Face down and put your hands behind your back, deadbeat."

Anthony was down but not out. "You can't arrest me. You're not cops."

"Call it a certified citizen's arrest," Edna said, tipping him onto his side and deftly binding his wrists with a zip-tie from one of her many pockets. "No point smothering you, though. I want you to sit with what you did to Hester Belcher."

Gertie kept the rifle trained on him while flipping up the seat on her snowmobile and pulling out a coiled rope. "We've got leg irons, but he needs to be able to get around in deep snow."

"No problem." Edna took the rope and tied a few fancy knots that left Anthony with enough mobility to shuffle. Then she rolled him onto his back.

Before she could hoist him to his feet, Percy dropped to the ground and scraped snow over Anthony's face. The man sputtered, "Is that necessary?"

"It means you're dead to Percy," I said. "And the rest of us."

Gertie lowered the rifle but kept it at the ready. "Shall we deploy?"

I stared from Anthony on the ground to the snowmobiles. "Sure. I'll walk with the animals. Who wants the pleasure of riding with a killer?"

No one volunteered.

"We'll use the toboggan," Edna said, walking around her machine and unloading her equipment from the plastic sled she'd dragged in.

"That's not safe for human passengers," Jilly protested.

"One could argue he's inhuman for what he did." Edna hauled a duffel bag to the door of the museum and dumped it inside. "At any rate, my sled is plenty good enough for him."

Coming back, she hoisted Anthony to his feet as if he were a child and then got him settled onto the sled. He fit with a little manhandling and some additional rope to secure him.

"I'm not riding in front of him," Jilly said.

"Me either," I said. "He just tried to kill me again. I'll walk with the pony."

"Girls, we can't stand around gabbing. Hypothermia waits for no one." Edna waved directions with her camo gloves. "Gertie and Minnie ride with me. Jillian drives the other machine, leaving Ivy's hands free for cat and pony. Mount up, soldiers."

Only Edna was satisfied with this arrangement, I was sure of that. She tried to place a spare helmet over Anthony's head, but he screamed again. His scalp was pretty raw.

"Suit yourself," Gertie said. "If you want to be exposed during the ride of shame, be our guest."

"This is humiliating," he said. "I know my rights."

Edna shrugged. "Like revenge, justice is a meal best served cold."

With minimal instruction, Jilly got us rolling slowly, and our little parade crept down the unplowed road and into town square. Weaving around all the emergency vehicles was the hardest part, but my bestie did well, considering how infrequently she drove.

When we arrived in the square, Percy immediately freed himself from my jacket and climbed to my shoulder to cover the last few yards in style.

The crowd, now dispersing or drinking hot cocoa from a food truck, stepped back, mouths gaping.

Meryl Martingale was standing on a podium beside the fallen tree. "Ivy Galloway," she hollered through a megaphone. "Explain yourself."

Edna rolled to a stop, cupped her mouth and shouted back, "Can we get a cop here?"

CHAPTER TWENTY

A police SUV rolled over the curb and into the square. Asher leapt out of the passenger seat and yelled, "Where is she?"

Jilly flipped up her visor. "Right here, honey. We're all fine."

"You drove the snowmobile?" A grin spread across his face. "I'll upgrade mine, and we can go winter camping."

Laughing, she dismounted and pulled off the helmet to release golden curls. "Never going to happen. Desperate times called for desperate measures."

Kellan left the driver's seat and directed a handful of his staff to move Anthony from the toboggan and read him his rights. The young man struggled on the way to the police van, but not too hard. His fight had mostly ended with the pony's teeth.

Once the doors closed on Hester Belcher's killer, Kellan came over and hugged me. It was a rare public display of affection and earned him a cat in a transfer. "I'm so sorry I didn't make it," he said, brushing orange fluff out of his eyes. "That was the most stressful night of my life. You didn't answer my texts to say you were safe."

"That's because I *wasn't* safe until fifteen minutes ago. Anthony came after me again and got a taste of Peppermint's dark magic."

"Magic?"

"Only the kind with teeth and hooves. She basically took him down, and our prepper friends did the rest."

"You know how you can thank me," Edna said. "I'll take my driver's license back, Chief."

"You seem to get around well without it," he said, releasing me but still touching my sleeve. "ATVs, golf carts, snowmobiles. What else?"

"Dirt bikes," Jilly supplied. That had been one of our scariest rides.

"Each has its use," Edna said. "A truck can only take you so far. But far enough that I'll take that license."

The mayor's arrival spared Kellan from answering.

Meryl swept a fur-trimmed glove around and said, "This is all your fault."

"Mine?" he said. "I was dealing with a collision and near-fatality outside of town. There were plenty of police on hand to deal with your riot. You got everyone riled up yelling through your megaphone to 'behave.'"

"The riot was Ivy's fault," Meryl said. "I told her that if she didn't nail the killer fast, Christmas would be ruined. Now look what happened. The tree is crushed."

"My fault?" I asked. "How is a riot my fault?"

"People have been pushed to the limit by the number of recent murders. Losing their tree lighting was one step too far. I warned you."

Keats stepped between us, grumbling, and Kellan joined him. "Mayor, with all due respect, Ivy is a regular citizen. The weight of crime in our region cannot fall on her shoulders, or on Keats and Percy."

"Do dogs and cats have shoulders?" Gertie asked.

"Yep," Edna said. "My shoulders are arthritic, and I don't hear Meryl thanking me for my volunteer service to this great metropolis.

Who towed the killer into town, Your Worship?"

The mayor shot her a withering look. "'Mayor' will do just fine, Edna. And thank you."

Edna cackled. "See if you still feel the gratitude when you find the remains of the original city hall chandelier. The killer got spicy."

Kellan wasn't finished. "Mayor, we were closing in on the killer the boring legal way, with help from our dark web informant and researchers. That takes time. I don't appreciate your undermining my authority and sending Ivy and her friends into danger. She could have been killed."

Flicking her fingers toward the tree, Meryl frowned. "The needs of the many outweigh the few. And I knew the dog would keep her alive. He always does."

"Don't discount the cat," I said. "And in this case, the pony. Peppermint was a hero."

"The pony. Yes. I found her owner. Silas Mullally. He's off the grid and had to hike to a neighbor's house to report the loss. She goes missing for a day or two regularly."

"That doesn't surprise me. Peppermint let herself out of the museum earlier to keep the door open for us."

The mayor looked skeptical. "I'll await my full briefing. Her real name is Daisy, by the way."

I wanted to argue about that, but it sounded like the pony wouldn't be around long enough to compete with my sister. Running my hand over her fur, I sighed. "I hoped she could stay."

Kellan rolled his eyes. "Like you need another animal. I just found you a new cat, trapped in a pantry by a suspect who should be brumating."

"Brumating?" Meryl asked.

"You don't want to know," Kellan said.

Jilly shook her head. "Respect my moratorium, or learn how to cook, folks."

Grinning, I rubbed the pony and caught Kellan's eye. "I have a good home in mind for Hester's ginger. One is plenty for me. As for the pony, I want her to stay with Reid Brisco and his daughter. They need a bright little girl like Peppermint."

Edna took the pony's lead rope and scratched her behind the ears. "Talk to Silas. For a reclusive homesteader, he's a reasonable man."

"We have so many of those," Meryl said. "Silas told Animal Services the pony is bored and lonely. Called her the 'Houdini of Shetlands.'"

I laughed, and my friends joined in. "The pony is smart. I'll drive her home tomorrow and offer to buy her." Staring around, I added, "Or you could have the tree lighting tomorrow and I could speak to him here."

Meryl turned to Kellan. "Dare we? It was utter chaos tonight."

"Lighting the tree symbolizes peace," I jumped in. "It's a return to normalcy."

"Or what passes for it in Clover Grove," Edna added.

Kellan thought about it for a minute, lips pursed. "I can call in a few favors with other towns. Staff up to get through the investigation quickly and roll into the event." He turned to me. "You recorded the confession? Cell reception was spotty. I heard only about half of it."

Nodding, I pulled out my phone and tapped. "Sent. It's a tough listen. I'm going to spend all day tomorrow on my manure pile trying to forget that one."

"What about your last-minute shopping?" Jilly asked, grinning. "Christmas Eve is your day."

"Got it covered," I said. "Hired a personal shopper Teri Mason recommended. You might actually like your gifts this year."

Kellan wrapped his arm around my shoulders and pulled me away from the group. Percy stuck with Kellan, proving the higher ride was always the best. "I've got all I need. Except I wish the mayor would stick to her job instead of impeding mine. She has no right to send you in where the police should go."

He jumped as Keats delivered some discipline to a uniformed shin. Winter boots were no hindrance to a diligent sheepdog.

"Leave it, Keats," I said. "Kellan is right, but he's forgetting we would have gone, anyway. With Iris still on the hook, what else could we do?"

"Let me take care of it?" His arm was still around me, so I knew it was coming from concern rather than annoyance.

"You had your hands full tonight, Chief. We were just lending a hand, paw and hoof."

"We'll talk tomorrow. And the day after."

"That's Christmas. Can we save the lectures for the new year?"

"No. I want to start the new year with a better understanding between us of how policing works in hill country."

"Oh, goodie. Cop school at last. Will I get a uniform and service weapon?"

"Definitely not."

"Ivy!" The shout came from Edna. "Are you just going to leave me with your pony? Wasn't saving your life enough for one night?"

I stood on tiptoe to kiss Kellan and then slipped out of his grip. "Gotta run."

"Where are you going?"

Easing away, I counted off my fingers. "Snowmobile back to the truck. Transport pony to Reid Brisco's. Home for dinner and a little manure therapy before bed. See you there?"

He grinned at me. "Save me a place by the fire."

"Always." I grinned back before eluding the dog's teeth and then clomped back to my friends through the snow.

"Can you help get the tree upright?" Mayor Martingale asked as we gathered around the pony.

Edna laughed. "Nope. I'll save your town, but I won't do your grunt work, Meryl. Sounds like a job for someone on salary."

"No room in the budget for staff," she called over her shoulder as she walked away. "But there may be more than coal in your stocking this year, Edna."

"That'll be a first," Edna bellowed back.

"Not true." Gertie grumbled as we got on the snowmobiles. "I gave you a live imaging sonar system last year. Cost a bomb."

Edna nodded before dropping her visor. "Very thoughtful gift. We should go ice fishing tomorrow. Walleye and trout for Christmas dinner."

Jilly climbed onto the back of Edna's machine. "Humbug. You drive the snowmobile. I'll drive dinner."

"Deal."

CHAPTER TWENTY-ONE

The town square was full the next night, and the vibe was as calm and bright as it should be on Christmas Eve. Despite everything that had happened—murder, chaos, a toppled tree—Clover Grove had rallied. The massive fir stood upright again, braced and tied off. Half the branches looked like they'd been through a wood chipper, but someone had cleverly strung extra lights over the damaged sections. It was a conversation piece even before being lit.

I stood near Aline Tupling's toy donation table with Peppermint's lead rope in my hand. The pony shifted beside me, her cream-colored mane almost luminous in the glow of white lights overhead. Reid Brisco had thoroughly groomed her and tied bows to her halter. If anyone deserved to look her best tonight, it was this girl.

Keats sat on my left, mismatched eyes tracking every movement in the square. Percy had claimed the high ground atop a stack of donated toys. Both pets were on their best behavior, which made me suspicious. They were probably plotting something.

Keely Brisco ran back from visiting the children's play area, wearing a tiara over her hat that she got from Aline. Reid followed at a more measured pace, his hands shoved in the pockets of a canvas jacket that had seen better days.

Peppermint's ears pricked forward as she nickered a greeting. The little girl wrapped her arms around the pony's neck. "I missed you so much! Did you miss me? Of course you did. We're best friends now."

The pony's agreement was obvious in the way she leaned into the embrace. Reid caught my eye over his daughter's head and smiled. It was a pleasant smile, warm and a little shy. The kind that made you doubt the speculation circulating about him and his mysterious missing wife.

"She's a very good pony," I told Keely. "Helped take down a bad guy yesterday."

Keely's eyes went wide. "How bad?"

Reid caught my eye, and I slowed my roll. "It was someone who didn't respect our town enough. We're a community that looks out for each other."

"When we're not rioting," Edna said, joining me with Jilly and Gertie.

Jilly intervened. "We are a riot here. So fun. I can't believe I lived anywhere else."

"Me either," Keely said. "Are we staying forever, Daddy?"

Patting her shoulder, Reid shrugged. "Maybe. If they'll have us."

"Of course we will," Jilly said. "We'll have you for Christmas dinner, for starters. If you're free."

"Well, uh... I guess so." Reid was utterly trapped by Jilly's gravitational pull. "We'd like to meet the alpaca."

"Yay!" Keely shouted the word, but Peppermint didn't flinch. I had the feeling this wasn't the pony's first exuberant child. Silas Mullally might fill us in on her history.

"How's business?" Jilly asked Reid. "Bet there a run on your products after the Founder's sleigh was recovered."

He nodded sheepishly. "Sold out in an hour. Taking orders for next year now."

"That's wonderful," I said. "See? I told you the Langmans' smear campaign wouldn't stick."

"They're the ones getting smeared now," Edna said.

Jilly shushed her before she shared that Heddy and Kaye had spent much of the day being grilled by the police. The sisters were having a hard time convincing anyone they didn't know exactly what they were buying from their anonymous seller on the dark web, no matter how complicated the arrangement. It would take time to establish how it all went down. I had some hope that the Langmans' true legacy would be a cautionary tale for other swindlers.

In the meantime, Heddy was on the hook for breaking and entering, and had surrendered the purloined cat. At my request, the Mafia had placed the ginger male with Isaac Gherkin and found another good home for the two gray tabbies. Hester might have had something to say about Isaac, but it felt right to let their old grudge die with a purr.

The surrounding crowd grew, filling the square with laughter and conversation. A small group of carollers in the red cloaks Mom made gathered near the tree. I spotted Iris among them, her dark hair tucked under a white hat. She looked radiant and when she caught my eye, gave me a little wave. It was all the thanks I needed. My big sister had her museum and reputation back. All was right in our world... until the next tempest in the family teapot.

"Ivy Galloway?"

The voice was creaky and unfamiliar. I turned to find an old man in a coat more bedraggled than Reid's. A thick beard mostly hid his weathered face, and a cap covered his ears, but his eyes were sharp.

"That's me," I said. "And you must be Mr. Mullally."

"Call me Silas. We're practically family, from what I heard

about you and Daisy." He nodded toward Peppermint, who took a step toward him and then another step back.

"Daisy?" Keely wrinkled her nose. "The pony's name is Peppermint."

Silas chuckled, a sound like gravel in a bucket. "This one's answered to a few names over the years. Doubt she cares much, little miss."

I introduced Mr. Mullally to our group. He exchanged hearty handshakes with Gertie and Edna, whom he already knew.

"Does the pony escape often?" Reid asked.

"Often enough. She's a magician." Silas reached out to scratch Peppermint's neck, and she didn't resist. "Slips her halter, picks locks with her teeth, snips wire and more."

"Why does she run away?" Keely asked, clearly worried. "Doesn't she like you?"

"Oh, she likes me fine. Just gets lonely, I think." Silas' smile had more than a few gaps. "Truth is, she was never really mine. Turned up at my place about five years ago. I asked around, put up notices, but nobody claimed her. She needed a home and I gave her one, but a crusty old hermit isn't much company for a social creature like her. I didn't want to take on even more animals at this stage in life. It's a big commitment."

Edna nodded. "Wish more people had your sense, Silas. You might live forever, but do you want to be tied down by livestock?"

"Not if they're as lively as this one. This pony's got a mind of her own. Keeping her penned up is like trying to cage the wind."

This confirmed my suspicion that Peppermint was a force of nature wrapped in fluff.

"Mr. Mullally," I said, "what if this pony had a home with plenty of stimulation and company? Where she'd be needed and appreciated?"

His sharp eyes moved from me to Keely to Reid and back again. "Is someone offering to buy her?"

"Name your price," I said.

"Daddy!" Keely grabbed Reid's hand. "Can't we buy her? Please? I promise I'll take care of her and brush her every day and clean out her stall."

"Sweetheart," Reid said gently, "I didn't sell enough sleighs to cover that. Ponies aren't cheap."

"Actually," Silas said, "I don't think I can sell her."

Keely's face fell. My heart sank. Even Peppermint seemed to droop.

"Can't sell what was never really mine," he continued, a smile playing at the corners of his mouth. "But I can *give* her to someone who'll appreciate her properly. Someone who'll let her be the hero she wants to be." He glanced at me and winked. "Meryl told me what happened at the museum. It proved Daisy is too much pony for this old homesteader."

"You're not that old, Silas," Edna said. "Some training would do wonders. Have you heard about my survivalist classes?"

"I've heard a lot about you, Edna," he said, grinning. "You always were a sparkplug."

I caught Reid's eye and confirmed his willingness to take on a sparkplug of the equine variety. Then I bent over and told Keely, "Mr. Mullally is letting you keep Peppermint."

Keely ignored the lead rope I offered and ran to wrap her arms around the old man. "Thank you, Mister Silas."

"You're welcome." He blinked a few times and patted the pink parka. "Merry Christmas."

When the little girl released him, Reid pumped Silas' hand. "That's so generous, sir. We'll take good care of her."

Silas simply nodded. "I know. This pony's been looking for her people for years. Seems like she found them."

Peppermint leaned into Keely's shoulder, and if there was a dry eye in our group, I couldn't see it. Even Gertie had to pull up her poncho to pat her cheeks, revealing enough of Minnie to make Keely's eyes widen again.

To add to the warmth of the moment, the carollers began singing Joy to the World. People joined in and pressed closer to the tree, clutching cups of cider and cocoa.

Edna shook off emotion and went over to conduct the carollers, who had been doing just fine without a camo-clad index finger counting out the beats.

Iris' voice rose clear and strong over the other carollers. She looked away from Edna to watch Reid and it seemed that he was watching her, too. Was this just a Christmas twinkle or the start of something that might bloom over our holiday dinner?

The mayor stepped onto her podium near the tree. The megaphone was nowhere in sight, thank goodness. Instead, she held a wireless microphone and waited for the carollers to finish their song.

"Good evening, Clover Grove," she began. "What a week it's been."

Nervous laughter rippled through the crowd.

"We've faced betrayal. Loss. Fear. But we've also seen the very best of our community. Neighbors helping neighbors. Friends supporting friends. Even a certain pony contributed to justice."

More laughter now, and people turned to look at Peppermint, who pranced a little beside Keely.

"Tonight, we light this tree as a symbol of hope and resilience. Whatever happens, we endure. We celebrate. We come together." Meryl paused, her gaze finding mine in the crowd. "Thank you to everyone who worked to keep our town safe. To our police force and our very special volunteers. You know who you are."

"We sure do," Edna said, rejoining us and fist-bumping Gertie. "Meryl can keep her faint praise."

"And now," the mayor continued, "let's bring some light to this beautiful night."

She signaled and suddenly, the tree blazed to life. A thousand or more colored lights twinkled against the dark sky, turning the battered fir into something magical. Even the damaged side looked beautiful, the extra lights creating a colorful shield against civic unrest. The crowd erupted in cheers and applause.

There was a single boo somewhere in the distance. Isaac Gherkin was adding a sour note to balance all the sweetness.

"It's perfect," Keely said.

We all nodded in agreement. The battered tree represented the essence of Clover Grove, with its imperfection, resilience, and undeniable charm.

"Daddy." Keely's voice cut through the noise. "Can we take Peppermint on a ride? You have my sleigh in the truck."

"I don't think so, sweetheart. Your sleigh is meant for *me* to pull. We'd need a properly fitted harness for the pony."

"Her harness is in my truck," Silas said. "Had a feeling she might not be coming home with me and the gear would be needed."

"All right, then," Reid said. "One short ride around the square, Keely. Then we'll get this pony home for good."

Reid and Keely walked off with Silas, while Gertie went to find Edna. That left Jilly and me to enjoy a quiet moment with Keats and Percy. The lights and the camaraderie chased away the last of the tension from last night. The confrontation in the taxidermy wing already felt distant, like something that had happened to someone else. Yet I couldn't deny being tired.

Aline Tupling emerged from the crowd, her face pink from cold and possibly tears. She wore a cream-colored coat and a red scarf and hat. "I've been looking for you, girls. To thank you in person. For everything."

"No need to thank us," I said. "It was all in a day's hike."

"But if you hadn't persisted, who knows what might have happened with Powell Nobbs?" She twisted her gloved hands together. "I can't believe he went to such lengths. All those letters. The planning. It's overwhelming."

"He cares about you," Jilly said, ever the diplomat.

"He barely knows me. We've only had about three real conversations."

"Sometimes three is enough," I said. "Although I'll admit Powell's methods were questionable."

"Borrowing a priceless antique and fleeing a crime scene?" Aline shook her head. "That's beyond questionable."

I patted her arm. "Powell's heart was in the right place, even if his judgment took a holiday. Aline, he's not the only one in town who admires you."

Her face flushed bright red. "What?"

"Isaac Gherkin spoke highly of you the other day. That's all I'm at liberty to say."

The woman's mouth opened and closed. "Isaac? He protests everything."

"Every activist has an Achilles heel," I said. "Maybe that's you. Beneath righteous fury about deforestation and consumerism, there's a man who appreciates a woman who rings a bell for charity."

"I don't know what to say."

"Say you'll keep an open mind," Jilly suggested. "The holidays are full of surprises. Some quite pleasant."

Aline looked dazed as she drifted back into the crowd. I hoped she'd give Isaac a chance. She deserved the companionship of someone who saw past her shy exterior to the kind-hearted person underneath.

Keats mumbled something approving. The dog had strong opinions about romantic pairings. It wasn't really about romance, I suspected, but about creating balance and order.

Before Jilly and I had time to chat more, Mayor Martingale arrived. Her hair looked impeccable under a red faux fur hat and coat probably chosen to raise my mother's blood pressure. A friendly rivalry kept the ladies on their toes.

"Larry and I are looking forward to spending a few days at Runaway Inn," she said. "We'll check in with my brother and his family by noon tomorrow." She looked over her shoulder and then did a full turn for good measure. "There's something I want to discuss beforehand. I have an issue. Off the books."

"Off Kellan's books?" I asked. "I've already pushed my luck this week, Mayor. It may not always look like it, but I value my relationship. He's threatened me with cop school, only without the bells, whistles and guns."

Jilly laughed. "It would break Asher's heart if you got a badge. That's his way of shining in a big family."

"No worries. I prefer not to know all the rules the police live by. Makes life more fun."

The mayor raised one red glove and twirled it, reminding us she'd commanded an audience. "Exactly. I need someone flexible to help me with a little problem."

I stared across the square at a clutch of cops watching over everyone. My beloved was among them. "Can't do it, Meryl. For the foreseeable future, I'm focusing on rescue."

She beamed. "Exactly what I hoped to hear. Take the week off, and we'll talk in the new year. Do not mention our arrangement in front of Larry or the Chief."

"We don't have an arrangement," I said. "Sometimes you need to take no for an answer, Meryl. Especially at Christmas."

"Impossible." She watched Reid and Keely come back with Peppermint towing the sleigh. The little girl walked directly to Iris and began an animated dialogue with hand gestures. It looked like an invitation to ride the sleigh. My sister kept shaking her head but smiled warmly. "Oh, dear. I hope Iris doesn't get too attached to that child."

I turned quickly to stare at the mayor. "Why not?"

She waggled her fingers and walked off. "Come to my office in the new year, Ivy. We're off the clock now."

I huffed in disgust before turning to Jilly. "Meryl did it again. Hooked me like a fish on a line. Iris just got out of a bind. How can I leave her hanging?"

Jilly looked down at Keats, whose mouth dropped open in a pant-laugh. "Does he look concerned about Iris gaining an insta family? Does Percy?"

"I guess not. They'll all be together at Christmas dinner. Boys, you have my full permission to monitor Reid Brisco. And Meryl." I sighed. "Can't we take a day off?"

The dog mumbled to me, affirming his disinterest in downtime. I didn't need much myself, but a few days would be nice.

"Look at the sleigh Reid made," Jilly said, redirecting my attention. "It's practical and sturdy yet pays homage to the Founder's sleigh."

It was wide enough to seat two children side by side, and another behind. Reid folded himself into it now, with Keely on his lap. Silas handed him the reins and they set off around the emptying square. The gentle thud of hooves and tinkling bells chased the mayor's twisty hints out of my mind.

The pony trotted with a smooth gait that suggested she knew her way around a sleigh. Keely's laughter rang out, pure and bright.

They made one circuit of the square and the people lingering stepped back to watch and cheer. Peppermint seemed to swell with the attention, her head high, her stride confident. This was what she'd been looking for all along, I suspected. Not adventure for its own sake, but purpose. A job. A family. A place to belong.

By the time they'd finished another full turn, Silas Mullally had rejoined us.

"She's happy," he said. "Warms my heart to see it."

"You gave the pony a wonderful gift," I told him. "Keely, too. They need each other."

He nodded. "Brisco invited me to visit. I probably will, even though I'm not the visiting type."

Jilly tried her luck. "How about joining us for Christmas dinner? Get in a practice round?"

At the rate she tossed out invitations, we'd have to extend the dinner table onto the porch. I couldn't believe that only a few years ago, Jilly and I regularly worked through Christmas. It was a non-event, whereas now our holidays were busy and happy.

"Might consider it and even bring my homegrown cranberry sauce," he said. "But only if you girls take a spin behind the pony."

I watched it glide in. Edna and Gertie had to help Reid out of the seat.

"I don't think so, Silas," I said. "That thing is built for the kids we don't have yet. Reid had to be extracted."

His bushy eyebrows rose. "Meryl said you're both quite brave. I guess you city girls are more comfortable in suits."

Jilly's chin came up. She'd left the city far behind, and the comment rankled. "Fine, we'll do it. But if I break my arm, you'll have nothing to eat with your homegrown cranberry sauce."

I was more concerned about the pony. "Pulling two adults is a lot, Silas."

"Pit ponies can haul around eight hundred pounds. You gals weigh more than that?"

"Not before the holiday," I said.

Edna helped Jilly get seated at the back of the sleigh, and I squeezed in front. It was definitely a tight fit for two grown women in bulky coats and ski pants. My elbows jabbed Jilly's ribs, and her knees were in my armpits.

"This is a terrible idea," Jilly said.

"Ivy Rose Galloway." My mother's voice soared across the square. "Get out of that sleigh this instant. You'll break your neck."

I had no choice but to follow through now. Family dynamics were like that.

Reid handed me the reins. "Keep it loose. The pony already knows what to do."

"Loose. Got it." I gripped the rope with both hands and called, "Let's go, Peppermint. Nice and easy."

Keats trotted along beside the sleigh, offering a mumble that sounded like "idiots."

The sleigh glided over the packed snow in the square, bells jingling. People parted to let us through, and I heard laughter and the occasional cheer.

Peppermint moved with the steady, confident gait of a pony who knew exactly what she was doing. We made the first turn around the square without incident. The lights from the tree cast reflections on the snow, and the carollers started singing We Wish You a Merry Christmas.

"Muscle spasms aside, this is actually quite magical," Jilly said.

"Don't jinx it. Nice moments in this town have a shelf life of about forty seconds before something goes sideways."

She laughed as we rounded the second turn and headed back toward our starting point. Maybe this would actually end without emergency medical intervention.

That's when Peppermint got frisky. The pony's pace sped up from a walk to a trot to a canter.

"What's she doing?" Jilly asked.

"Feeling her oats." I gripped the side rail with one hand and called, "Whoa, girl. Whoa!"

The sleigh bounced over uneven patches of snow. Bells jangled wildly. Keats let out a rare alarm bark.

That's when we hit a clear patch of ice. The sleigh slid sideways before tipping and tossing us onto a snowbank.

We both fell out and landed on our backs, staring up at the crooked Christmas tree. Then we laughed so hard we could barely breathe.

Keats climbed onto my chest to stare into my face, making me laugh harder still. Percy did the same to Jilly, using his claws to grip her parka.

"Can you believe this is our life?" Jilly said.

I lifted my head and took in the spectacle. Our town had survived another crisis with its spirit bruised but intact. Snow fell heavily now, as if determined to mask our communal flaws. "It's something straight out of a snow globe."

"With a little more murder," she added.

We were in no hurry to be responsible adults, but eventually the long arm of the law came to help me up. Kellan pulled me close, kissing my forehead in bemused fondness.

Asher did the same, hugging his wife with the cat squeezed in between.

Then the dog herded us away into our personal winter wonderland.

When a grave in Clover Grove Cemetery is disturbed, old scandals and fresh outrage threaten to derail Ivy's bachelorette party. Join the gang as they get to the very bottom of a new mystery in **Beg, Burrow or Steal**.

Bones where they don't belong

A bachelorette party gone wrong

Can Ivy solve it all before "I do"?

FIND OUT NOW!

Interested in hearing more about my books or my pets? Join the Ellen Riggs newsletter at **ellenriggs.com/opt-in**.

RUNAWAY FARM & INN RECIPES

Crime Scene Chocolate Chunk Shortbread

Ingredients

- 2 ½ cups all purpose flour
- 1 lb. butter, room temperature
- 1 cup fruit sugar
- 1 cup rice flour, sifted
- ½ lb. Belgian chocolate

Directions:

Spread the all-purpose flour on a cookie sheet and place under a pre-heated broiler about 4-5 inches from the element.

Roast the flour, watching it all the time until it is medium brown. Turn the flour with a spatula to brown the other side. The entire procedure takes about three minutes.

Let the flour cool.

Mix the soft butter with the fruit sugar and add the sifted rice flour.

Fold in the roasted flour and blend well.

Chop the chocolate into small chunks.

Mix them quickly into the dough.

Drop by the tablespoon onto a parchment-lined cookie sheet.

Bake at 300F for 1 hour.

More Books by Ellen Riggs

Bought-the-Farm Cozy Mystery Series

- A Dog with Two Tales (Prequel)
- Dogcatcher in the Rye
- Dark Side of the Moo
- A Streak of Bad Cluck
- Till the Cat Lady Sings
- Alpaca Lies
- Twas the Bite Before Christmas
- Swine and Punishment
- The Cat and the Riddle
- Don't Rock the Goat
- Swan with the Wind
- How to Get a Neigh with Murder
- Tweet Revende
- For Love Or Bunny
- Between a Squawk and a Hard Place
- Double Dog Dare
- Deerly Departed
- Think Outside the Fox
- Mouse of Ill Repute
- Bee All and End All
- Sheep with One Eye Open
- Roo the Day
- Till Death Zoo Us Part
- Hit the Road, Quack
- One Horse Open Slay
- Beg, Burrow or Steal

Bought-the-Farm Mysteries - Boxed Sets

- Bought the Farm Mysteries - Books 1-3
- Bought the Farm Mysteries - Books 4-6
- Bought the Farm Mysteries - Books 7-9
- Bought the Farm Mysteries - Books 1-10

Dog Town Series

- Ready or Not in Dog Town (The Beginning)
- Bitter and Sweet in Dog Town (Labor Day)
- A Match Made in Dog Town (Thanksgiving)
- Lost and Found in Dog Town (Christmas)
- Calm and Bright in Dog Town (Christmas)
- Tried and True in Dog Town (New Year's)
- Yours and Mine in Dog Town (Valentine's Day)
- Nine Lives in Dog Town (Easter)
- Great and Small in Dog Town (Memorial Day)
- Bold and Blue in Dog Town (Independence Day)
- Better or Worse in Dog Town (Labor Day)

Mystic Mutt Mysteries Paranormal Cozy

- I Want You to Haunt Me (Prequel)
- You Can't Always Get What You Haunt
- Any Way You Haunt It
- I Only Haunt to be with You
- All I Haunt Is You
- Do You Haunt to Know a Secret?
- All I Haunt for Christmas
- I Haunt You Back